1ˢᵗ us ed
5 —
m

Scratchproof

Scratchproof

MICHAEL MAGUIRE

ST. MARTIN'S PRESS
New York

This is a work of fiction. Although reference has been made to actual races, sponsors, and organisations for the sake of verisimilitude, any use of real names either human or equine is purely coincidental.

My thanks to Stuart Lyons for his invaluable help in editing the film content of this story.

All rights reserved. For information write:
St. Martin's Press Inc., 175 Fifth Ave., New York,
N.Y. 10010
Printed in Great Britain
Library of Congress Catalog Card Number: 76-45771
First published in the United States of America in 1977

Library of Congress Cataloging in Publication Data

Maguire, Michael.
　Scratchproof.

　I. Title.
PZ4.M189Sc　(PR6063.A332)　813'.5'4　76-45771

For Nicola, with love

Chapter One

'You look wonderful, Catherine. Truly wonderful!' Howard Grant pushed his way through the dinner-jacketed devotees to bestow a kiss on her languorous white hand.

'Why thank you, Howard.' She rewarded the courtly gesture with a vivacious smile.

'Love the gown, Cathy,' the accent was undoubtedly Harrovian.

'Bless you, Keith.'

'Can't wait for the picture.'

'You've all been so marvellous. Bless you all.'

The hi-fi was playing tunes from the twenties and thirties, the Bollinger '69 was flowing pretty freely, and Catherine Forrest was enjoying all the attentions being showered upon her. People on the selvedge of society and slightly passé showbiz types crowded around the immortal screen goddess as though she was a priceless piece of porcelain which was about to be covered with a dust sheet and locked away in a museum vault.

Kisses were blown, the smile repeated itself again and again, and a calculated swing of the hips set her clinging multi-coloured evening gown shimmering exotically. She looked cool, lush. It was almost as if she was playing out a scene. The guests were merely a retinue of ad-libbing extras. The exultations, the subtle laughter, the gushing compliments.

'Scrape off the six coats of Revlon and you'll see the real Catherine Forrest.' The words were whispered through clenched teeth of a smile. They came from a bored-looking woman who stood well clear of the worshipping menagerie. 'There's nothing so pathetic as an actress who's outgrown her image . . .'

I moved through the clanking jewellery, the tight faces, the tethered torsos. I sampled an anchovie canapé, as a waiter re-energized the flagging bubbles in my glass. I felt a little out of place. I wasn't 'society' or 'showbiz' and the reason I'd been summoned to this birthday-cum-dinner party wasn't at all clear.

'*Fiona's dying!*' A voice suddenly turned the elegant dinner party into a fiasco.

I saw Catherine Forrest's body go rigid and sway slightly. Glasses rattled then shattered as she collided with a silver salver. A look of stupefied horror had replaced the smile and her lower lip trembled as she cradled the frail little body in her arms.

'Fiona's dying,' she said again.

She was right, Fiona *was* dying. And not peaceably either. The pink satin bow on her head danced like a butterfly trapped against glass. Her mouth quivered showing tiny white teeth and her eyelids fluttered spasmodically. There was a final half-broken gasp for air and she lay still.

'Oh, God . . .' Catherine shook her head from side to side. Slow. Stricken. 'My baby—my poor, poor baby . . .'

Doleful expressions replaced party grins. Voices suddenly sobered into conspiratorial whispers. The last few bars of Rhapsody in Blue trickled indelicately from the hi-fi.

'Somebody call a vet!' The command rang out.

'What the hell's happened?'

'Stand back, *please*!'

'Give the dog some air!'

The ejaculations were numerous, but futile. The tiny white poodle was dead and Catherine Forrest knew it. She pushed away a cluster of inquisitive fingers and wrapped the lifeless ball of fur in her sable cloak. Her face was a synthesis of emotions. Abandonment, need, tremendous solitude. She was surrounded by an ocean of people yet marooned in a dimension of grief. Blinded by tears, she groped her way towards Howard Grant, a reliable lifelong friend. He wrapped a comforting arm around her shoulders and nursed her out of the room.

There was an embarrassing silence, broken only by a few nervous coughs, the odd click of a cigarette lighter, the swish of a lurex gown. Somebody fiddled with the hi-fi in an attempt to rejuvenate the lost party spirit. Heads that had been lowered morosely were raised, relieved. True to that famous theatreland maxim, the show had to go on.

'Simon?'

'Yes?' I turned, traced the enquiry to a pair of hazel eyes, a head of long chestnut hair and lobes that supported large gipsy ear-rings.

8

'I'm Karan Langford,' she said smiling, offering her hand. 'Miss Forrest's girl-Friday.'

'Hello.'

'I've been sent,' she added.

'Sent?'

'By Howard Grant. He wants to see you in the study.'

'How did you know that . . .?'

'You were Simon Drake? Easy. He'll be standing alone, probably looking bored, and he has——' She lowered her eyes an inch.

'A broken nose,' I grunted.

'Yes, but I would have found you anyway. Truth is, you're the only one here I don't know. You see, I usually mix with middle-aged drones, eccentrics, egoists and inflated windbags. A new face is a refreshing change.'

I grinned. I liked her breezy manner, her overwhelming torrent of chatter. She was young—twenty-two, twenty-three, maybe, not over pretty, but unquestionably attractive. Her skin had a coppery sheen, a dusting of freckles, and the only make-up she wore was a trace of turquoise eyeshadow. I expected I was about to find out the reason for my presence. Either that, or I was going to be asked to bury the dog. 'Lead on,' I said.

As I reached the study I nearly collided with Catherine Forrest. Her eyes were squeezed shut in a great show of suffering as she floundered towards the bathroom. I rapped a knuckle on the study door.

'Enter.'

Howard Grant had a face for every occasion. At this precise moment he was wearing his famous weltschmerz expression. He coughed out a greeting, waved at a chair.

'Sit, Simon. We've business to discuss.'

I sat.

'Thank you, Karan.' His eyes dismissed the girl.

'Is Miss Forrest . . .?'

'Powdering her nose, as you ladies say. She might be glad of your company.'

Karan Langford nodded. I winked as she palmed the door handle and expected an engaging smile in return, but she simply looked at me with an expression that would keep anybody at arm's length and departed.

'I'm going to ask you a favour,' Grant said, as with an almost indiscernible manoeuvring of his features he showed me the tough, relentless face that had taken him to the top of the Security Division promotion ladder. He sniffed, massaged his temple, and sat behind a desk that was large enough to dummy for a billiard-table. 'I asked you here this evening to meet Catherine Forrest. She needs help, Simon.'

'Official T.S.D. help?'

'Unfortunately the Division can't get involved.'

I raised my eyebrows.

'She's making a film, her first for ten years. Have you read about it in the Press?'

'*Devil Take The Loser.*'

'Right.'

'So?'

'Things aren't at all well at the studios. Catherine thinks somebody is deliberately trying to wreck the picture. Accidents have been happening—slightly bizarre accidents which are having a damaging effect on Catherine's health. That's why she sought my help, and that's why I'm now seeking yours.' He lifted a cardboard box from the top drawer of the desk and pushed it towards me. 'This latest incident with the dog would seem to indicate the need for immediate investigation.'

I didn't follow the tag. It seemed to have an oblique logic all its own. 'How old was the poodle?' I asked.

He evaded the question. 'It was a present from some film director or other. The sentimental value of the animal was immeasurable.'

'How old?' I said again.

'Fourteen.' It came out as a murmur.

'*Fourteen?*'

'I know what you're going to say, but——'

'That's ninety-eight in human terms. A pretty good innings for——' I stopped short as he extended a finger and flipped open the lid of the box.

'Have a good look, Simon,' he said. 'Catherine brought this to me five days ago. She found it on the seat of her car.'

A wax effigy of poodle Fiona stared up at me. It was complete with pink satin bow and it was riddled with pins.

'Voodoo,' he added gently.

'You're not serious?'

'Are you a sceptic?'

'Are you?'

'The dog did die, Simon,' he parried.

'Yes, but at fourteen years of age the inevitable happened. Death by natural causes, not bloody pins.'

'Within a week of the effigy's arrival?'

' O.K.,' I conceded. 'Well if you're ruling out natural causes and I'm ruling out pins—how about poison?'

'Very possibly.' He sat back, complacently lacing his fingers behind his head. 'Somebody plants the voodoo doll and then helps the magic along by administering some sort of toxin. It seems logical but I'm afraid you won't convince Catherine of that.'

'She's siding with the supernatural.' My voice was gently sardonic.

'And with what's happened of late I can't blame her.'

He rose stiffly and began toying with a large globe of the world which stood beneath an array of tasteful water-colours and etchings. He silently spun the globe for maybe ten seconds, then stopped it with a jerk and launched into a graphic description of what he'd previously summarized as bizarre studio accidents. They were all aimed at Catherine, and included a faulty staircase prop which had nearly broken the actress's ankle, and a spotlight which had mysteriously unhitched itself during a rehearsal, missing Catherine by inches. Shooting schedules were being delayed and people were beginning to say the film was jinxed. He added hesitantly, 'She's also seen things which can only be interpreted as apparitions.'

'Spiritual or inebrious?' I ventured dryly.

'She doesn't drink.'

'Spiritual then.'

'I'm levelling with you, Simon. She claims to have seen things which defy description.'

'Such as?'

'Nightmarish things. Incredible things.'

'Phantoms, vampires, the devil incarnate?'

'Don't be flippant. It's all very distressing.'

'I'm trying to be practical,' I countered. 'Neurotic actresses just aren't my pitch. Catherine Forrest doesn't need me—she needs an exorcist or a bloody good head-shrinker.'

He slicked a hand over his silver hair and doggedly pressed on. 'I've known Catherine for years. Admittedly at the height of her career she had a reputation for being stormy and highly strung, but not any more. She's calmed down over the years. Any neurosis is a direct cause of these . . .' He faltered, 'These inexplicable incidents.'

'You've got the wrong guy,' I said bluntly. 'I deal with horses not hallucinations.'

'There's nothing hallucinatory about *that*.' He indicated the effigy.

'Let's carry out an autopsy, prove it was something other than old age that killed the poodle, and then maybe——'

'She won't have the dog cut up,' he interjected, 'her finer feelings won't allow it. I'll keep trying to persuade her otherwise, of course, but if I know Catherine, it'll be flowers and a casket burial in a dog's cemetery.'

'Then you can't persuade me either.' I headed for the door.

'You're not taking the case?'

I shook my head like a taunted boxer.

'The racing scene is very quiet,' he went on inexorably. 'The Division is twiddling its thumbs. Investigators are idle. No hope of work for freelance operators . . .'

'Goodbye, Howard.'

'I'm asking as a favour, Simon.'

I turned. 'I don't owe any. I was manipulated on my last assignment. There'll be no repeat performances.'

'But that's water under the bridge——'

'People tend to drown under your bridges,' I said with finality.

I'd barely got a finger to the handle before the door swung inwards to reveal Catherine Forrest. She'd donned dark glasses and she looked at me with her head held high, entirely the composed actress again. There was only the remnant of a quiver from her lips as she smiled, showing large very white teeth. A little too large, a little too white. At this range the crowning was just about discernible, which indicated she'd spent a lot of time and money in a Harley Street chair.

'You must be Simon,' her voice was low, controlled. 'I've heard such a lot about you.' My right hand was suddenly engulfed by two smaller ones, fervent and heavy with jewellery.

'Miss Forrest.' I nodded politely.

'Call me Catherine from now on. I might be your new employer but we'll waive the courtesy titles. You don't mind, do you?'

Suddenly I found myself minding very much. It was blatantly

bloody obvious that Grant had accepted this abnormal assignment on my behalf. 'If you'll excuse me,' I said, making to get the hell out of there.

'I don't understand.' Catherine looked from me to Grant as if sensing the coolness between us. 'Is something wrong, Howard? Why is Simon leaving?'

There was a heavy silence as Grant and I regarded each other. He was back behind his desk and had adopted his indomitable pose. The questions went unanswered as he idly rolled a pencil between his palms.

'Why is Simon leaving?' she said again.

Grant's lips barely moved. 'He feels that your problems are a little out of his field.'

'He isn't going to help me?' It was almost a plea.

'I'm afraid not.'

'I'll double the donation,' she said suddenly.

Grant's pose slipped slightly.

'What donation?' I queried.

'To the Injured Jockeys' Fund.' The pressure from those small hands had a determined pull about them as they coaxed me away from the door. 'Howard did tell you?'

'We never actually touched on the subject,' Grant murmured rather inadequately.

'Dear Howard, you do tend to omit the relevances.'

'Simon isn't easily swayed. He might well have interpreted the donation as some kind of bribe.'

'What nonsense.' She gave my hand a final pat, removed the dark glasses, and sank gracefully into the depths of a plush swivel chair. 'Do I look like an inveigler, Simon?'

She looked quite incredible. It was easy to see how her exquisitely-boned face had wowed the cinema-goers of the thirties and forties; how those smokey-sapphire eyes had parched many a throat, fluttered many a male heart. The years and the cosmetic surgeon's scalpel had been kind to Catherine Forrest. Perhaps the eyes had grown a little duller and a fine henpecking of lines was at last beginning to infiltrate the flawless complexion. But from the tip of her dusky blonde head to the toes of her neat sequined shoes she undoubtedly looked a star, loaded with that intoxicating quality that only the 'greats' can exude.

'Howard was right not to mention the I.J.F.' I said. 'It's a very worthy cause and I'm sure the donation will be welcomed, but it won't make me change my mind.'

'I'll pay you three hundred a week, plus expenses.'

'You can get a good private investigator for a third of that amount.'

'I don't want a private investigator—I want you. You have a price, surely?'

It sounded like a line from one of her old films. 'Everyone has a price, Miss Forrest, but scruples prevent me stealing from elderly actresses with more banknotes than brains.'

She smiled fleetingly. 'Does the inclusion of the word "elderly" indicate that you think I'm senile?'

'Of course it doesn't,' Grant put in quickly.

'How old do you think I am?'

'Fifty,' I said, meaning fifty-five.

'Today is my sixty-first birthday,' she leaned forward and delicately removed a king-size from the open cigarette-box in Grant's out-stretched hand. 'So you see you're right. By most young people's standards I'm rapidly approaching, or already in, the senility bracket.'

'Let me try another tack,' I said, grinning, liking her a little better. 'I know nothing about the film industry. Actors, actresses, and the rest of the celluloid species just aren't my bent. Asking me to help you is rather like asking a plumber to wallpaper a ceiling.'

'Horses for courses?'

'Exactly.'

Grant snapped a lighter into flame, adding succinctly, 'Simon underestimates his capabilities.'

'On the contrary,' I countered, 'I know my limitations. Crooked jockeys, trainers, doping, betting coups—that's my line of business.'

'How much or how little do you know about me?' Catherine emerged from behind her cigarette.

'You're an American actress now living in England,' I said, trying to keep the tedium out of my voice. 'You've survived three husbands, about the same number of nervous breakdowns, and you've recently been cast as the leading lady in a horseracing thriller which the pundits are forecasting as a godalmighty flop.'

Grant clawed open his collar and made a few worried noises. 'Simon's never learned the art of diplomacy,' he grunted.

'I admire forthrightness in a man. What he says is correct and it will give me great pleasure to prove the experts wrong. The *public*

14

are asking for another Catherine Forrest picture. They will get a performance worthy of their demands. Box-office receipts will soar, you'll see.'

I detected a slight note of desperation in the statement. Even Grant's agreeing nod was a trifle apathetic. I had the feeling that the only person Catherine Forrest was deluding was herself.

Smoke wreathed from her lips as she went on, 'Nevertheless, I am a little disappointed with Simon's précis. As some of my racehorses rank among the finest in the country I hardly expected him to gloss over the fact.'

'I apologize,' I said humbly. 'I was thinking of Catherine Forrest— star of the silver screen, not Catherine Forrest—celebrity of the winners' enclosure.'

'But are you aware they're using my horses in the film? They're also using real jockeys, training establishments, and racecourses. Altogether very much your kind of environment, surely, Simon?'

Between the two of them they were gradually shading off the logic of my resistance. For some obscure reason she wanted me, and only me. I couldn't understand it. 'I repeat,' I said, 'what's wrong with a good private investigator?'

She looked towards Grant. 'Howard is a loyal and trusted friend, and as you are one of his best operators——'

'It won't wash,' I retorted.

'A private investigator is going to be obtrusive, Simon. I want someone who will fit in with the surroundings.'

'And I'll "fit in", huh?'

'As racing adviser, most certainly.'

Before I could answer, Grant cut in. 'You have both the knowledge and the guile to play a double game. As co-producer it's easy for Catherine to put you on the film's pay-roll. That way you'll be accepted by the acting fellowship and be on tap, so to speak.'

'Racing adviser . . .?' I could feel the muscles in my throat involuntarily contracting. 'I've had no experience——'

'Crooked jockeys, trainers, doping—your very own words,' Catherine reminded me. 'The film has all those ingredients, plus a little blackmail mixed in for good measure. You'll be invaluable to us. What do you say?'

There wasn't anything left to say. She'd taken the words out of my mouth, twisted and turned them, gutted them and thrown them right back in my face. She had me feeling that I was in need of the head-shrinker for hesitating. She even had my scruples admitting that three hundred quid a week was money for old stagers. I'd like to think I was finally won over by the intelligence, the subtle persuasion, and the undeniable obstinacy of the woman. All I know is I found myself grudgingly agreeing with something that sounded like a strangled, 'O.K.'

'You'll help me?' She extinguished her cigarette and for the first time gave me a truly relaxed smile. 'Simon, you're an absolute darling.'

'I can't promise——'

'No, but you'll try.'

'All I can hope to do is find a credible answer for these apparently incredible happenings.'

'And that hideous *thing?*' Her eyes flickered towards the box.

'Surely all actresses are easy targets for this sort of freakishness. Cranks must have a field day sending obscene letters or——'

'No, no, no.' She shook her head violently. 'That thing is evil, positively evil. Or should I say *was.* It's harmless now. It's completed its mission. Oh, God!'

Grant was giving me frantic hand-signals. The kind which meant cut the questions, change the subject, or you'll re-open the sluice-gates. But Catherine had no intention of repeating the tears. She made a brief check to see that her eyelashes were in place, switched on her smile, and buried the effigy under a torrent of words.

'You'll come to the studios tomorrow and I'll introduce you to the crew. Rex will want to see you. You'll like Rex—I've known him almost as long as I've known Howard. Then there's the production manager, of course, and Sidney . . .' She bubbled on and on with the gushing enthusiasm of a child bride, making it hard to recognize the shattered, grief-stricken woman who had wept for poodle Fiona.

Grant pursed his lips thoughtfully. 'None of the racing sequences has been filmed as yet, so Simon's arrival is perfectly timed.'

'Perfectly,' Catherine echoed. 'Nobody could possibly guess the real reason for his presence.'

'I'm not exactly unknown in the racing world,' I pointed out. 'If I'm mixing with jockeys, etcetera . . .'

'Then you could well be recognized,' Grant provided. 'Don't let it worry you, just turn it to your advantage. You're a Turf Security freelance making a bit of extra money in between assignments. If anything, your background enhances your status as racing adviser.'

'I'll need a link man,' I said. 'It will look highly suspicious if I'm seen frequenting the star's dressing-room.'

'How about a link woman,' Catherine mused. 'My private secretary, Karan. She's the one person I trust implicitly.'

'Does she know about the effigy?'

'I've told her everything.'

Grant looked pensive. 'She's very young. I was thinking more along the lines of your husband.'

'Luke?' She laughed. 'I love him dearly, but the poor darling couldn't keep a confidence to save his life. The Aston Martin in your driveway was supposed to be a birthday surprise—I've been driving it for five weeks.'

Catherine prattled on about the racing sequences and the sort of things a racing adviser is supposed to advise on. It all sounded fairly elementary, the kind of thing any self-respecting T.S.D. operator would be able to recall from memory, bluff through, or swot up on, although Catherine had a way of making everything sound easy. 'The most important thing is to look as if you know what you're doing, even if you don't. You'll be marvellous at it, Simon, I'm sure.'

Was that a compliment? I was damned if I knew. I didn't have time to analyse it. There was a sharp rap as the door nearly lurched off its hinges to expose a thick-set, unsmiling, expensively dressed individual.

'I'm taking you home, Catherine,' he announced without preamble.

He had a small crescent-shaped scar on his cheekbone, and the kind of bronzed features which romantic magazines call 'ruggedly handsome'. His eyes were hostile and so dark they partially merged with the pupils. His hair rolled over his collar and tapered into sideburns which ran a couple of inches below his ears. The all-American image, almost cowboyish. He was older than me, by nine or ten years at a guess, which put him in his late thirties. He towered over Catherine and topped me by a good three inches. He also outweighed me by at least thirty pounds.

'Luke, I'd like you to meet Simon Drake,' Catherine said, 'our new racing adviser.'

17

I detected an inward oh-bloody-Christ sigh of frustration as we crushed hands. Those dark eyes flashed towards Catherine. 'Aren't you being a trifle extravagant, honey? Surely the horse manager——'

'The horse manager manages the horses. Simon supplies the expert advice.'

He grinned a little crookedly at me. 'No offence, buddy, but this wife of mine is stretching the budget to breaking point.'

'Rex and I will worry about film budgets,' she assured him. 'You just concentrate on your rich Olympus clientèle.'

'O.K.' He made a gesture of resignation. 'On the set you wear the pants, but off the set—I do—and I said I was taking you home.'

'Fiona?'

'She's in the boot of the car. I'll take her to the dogs' cemetery in the morning.'

He made brief apologies, saying he wanted Catherine home and in bed before delayed shock took over. Catherine called him a darling, me a darling, and Grant an absolute darling. She blessed us both and made a graceful exit. Luke drawled a, 'Yeah, see you guys around.' The door clicked shut.

'A truly remarkable woman,' Grant sighed.

'With truly remarkable emotions,' I added cynically. 'What do we know about Taylor?'

'Like the husbands of most famous women, he tends to stay in the background. In a sentence—he's been married to Catherine for six years, has a son by a previous marriage, and has been running a health farm at Sunningdale since he arrived in the U.K.'

'Not good enough. I'll need to know his American history. Everything—right down to how he got the scar on his cheek.'

'That's a tall order, Simon . . .'

I remained silent, just looked at him unflinchingly. He took a few seconds off for meditation, then nodded resignedly. 'I'll try.'

That meant I'd get it and I knew it would make interesting reading. Nobody could look the way Luke Taylor looked and not have a colourful past. I switched to the topic of the film.

'Catherine kept mentioning a character called Rex.'

'Rex Delgado. He's co-producing the picture. He'd head of a company called Lapwing Films.'

'Successful?'

'In the thirties he was one of the biggest.'

'And in the seventies?'

'He needs Catherine as much as she needs him.'

'So you're trying to tell me that a pair of nostalgic has-beens are wasting a lot of backers' money by making a film that hasn't a hope in hell of being a good box-office proposition.'

Grant gave a vexed sigh. 'I'm trying to tell you that Delgado needs Catherine because Catherine is financing the picture. To the tune of £650,000 to be exact.'

I whistled through my teeth.

'Catherine needs Delgado because the reason she hasn't made a film for the past decade is because she hasn't been asked. Delgado bought the film rights of a novel, put up a little front money for development, and then offered Catherine the leading role. She's a wealthy woman, Simon. She's doing it for prestige of course, but she'll also get a huge slice of the film's profits.'

'If there are any,' I murmured more to myself than to him. 'Catherine Forrest pictures went out with straw boaters and Oxford bags.'

'Fashions change,' he grunted. 'Besides, Oxford bags recently had a revival, didn't they?'

'True,' I conceded, 'but don't let's kid ourselves. The Hollywood era is over. Take a look at the cinema hoardings. All you need today is a bloke, a blonde, and a brass bedstead.'

Grant grunted, and dispensed his best Napoleon brandy into two glasses.

'*Devil Take The Loser*,' he said.

Quite a title considering the circumstances. As the brandy clung a little unpalatably to my throat, I had the feeling he very well might.

Chapter Two

I ARRIVED at Alverton Studios a little after eleven. The curlicue iron-work and impressive pillared entrance housed a complex of avenues and towering Nissen-shaped buildings. A factory whose end-product bought ninety-five minutes of smiles or heartache; where dreams came off the production line, and where all things were possible. The gateman checked my identity and directed me to Rex Delgado's office.

Catherine Forrest's Aston Martin Lagonda was parked outside. Its glistening silver paintwork was nuzzling a little wooden sign which bore her name. I backed my M.G.C. into a vacant space and sat looking at the Aston. The resplendence of the thing at close quarters was stunning. It was also a little frightening.

'Mr Drake?' A voice, sharp and peremptory broke into my thoughts. It was a command rather than a question, with a hint of urgency in it. 'Mr Simon Drake?'

'Yes?'

'Delgado.' He walked towards me, right hand out-thrust, diplomat-style. 'Catherine phoned me last night—said to expect you. I briefed the production manager. You'll take your instructions from him.'

'Fine.'

For a man in his sixties, he was wearing well. His bullet-shaped head was close cropped, with only a whisper of grey at the temples. The three-piece suit which hung on his slender frame was a little young in style, but he carried it superbly. A cravat and fashionable shoes completed the ensemble.

'You were admiring the car.' He tilted his chin towards the Aston.

'Yes, I was.'

'You were thinking it too powerful an animal for someone like Catherine.'

'You read minds, Mr Delgado?'

He smiled briefly. 'I read faces, Mr Drake. I've seen your expression duplicated a dozen times over in the past few weeks. Let me assure you that Catherine is a very capable driver.'

I pondered on the four overhead camshafts and ditto number of double-choke carburettors which nestled under the bonnet. I returned the smile without comment.

'Let's head for the set,' Delgado suggested. 'They're shooting a stable interior. As racing adviser you might well find it interesting.'

I nodded agreeably, letting him talk as we walked. He never touched on the matter of studio accidents, or delayed schedules. He spoke only of Catherine's acting ability. On that subject Rex Delgado didn't believe in minimizing the superlatives.

'Ellen Terry put it in a nutshell when she described star quality as "that little something extra". Actresses with Catherine's photogenic qualities are indestructible. Never, but never, do they die.'

'There's been some controversy in the Press——' I began.

'Those puerile pen-pushers?' His Adam's apple bobbed furiously as he choked out the words. 'They don't know the meaning of the word *STAR!* Catherine Forrest's name alone gives us a box-office head start over other studios.'

The verbal flurry had caused him to colour considerably. It sent probing fingers to his waistcoat pockets. He pulled out a little silver box and popped a lozenge into his mouth.

'Sorry,' he said shortly, 'as you can see, the Press isn't my favourite topic for discussion. For my health and your own peace of mind, Mr Drake, I suggest you remember that.'

We stopped at B stage. Delgado waved a hand vaguely towards a red light over the door and gave brief instructions as to its purpose. It wasn't illuminated, so we entered.

People appeared to be milling in all directions. Chaos was all around us, but Delgado seemed imperturbable. He rapidly categorized this hubbub of humanity as the carpenters, the electricians, the swing gang, the camera crew, the continuity girl, the hair-dresser, the make-up man—the list was endless. We picked our way through the troupe and over the snaking lengths of cable which straggled the floor. A brilliant array of arc lamps bathed the set with high-intensity light. It depicted the interior of a racing tack-room. A couple of assistants were eagerly applying a high-gloss substance to saddles, bridles, and anything leathery in view of the camera. In a conventional tack-room, I reflected, the substance would have been neatsfoot oil applied with a cloth and loving care. This varnishing stuff was applied with a paintbrush and gave the maximum shine with the minimum of effort. The visual effect, of course, was quite incredible.

'Max, Raymond, Oliver . . .' Delgado nodded to several faces as he took up a position behind the camera.

'*Good morning R.D.*' The replies were almost in unison.

'Sidney looks harassed.' Delgado's eyes strayed towards a small, bald-headed guy. He acknowledged with the briefest of hand signals and began thumbing through an inventory clipped to a board.

'Julian's in one of his moods,' said an assistant.

'Boyfriend trouble I think,' mocked another.

'The prostration of being gay, dear.'

'I'll handle Julian.' Delgado sighed heavily and strode briskly towards a swarthy-looking actor garbed in jodhpurs and polo-neck sweater.

The set was a conglomerate of sound, dominated by the strident voice of Catherine Forrest as she querulously complained, 'If Julian intends to play this scene looking like death warmed up, then I suggest we switch to the corpse sequence.'

Everybody grinned at that—except Delgado, while Julian countered with his own brand of flippant sarcasm.

'And you should know, darling,' he said, throwing back his head. 'You've been warmed up so often you're beginning to decompose.'

'That will do, Julian!' Delgado's command was harsh, loaded with cool authority. 'Are you unhappy with the part or what?'

'With my part in *this* scene, yes. It just isn't me.'

'Do you know your lines?'

'Of course I know my bloody lines—such as they are.'

'Well we haven't time for re-writes. Play it the best way you can.'

'I'm a method actor. I have to feel my way into a role.'

'Well feel your way into this one—*now!* Or feel your way off the salary list.'

He gazed at Delgado with silent contempt, thumped his boot against a light stand, and lurched arrogantly away. The bald-headed guy looked relieved. He waved his clipboard at a pneumatic blonde who was being chatted up by a couple of technicians. At least, one was chatting her up, the other was looking at her legs as if he could imagine them round his waist. The stand-ins were called for. The shot was lined up.

'Hi!' A voice purred into my left ear.

'Karan.' I whispered the name, watching as a smile formed on that small cherubic mouth.

'Why are you whispering?'

'Isn't one supposed to whisper?'

'Only during an actual rehearsal.'

'I see.'

She grinned engagingly. 'Don't look so wounded. A couple of days on the set and you'll be strutting around like a pro. What do you think of our tack-room interior? Have props done a good job?'

My eyes flitted over the leather hardware. 'See that bridle on the far peg,' I said, 'it's fitted with a Buxton bit and winkers.'

'Is that bad?'

'It is unless the stable happens to have a couple of draught-horses and a cart.'

She blinked. 'Good heavens. You'll have to tell S.N.S.'

'S.N.S.?'

'Sidney Newton-Smith, the director. Well done, Simon, you're going to make an impression on your very first day.'

Any enthusiastic lift I might have been feeling was instantly quashed by Karan's repetitive yell of, 'Sidney! Sidney! Sidney!' I felt myself physically shrink. Catherine's stand-in had been replaced by the genuine article and she was listening intently to Newton-Smith as he read lines from a script and explained the action. He stopped abruptly, cupped a hand to his forehead, and squinted in our direction.

'I hope this is important, Karan,' he said.

She pointed out the tack discrepancy and then she pointed to me. 'Simon Drake—our new racing adviser.'

'Pleased to meet you, Mr Drake. And thank you.' He finger-snapped an assistant to remove the offending bridle.

'Authenticity Simon. Well done.' Catherine applauded lustily.

'Let's get on with it,' growled Julian.

The blonde flicked back her peroxide curls and smiled sweetly. She was another discrepancy. I'd never seen a torso like that in a racing tack-room. Her jodhpurs housed long, long legs, and were topped by a tight denim blouse which accentuated the kind of form any red-blooded trainer would have been anxious to develop. I smiled in-wardly on seeing my own feelings endorsed by nudges and sly winks from the technical staff. Only Julian looked bored. Knowing his sexual inclinations, it figured to see him standing with arms folded and eyes averted.

'Right, children,' Newton-Smith barked, 'let's briefly run through the scene.'

Delgado, seemingly satisfied that everything was under control, sank into a canvas chair. He adopted an air of casualness as he began flipping through several sheaves of script. As the lines were said, the atmosphere began to build. I watched, slightly amused, as the ever-persevering director cajoled, coaxed, and prised the best possible performances from each individual.

'Catherine's good, isn't she, Simon?' Karan nudged me back to reality.

'Very,' I said.

'Just watch her reaction when Julian rips Amanda's blouse.'

'Rips . . .?'

'Amanda Stewart, the blonde. She's playing Catherine's daughter, and Julian rips open her blouse as a gesture of defiance . . .' She studied me critically. 'You have read the book?'

'I don't read very much fiction.'

'Here.' She reached into her shoulder-bag and handed me a slightly tatty script. 'I haven't read the book either,' she confessed softly, 'so we'll both have to make do with the screenwriter's version.'

Newton-Smith was showing Julian the small scissor-cut in Amanda's blouse. 'There—at the top of her cleavage—see?' He did see. He regarded the incision with an expression of distaste, and nodded. 'Just grab , pull, and the whole thing will fall apart,' the director added. 'And please try to look as if you're enjoying it, O.K.?'

'Poor Julian,' Karan smothered a giggle.

'Is the boyfriend here?' I asked.

'Not unless Julian's found someone new. Catherine sacked the last one a few days after starting the picture. He was a middle-aged director with a weakness for virile young men. Sidney's the replacement.'

'And strictly heterosexual, huh?'

She nodded.

I chewed my lip thoughtfully, trying to ignore the verbal thrusts and parries which didn't appear in the script but which had now developed between Catherine and Julian.

'Are they always like this?' I asked.

'Like what?'

'At each other's throats.'

'Invariably. There's no real malice, it's known as friendly repartee.' She could have fooled me. Catherine was waving a hand at Amanda's blouse and giving Julian some private tuition, 'They're called mammary glands, darling, or haven't you seen a pair since you were weaned?'

'At least I *was* weaned, Catherine *dear*. You were bloody quarried!'

'But with the correct hormone balance, darling, that's the difference.'

'Damn bitch!' Julian glared, almost stammering. 'Damn invidious bitch!'

As the invective raged, Karan looked from me to Julian and then back to me again. 'You're looking very serious,' she said.

'First day on the set and I'm already fitting up a suspect,' I admitted.

'Julian?'

'He looks promising—it's certainly an interesting situation. Look at it from a conventional angle. Cast yourself as the co-star and your boyfriend as the director. How would you feel if the leading lady flexed her co-producer muscles and sacked him?'

'I haven't got a boyfriend.'

I grinned, pleased. 'Whether you have or you haven't is irrelevant,' I said. 'Hypothetically how would you feel?'

'Pretty bitter I suppose, but it's hardly comparable——'

'In their world the relationship is identical.'

'No.' She shook her head emphatically. 'It doesn't make sense.'

'It does if you work on the premise that the accidents are being directed at Catherine as a person and not at the film as a whole.'

'With what end in mind?'

I didn't reply. The voice of Sidney Newton-Smith put paid to any further speculation.

'All right, quiet everybody! I want to get this in ONE take!'

The camera started.

'We're rolling.'

'Catherine's hair!' Delgado frantically waved a woman on to the set.

An expert flick of a comb. A puff of an aerosol.

'Scene numbers.'

'*Devil Take The Loser*—scene twenty-four—take one . . .' The clapperboard jumped.

'Action!'

It started well. The pretence of playing a lusty all-masculine jockey certainly seemed real enough as Julian, bridle in hand, wrapped the reins playfully around Amanda's throat and dragged her towards his lips. The girl's reactions were good, too. Her facial expressions, the mock struggling as she beat her tiny fists against his chest, the unwilling yet challenging cries of: 'You're hurting me, Bob . . . Not here, not now . . . If mother sees us . . .'

Mother *was* seeing. The camera dollied in to show the embittered look on Catherine's face as she stood in the doorway, screened behind a pillar of racing hampers.

I felt Karan's mouth against my ear as she whispered, 'Catherine plays Sheila Crossland, a frustrated trainer's wife who has an unhealthy passion for young jockeys. Julian—Bob Drury in the story, is in the pay of a betting syndicate and has been throwing races. Sheila has found out——'

'And is dabbling in blackmail to satisfy her libidinous needs,' I whispered back.

'You *have* read the book.'

'Not "the" book. Just others with a similar plot.'

'Well I think it's good,' she pulled a face. 'Besides, the oldest cliché in the world can still work if you have an actress of Catherine's calibre.'

The part suited her personality well enough. Even I found myself holding my breath as she stepped from the shadows and unleased her neurotic energy at Julian.

'How very cosy,' she said, her eyes flitting over the aggregation o í tack. 'Have you a fetish for leather, Mr Drury? Does the smell and feel of it arouse your innermost passions? I shall have to remember that—yes, yes, indeed.' A calculated pause, a widening of the eyes, then, 'Perhaps for the moment at least, you'd care to curb your desires and *take your filthy hands off my daughter!*'

'Mother . . .' Amanda began.

'Get out you little slut!'

'She stays.' Julian's fingers tightened around the reins.

'You dare to contradict——'

'Yes, Sheila—I dare! I don't care about your threats, and I don't

26

care about you. I'm in love with Trudy and . . .' he faltered, dropped his hands in disgust and turned to Newton-Smith. 'I can't say this schmaltz, Sidney. It just isn't me. This crappy dialogue went out with two and ninepenny cinema seats.'

'Cut it! God al-bloody-mighty, cut it!' Delgado blustered, reaching for his tin of lozenges.

Catherine sighed elaborately.

'Keep that camera rolling!' Newton-Smith countermanded the order. He said to Julian, 'O.K., so the writer's stretched it a little—so let's see how you can handle it, huh?'

'Stretched it? Christ this dialogue will rupture the whole scene.'

'I thought it was quite romantic,' Amanda put in.

'Romantic? Bloody-hell, this is supposed to be a thriller, not a re-make of *Wuthering Heights*.'

'Might the leading lady be consulted?' Catherine asked icily.

A look of strain passed over the director's face.

'If I were Bette Davis I'd probably produce my fabled line: And what am I supposed to do? Stand here with egg on my face?'

'A moment Catherine,' Newton-Smith pleaded.

'But as I'm not Bette Davis,' she pressed on resolutely, 'I'll wait patiently for Sidney to decide whether it's the dialogue that's suspect, or Julian's inability to deliver it.'

'Thank you, Catherine,' Newton-Smith ran a hand over his naked scalp. 'Pick up the line Julian—*please*.'

As poses were regained and the grip on the reins re-tightened, I had the feeling that had the leather choker been around Catherine's neck Julian would have felt no compunction in strangling the last breath from her body.

He cleared his throat. 'I'm in love with Trudy . . .'

The ensuing dialogue *was* a load of schmaltz. Julian valiantly battled his way through every poetical love-and-the-world-well-lost sentence of it. Catherine carried herself arrogantly, delivering her testy lines with professional conviction. The lovely Amanda enhanced the mélange of emotions by offering a few reconciliatory words, and of course the inevitable tear.

'So threaten away, Sheila,' he wound up, his fingers hovering over Amanda's cleavage. 'Curse, snarl, and bite as much as you like. Expose me to the Jockey Club for all I care. I want your daughter and by God I'm going to have her!'

27

The tear was savage. The effect startling. Julian looked aghast as the denim split apart to reveal Amanda's breasts in all their naked glory.

'Cut! Cut!' Newton-Smith's voice was hoarse. 'The silly cow's not wearing a bra!'

'I'm sorry . . . I thought . . .' Amanda blushed and did a hasty cover-up job.

Delgado lifted his clenched fists to a heaven that didn't give a damn about producers with schedules to keep and a budget to meet. 'What does she think we're making here?' he ranted. 'A bawdy boob movie? The script calls for taste—not a screenful of tit!'

Technicians and assistants grinned. I felt Karan giggle as she hid her face against my shoulder. Julian, lacking the poise to carry off the situation with dignity, accused Catherine and Amanda of conspiring to make him a laughing-stock. Amanda began to cry again, this time for real.

I had to admit to being amused by it all, but at the same time I was already beginning to regret my involvement. They say the old platitudes are the best; so bitten off more than I could chew just about summed up my feelings. I'd accepted the terms and like it or not, I was just going to have to smile as I swallowed them.

Sidney Newton-Smith had something a little more palatable in mind. He waved his arms in the air and in a strangled voice meant to silence any further outbursts, shouted, 'Lunch!'

It was a very gastronomic affair. Alverton Studios boasted a good menu and produced one—complete with wine, waiters, the works. Piped music provided a melodic background for the sporadic chatter which emerged in between the mouthfuls of *Sole Colbert*. Luke Taylor and son Anthony had arrived for the afternoon's shooting, and were tucking into American-size steaks.

'Of course things were very different when I worked for Metro,' Catherine reminisced, patting her mouth delicately with a napkin. 'In the mid-thirties Hollywood was bursting at the seams with young starlets who were snapped up and signed up by the major companies. Only a few survived. The rest, poor dears, were dropped from contract.'

'And here is one of those survivors.' Delgado reached across to stroke Catherine's hand. 'In the early days her need to be the best was almost a self-destructive passion. It still is to some extent.'

28

'Rex worries about her working too hard.' Luke looked up from his steak.

'Nonsense.' She flicked him a smile. She said to me, 'Rex groomed me you know, Simon. Today there is no grooming—more's the pity.'

The rider was added with some emphasis and was meant for Julian's ears. He sat with another group of actors, two tables away. He didn't turn around.

'You mustn't push him too hard, Catherine,' Newton-Smith's eyes strayed towards the group. 'We all know Julian can be temperamental, but he's a good actor and an asset to the picture. The younger generation go for him in a big way—am I right, Anthony?' He tossed the question to the boy.

'Sure thing,' he said, with an accent that matched his father's. 'Most of the chicks I know have pictures of him in their bedrooms.'

'What did I tell you, Catherine. Didn't I say we were catering for all tastes.'

'The guy's a fag,' Luke said to no one in particular.

'Who or what was Julian Knight two years ago?' Catherine asked deprecatingly. 'He was an attendant at a gas station who did a little modelling on the side, that's who. He was spotted by a producer, a notorious queer, served his "casting couch" apprenticeship, and was duly launched. No incubation period, no build-up. He found favour with youth audiences and so that made him a star. God, it's sickening!'

'Times change, Catherine,' Delgado murmured softly.

'If you dislike him so much,' I interposed, 'why the hell was he ever given the part?'

'If pictures were made on the premise that actors had to love each other in order to act together, then——'

'Of course, but surely you could have found someone more compatible.'

'He was chosen because he has the looks and the build of a jump jockey,' Delgado said. 'He was free for the duration of the picture, and relatively inexpensive to acquire.'

'He was also the only screwball crazy enough to accept the part,' Luke announced. 'The other three candidates flunked out.'

'Luke!' Catherine's head came up sharply.

'I'm sorry honey, but it's the truth. Don't let's kid ourselves that this film will make money—it won't. The only thing that's guaranteed are the losses, your losses.'

'That's completely untrue!' Delgado fidgeted with his huge signet ring, his suave affable manner suddenly in tatters. 'Loose talk like that can ruin a production before it even gets off the ground.'

'We've been over this so many times . . .' Catherine sighed.

'Well once more won't hurt, honey. I know it's your cash and you're entitled to do what you want with it, but it needles me to see you throwing it away on this emulsified garbage.'

Delgado's eyes narrowed instantly. 'You have *read* the script, I suppose?'

'Half a dozen times. Each time it reads worse than the time before.'

'So what do you suggest, Mr Taylor—a re-write of certain scenes?'

'A cancellation. Chop it now—salvage what capital you can.'

There was a momentary silence. Everyone seemed to be at an impasse.

'Any film is a risky business these days,' Newton-Smith temporized.

'I think we'd better ask the financier, don't you?' Delgado said sharply.

Catherine looked at Luke. 'I had no idea you felt so strongly——'

'Frankly I'm worried about your health, honey.'

'Health?' Delgado broke in. 'I thought the point at issue was cash, not Catherine's constitution.'

Luke flashed back with, 'The point at issue is this goddamn picture . . .'

The duel was on. Catherine sat between the two conflicting points of view, looking from one to the other and siding with neither. Taylor, with his brash, lay-it-on-the-line manner had opted for the bludgeon technique. Delgado wielded a skilful rapier, stabbing at his opponent with figures and box-office statistics while at the same time shielding the heroine with honeyed phrases and self-righteous optimism.

Karan and Newton-Smith kept out of it. I just sipped at my white wine, smiled pleasantly, and kept a mental tally of how many points were scored. It was all very enlightening. If I had any doubts about which side of the fence Luke Taylor stood, I wasn't left with any at the finale. The last word came from Catherine, and she ruled in favour of Delgado.

'I'm sorry, Luke,' she said, 'but you can't expect me to cast aside Rex's forty years in the industry. I relied on his judgement for my first picture and I'm relying on it now.' She gave him a big smile to nullify her frankness.

He didn't return it. He pushed his half-eaten steak away in disgust and mumbled something about getting some fresh air. The table lurched slightly as he climbed to his feet.

'What about Ant?' Catherine asked, glancing at the boy.

Taylor shrugged indifferently. 'We're not shackled together, Catherine.'

'I know but——'

'Try acting out your stepmother role, honey. It isn't one of your best performances, but you'll just have to cope for half-an-hour.'

Catherine took a deep breath and glared. Taylor turned on his heel and went.

The boy said, 'I wish you wouldn't call me Ant. I hate it, I tell you—I hate it!'

'W-what, dear?' Catherine was fumbling with a gold cigarette case. The facets of a diamond monogram flashed expensively as she snapped open the lid.

'My name's Anthony—not Ant. I loathe that name.'

'Now don't be childish, dear.'

'I'm not being childish——'

'That's enough, Anthony. Now . . . now finish your lunch.'

She laughed, a laugh which overplayed the effect of casualness as it fluttered ceilingwards on a plume of smoke.

As the seconds melted into minutes, the atmosphere slackened noticeably. Heads were huddled as Newton-Smith shared a joke with Karan. Delgado and Catherine comforted each other with the idiotic pretensions and nonsensical verbiage that only film people seem to indulge in.

Then there was Anthony. He was a weird kid if ever I've seen one. Thick, black hair with a fringe hanging over his forehead. Owl's eyes, dark like his father's, but piercing and huge. He seemed to take a delight in pointing them in my direction. The scrutiny of his stare was unsettling to say the least.

'How old are you?' he asked suddenly.

'Twenty-nine,' I said with a grin.

'I'm seventeen and just left school.'

31

Seventeen? My mind spiralled at that. I'd taken him for fourteen, fifteen at the most. Obviously Catherine's manner, her talking down to the boy, had affected my judgement.

'What was your first job?' he asked.

'I was apprenticed to a northern stable.'

'A jockey?'

'An apprentice jockey—I was only fifteen.'

'But you didn't stick it.'

'It didn't stick me. I was a late developer—I started sprouting, putting on weight.'

'So you quit.'

I nodded. 'I went to work at a stud. Brood mares and breeding instead of bruised bums and blisters.'

He grinned wryly. 'My stepmother owns horses—a whole string of them. Eight I think it was at the last count. Have you seen My Liberty? Oh boy, he's a beautiful animal.'

His eyes echoed the enthusiasm in his voice and widened dramatically.

'He's obviously your favourite,' I said.

'I rode him last week. Only a canter on the gallops of course, but——'

'Anthony!' Catherine broke in ruthlessly. 'I hope you're not trying to woo Mr Drake with this ridiculous notion you have about working with horses.'

'I was only——'

'Your father and I will decide what's best for you.'

'But dad says——'

'Horses indeed!' she scowled at him then turned to me. The smile snapped on as if governed by a time-switch. 'I've been neglecting you, Simon. Has Anthony been boring you terribly?'

'Your stepson seems to have a natural spontaneity for horses . . .' I said, and then I didn't say any more. Her eyes had left my face to do a mesmerized pan over my right shoulder. Her mouth drooped open.

'Catherine—are you all right?' Delgado asked, anxiously following her gaze.

'Oh, God!'

I turned.

Amanda Stewart was wading through the tables, picking her way towards the far end of the room. I couldn't see anything amiss, apart from the change of blouse. This one was intact, clinging lovingly to her figure as she bounced her way past us.

I swung back to Catherine. The sight of the girl had had a devastating effect on her composure. Her face had suddenly been transfigured into an obscene white mask of hysteria. Her tongue retracted as if to scream, but nothing came. Her jaw muscles locked, her eyes rolled up, and she slumped flaccidly forward. The table shivered under the excess weight.

'Christ, is she dead?' Anthony looked dazed.

'She's fainted,' Karan said. 'Help me . . . help me get her outside.'

Newton-Smith and the boy offered assistance. The colour had drained from Delgado's face. He seemed rooted to his chair, unable to take his eyes from the lipstick-smudged tablecloth.

Within seconds the animated conversations had withered into silence. I stood looking at Amanda Stewart, my brain groping for some plausible answer.

There were two—and they hit me simultaneously. The bow and the music. I mimed the words as the visual and audible symptoms passed fleetingly across my consciousness.

Amanda's blonde hair was tied back with a bow, a pink satin bow, which shimmered as she moved. The piped music was Rhapsody in Blue. I caught the last melodic bars as the track faded and switched to a more up-tempo number. It was easy to see how Catherine's mind had been triggered back to the death of the poodle. Coincidence? It had to be. A hideous one, but coincidence nevertheless. I scanned the faces. They were tight, sombre. Only Julian Knight had a slight quirk on his lips. The kind of quirk that gave me doubts. Doubts I didn't want.

'She's recovering. She'll be all right.' Karan returned, looking relieved.

Delgado mopped his brow with a napkin. 'Amen,' he said.

Chapter Three

THE THIRTIES was an exotic decade and Catherine Forrest's bedroom certainly reflected that mood. It was coolly furnished in pale turquoise, Chinese carpeting, dripping with crystal chandeliers, and heavy brocade curtaining. The actress sat propped up in a massive chenille-upholstered double bed, her sable cloak draped elegantly over her shoulders.

I stood in the doorway, drinking it all in. Catherine looked pale, yet incredibly beautiful. Lacking the sheen of cosmetics, her facial structure had the ethereal perfection of a Botticelli painting. A vision that was instantly shattered as she beckoned me to her side. Her voice was sharp, with an employer to employee ring about it.

'Have you something to report, Simon?'

'Nothing tangible,' I said.

She stared at me, completely motionless. If her eyelids hadn't flickered I might well have believed she'd stopped breathing.

'I have been checking,' I offered.

'And?' Her lips barely moved.

'The restaurant buys tapes periodically. Rhapsody in Blue just happened to be among the last batch.'

'A batch of how many?'

'A dozen or so.'

'A dozen or so with what . . . twenty tracks on each?'

'About that.'

'Two hundred and forty tracks in all and that tune just *happened* to be playing while Amanda just *happened* to be walking by.'

Her tone was cutting. 'I've questioned Amanda about the bow——' I began.

'And she says that she just *happens* to favour pink. Not blue, not green, not red, but pink!'

'Yes.'

'And you believe her?'

'You don't?'

34

'She's capricious, undisciplined, and a bitch. She tries to steal my scenes—you witnessed it yesterday. That farce with the blouse. Typical Amanda Stewart tactics. The crew loved it.'

'But hardly relevant. That was more to Julian's detriment than yours.'

Her lips retracted. 'Don't tell me you're in love with her too?'

I smiled, made no comment.

'Under the goldilocks image is a steel trap just waiting to be sprung.'

'A steel trap with a motive?'

'She was involved in a scandal a few years back. Her boyfriend was a narcotics pusher. I exposed him to the authorities. She's never forgiven me for it.'

That seemed like a pretty good answer. It was one more to chalk up to the ever-growing list of suspects that were swimming around my brain like a heady French wine. I'd only been on the case thirty-six hours, but I'd learned one thing for sure. Catherine Forrest didn't make friends, she made enemies. By the time I'd mentally totted them all up, I was left wondering why she hadn't a mantelpiece full of effigies.

'I've checked out the staircase prop and the lamp,' I said. 'It's possible they were doctored but it's more probable they were accidents.'

'Accidents?' She looked at me open-jawed. 'That third tread would have crumpled if the director had sneezed. Have you seen the bruises——'

'The reinforcing bar had come adrift. An oversight on the part of the carpenters. It happens.'

'Not to Catherine Forrest it doesn't—not without someone's head rolling,' she gave a cold smile, adding in a barbed voice, 'what about the spot lamp? The clamp had worked loose, is that it? An oversight on the part of the scaffolding riggers, no doubt.'

'Didn't it happen during a fight scene?'

'It did.'

'There was a lot of physical action, you stepped in to break up the fight and that's when——'

'Oh my God! You're not going to tell me it was caused through vibration.'

'I'm not saying it *was*, I'm saying it could have been.'

35

'It *could* have developed eyes, Simon dear, after all X did mark the spot.'

I quirked an eyebrow at her.

'It landed on a chalk mark—my positioning for the camera. Had I reached that mark a second before . . .' She dribbled off, shuddered.

I hadn't known about the chalk mark. I'd examined the lamp and its fixing bracket and accepted the lighting cameraman's account of the incident. No cross-examination, just a few idle questions slipped into a chat and a laugh over a cup of coffee. The rational part of my mind kept telling me that the two 'accidents' were totally unconnected with the effigy of Fiona. That was up to a few moments ago. Now the rational part had me admitting that the accuracy of the damn thing added a new dimension to the saga.

'Have you a cigarette, Simon?' Her tongue crept out to moisten her lips. 'Luke's confiscated mine. Since yesterday's emotional upset he's been treating me like an Olympus client. Organic diets, herbal pills, ugh!'

I broke open a pack of Chesterfield, teased two out. 'He's very anti *Devil Take The Loser*,' I said.

She paused, the filter hovering half-way to her mouth. Her eyes probed mine for a double meaning. I kept my face impassive as I snapped a lighter into flame.

She pulled in a lungful of smoke and released it with indifferent grace. 'The dear boy worries too much. This antipathy towards the film stems only from his concern for me. If *Devil* turns out to be a failure then Luke thinks the blast of bad publicity will shatter me beyond repair.'

'And will it?'

'If you mean will it be a failure, then I'll give you an emphatic *no*. As for shattering me beyond repair—well I think my previous answer cancels that one out, don't you?'

'Sure.' I smiled weakly. 'When will you be back on the set?'

'Tomorrow.'

'You'll be fit enough?'

'I'll be radiant.'

'They've juggled today's schedules,' I told her. 'A little location work at Berkeley stables.'

'Then you'll be in your element. You know how to get there?'

'I'll be with Karan.'

She glanced uneasily at me. 'Do you find her attractive?'

'Very,' I said truthfully.

'So do most of the crew. If they'd been given half a chance she'd be on the bed circuit by now.'

Her tone of omniscient guardianship annoyed me. I said nothing.

'I'd sack any man who laid a finger on her,' she added.

My mind rebelled against the innuendo. 'Three hundred a week buys you my powers of detection,' I averred, 'not my chastity.'

'I've dented your pride.' She seemed amused. 'I was simply asking you to keep an eye on her in my absence. To keep her away from over-sexed predators.'

'Surely she's old enough——'

'She's had a very strict convent school upbringing. She's fresh, unspoiled, and a little naïve where men are concerned. Perhaps I'm over-protective but——'

'If you're looking for a chaperon, you've got the wrong guy.'

'Have I? Isn't there a gentle person under that slick patina of toughness? Surely Simon Drake isn't the "wham, bam, thank you ma'am" type.' She shuddered distastefully. 'What a horrible phrase that is.'

'I'm not any *type*,' I retorted, 'I don't have a set pattern of behaviour or a strict code of ethics. If you're worried that I'll rape Karan on the way to the stables, then substitute her for an AA handbook. That way I'll confine my sex drive to the highways and byways and avoid a possible tour of her erogenous zones.'

'Sarcasm doesn't suit you,' she snapped.

'A probe into my morality suits me even less.'

'Howard Grant told me about your wife. So young, so tragic. Leukaemia wasn't it?'

It was my cue for a tactful withdrawal. 'If there's nothing else . . .' I began to walk out.

'Simon—please . . .'

I turned.

'Forgive me. I can be very obtuse at times. I'm upset, confused——'

'And you're behaving irrationally?'

'I think I must be.' She studied the glowing end of her cigarette, then mashed it into an ashtray. 'My mind is upside down. This awful business . . .'

'The message is perfectly clear, Miss Forrest,' I said bluntly. 'If you catch me in bed with Karan, I'll be out on my ear.'

'I didn't say that!' Her eyes displayed emphatic innocence.

'You have a habit of making everything sound like an ultimatum.'

'Nonsense.' She gave a little laugh.

'You sacked a director under similar circumstances,' I pointed out. 'Rupert Gibson?'

'He was having an affair with Julian.'

'He was sacked because he was a bad director. He was entirely wrong for the picture.'

'Wrong for the picture or wrong for you. You love to be loved, don't you Miss Forrest? The centre of attraction. Gibson was fired because he was a poof. A poof director with designs on the co-star. You found yourself playing second fiddle and you didn't like it.'

'How dare you . . .!'

'Oh, I dare because I'm not under contract. I can cut out of this assignment any time I want to. I've learned a lot since yesterday, spoken to a lot of people. Leaving aside a handful, I've yet to find someone who doesn't bear you a grudge.'

'Rex and Sidney . . .?'

'They're included in the handful. Delgado because he worships your money and the ground you walk on, and Newton-Smith because the stress of two alimony payments and the strain of keeping a mistress on the side doesn't afford him the luxury of grudges.'

She bridled.

'You wield the big stick,' I went on, 'get everyone jumping through your whimsical hoop. The company has only been shooting for a month and already you've sacked five people. Not exactly the best way to win friends.'

'I'm paying you to look after my interests,' she snapped maliciously, 'not offer me primitive psychiatry.'

'I'm offering you a dole queue of suspects,' I countered.

She laughed, a laugh which took on a thin edge, a shrillness which dissolved into a sob. I'd cracked the star-spangled armour and she was trying to make me feel guilty for doing it.

I did. Those moist sapphire eyes had me hating myself and hating her because she was a woman. The male reaction of either acceptance of the situation or a punch in the mouth, I could have handled. But Catherine Forrest, like most women who were hurt by the truth, brought up that old but impregnable defence of taking refuge in tears.

'D-don't be angry with me, Simon,' she pleaded. 'If you desert me now . . .'

There was a touch of pseudo-helplessness in the voice. A tear-jerker line that would have had pre-war audiences weeping in the aisles. It left me cold. 'Tell me about Rupert Gibson,' I said. 'What was his reaction when he found out he'd been fired?'

'He was very angry.'

'That I figured on.'

'He was also abusive.'

'Better. How about threats?'

'Yes,' she admitted reluctantly. 'He cursed me to hell and——' She paused, searching my eyes and considering whether to go on. 'He said something about evening the score. We were both very heated, but Rupert's not the type——'

'He couldn't have rigged the studio accidents, anyway—he wasn't on the pay-roll,' I interrupted, 'but Julian could.'

'Julian? You think they were accomplices?'

I shrugged. 'It's early days and I'm groping, speculating. Grant ran some lab tests on the effigy but they don't tell us much. Common or garden candle wax, chain-store ribbon and hat pins stocked by most milliners. The only finger-prints on the thing were yours.'

'Mine?' Her lips quivered.

'Sure. Wax is a pretty good recipient and when you handled it——'

'But I didn't.'

'You must have done.'

'I'm telling you I didn't.'

'You picked it up——'

She shook her head violently. 'I could see what it was just by look-ing at it. I couldn't . . . I wouldn't touch the hideous thing.'

I began to seek flaws in my reasoning. I scratched my head a couple of times and took a slow walk to the door and back. 'Correct me if I'm wrong,' I said, 'but Grant did take your prints for elimination purposes?'

'Yes, yes, but there must be a mistake. The prints on the effigy aren't mine.'

'You're absolutely sure you didn't——'

'God in heaven, how many more times! Maybe it's difficult for you to understand a woman's feelings, but when I lifted that lid . . .'

'You looked, you saw, and you shut it again?'

39

She nodded, swallowed hard.

Microscopic fidelity told me it didn't make sense. Perhaps the boys at forensic had made a gaff. Perhaps the optical comparator was malfunctioning. Perhaps Catherine had a bad memory, or perhaps I wasn't really hearing any of this and it wasn't me but some other poor guy who was expected to untangle the lack of continuity in this nickelodeon production.

'I'm going to be late.' I dragged back my sleeve, studied my wristwatch. 'I'm expected at the stables in forty minutes.'

'You'll do it in thirty if you take the Aston.'

I politely declined the offer. Rolling up in the star's automobile wasn't the best way to advertise my apparent neutrality. I headed for the door.

'About those prints . . .' she began, 'you do believe I'm telling the truth, don't you?'

'It's unimportant,' I said, forcing conviction into my voice. 'The lab must have made an error. I'll check it out.'

Her strained features relaxed a little. 'We're still friends?'

'I don't work for enemies, Miss Forrest.'

'That's an ambiguous answer.' She flapped a hand at me. 'Leave me some cigarettes Simon dear, there's a good boy.'

I took one out and tossed her the pack. For a brief moment I thought I detected a distinctly satisfied smile cross her face. A faithful-dog-Simon look; a hound who could be sent bounding off to fetch and carry, to be whistled at will. Perhaps the flickering flame from my lighter was playing tricks on my eyes.

'Roll it!' The two syllables clacked in the cold morning air. Sidney Newton-Smith, hands jammed deep into his pockets, astrakhan hat snugly covering his bald pate, looked anxiously towards the groaning Julian Knight as he floundered then collapsed among the straw bedding. The camera lens viewed the scene through the gap of a partially open loose-box door. A bank of lights illuminated the glistening technicolour blood as it dribbled from Julian's matted hair to the rollneck of his sweater. He writhed and mumbled incoherently as he elbowed himself into a semi-vertical position.

'Bob! Bob!' Amanda Stewart shouted the name on a signal from the director. The camera pulled back as she dashed into shot.

'This is just a warning, Trudy,' Julian said dazedly, wrapping an arm around Amanda's neck as she supported his weight. 'Unless I throw that race on Saturday I'm going to wind up in the morgue for sure.'

'Oh Bob, who . . .?'

'Those bastards in the syndicate. What a mess Trudy, what a godawful mess.'

'Don't talk darling—we'll find a way, some way . . .' She stroked his hair, flinched convincingly as the slime of synthetic blood came away on her fingers.

'Cut,' Newton-Smith said softly. He turned a full circle, pinching his nostrils and shaking his head. 'You're gawping Amanda. Don't gawp at your hand. We all know Julian's bleeding to death so there's no need to telegraph it. A brief glimpse, nothing more. Look at Julian. It's him you're concerned for. Lift your head a fraction. Good, good. Keep your mouth closed, clench your teeth. I want the expression to come from your eyes . . .'

'I'm frozen,' Karan whispered, tugging at the sleeve of my sheepskin jacket and beckoning me away from the tableau.

I looked into those big fun-sparkle eyes.

'Coffee?' she suggested.

'Sure thing,' I agreed.

'Let's go again,' Newton-Smith was saying. 'Make up! Keep that blood flowing, sweetheart. That's it. Clapperboard please. Turn over!'

We weaved a course around the lengths of trailing camera and sound equipment cable and broke through a cordon of onlooking stable lads. I was overwhelmed by the size of the place. The stable complex was one of the biggest I'd ever encountered. There must have been at least ninety loose-boxes, all of them spotless and immaculately maintained. An indoor school, isolation units, modern harness and fodder rooms, double-railed paddocks and superb gallops and training grounds. Berkeley stables certainly had the lot, including some 300 acres of land.

'Quite a spread,' I said to Karan as she guided me towards the lads' rest room.

'Only the best for Miss Forrest,' she confessed softly.

I looked briefly back. 'Are you sure we won't be missed?' I asked.

'Uh, uh. They'll be shooting the loose-box scene until lunch.'

'And then?'

'Sidney hopes to squeeze in a couple of short sequences of Patch on the gallops. You know he's doubling for Julian?'

'Patrick Hunter, the stable jockey?'

'Mm. You've met?'

I shook my head.

'Well now's your chance,' she tilted her chin towards the far end of the yard.

I followed her gaze. A horse and rider were forging in our direction. An attractive black animal with an elegantly modelled head. He had a splendid physique, strong and low, and he was very much on his toes.

'That's Intruder,' Karan said.

'Owned by the producer-man.'

She looked amused. 'You've been doing your homework.'

'I've been studying the form book as an alternative to that lousy script,' I told her, chewing on my lip for a few seconds and adding with a show of racing expertise, 'Intruder arrived from France five months ago. Over there he was a good horse—won several high value races in fact. Over here he appears to have gone a little sour. Apart from one victory in a moderate race at Doncaster, he's been duck-egging.'

'Duck-what?'

'Not finishing in the frame. He was ninth in the Marlow Ropes, seventh in the Cheltenham trial, and fifth in the White Lodge.'

'Are they all races?'

'All hurdle races, yes.

'Ninth, seventh, fifth.' She did mental calculations. 'He's improving.'

I grinned. 'At the price Rex Delgado paid for the animal I doubt if he'd be impressed by your dialectics.'

'Big word, Mr Drake, are you trying to impress me?'

'Are you the impressionable type, Miss Langford?'

'No.'

'Then my noun, like Intruder's form, couldn't possibly impress anyone.'

She pulled a face and shook her chestnut hair in a cute little girl way. For a moment I felt drawn towards her seductively outlined body, warm, soft. I was engulfed on a wave of her perfume, intoxicated and transported far away from the clatter of film cans and the smell of horseflesh.

'Hello there,' a voice said with assumed familiarity, breaking the spell. 'You must be Simon Drake.'

I looked up at a leathery sweat-blistered complexion, a pair of alert blue eyes, and a set of very white teeth.

'Patch Hunter's the name,' he added, swinging a leg over Intruder's withers and sliding effortlessly to the ground.

'You know me?' I said, slightly at a loss.

'Know of you. Your reputation has preceded you.'

I lifted my eyebrows.

'Turf Security Division, right? Under normal circumstances I should be quaking in my boots.' He wiped his hand on his jodhpurs then jabbed it towards me. 'When Mr Delgado phoned to say he'd engaged a racing adviser called Simon Drake, well the name just clicked. I don't know where he got you from, but he certainly didn't know who you were. I put him right, of course.' He slapped my palm enthusiastically. 'Perhaps he doesn't read the Sunday papers, huh?'

He was referring to a couple of stories which had featured me as a sort of comic-strip hero who specialized in worming out and exposing the insidious villains who lurked in the depths of the racing underworld. (Their words, not mine.) That's why I was now inwardly wincing and working hard at returning his smile.

'I suppose you really are the racing adviser?' he said almost absently, handing the reins to a waiting lad. 'It wouldn't surprise me if you were using this status as a T.S.D. cover.'

That was a gut-twister all right. It rocked me.

'Simon's freelance,' Karan came to my rescue. 'The Security Division doesn't own him. For this type of film his knowledge is second to none.'

'I was kidding sweetheart—kidding see.' Hunter laughed good-naturedly, adding, 'Did you see the way she sprang to your defence, Simon? Jeez—what have you got that I haven't?' He clapped a hand on my shoulder and chuckled, 'I'll tell you what you *haven't* got, and that's Catherine Forrest. If she were here she'd be looming ominously between you, as threatening as "the Chair" at Aintree.'

He had such an easy manner, such a light-hearted way of saying things, that I couldn't help cracking my face and enjoying the joke.

Karan didn't share my amusement. 'That's not funny,' she said. 'Miss Forrest has been——'

'Like a mother to me,' Hunter interjected.

'Yes she has.'

'Well mother isn't here now. You're alone with three lecherous males bent only on——' he paused dramatically. 'Is Julian Knight around?'

'Yes he is.'

'Then I'll re-phrase that last bit. *Intent* only on having their way with you. So you're helpless my child . . .!' His fingers became claws as he did his pantomine villain impersonation.

'Go away.' Karan covered her eyes. 'You're incorrigible.'

Hunter laughed uncontrollably.

'*Three* males?' I queried shortly.

'Frankie Wade,' he said, guiding me towards the rest room. 'Not very masculine, but I'm conceding a point. I'll always give a guy the benefit of the doubt. Some say Frankie was so puny when he was born that they threw him away and kept the afterbirth.'

'Don't be horrible,' Karan said.

'Don't be so serious,' he tweaked her nose and booted open the door. 'O.K., Wade,' he lowered his voice and spiked it with an American accent, 'Turf Security—stay cool and nobody gets hurt.'

'Bollocks,' came the reply.

'Oh, beautiful. I hope you realize there's a lady present.'

He sat with his back to the door, thumbing through a copy of *Pacemaker*. 'You don't know any ladies, Patch—except perhaps the brick built bog in the High Street.'

'I'm standing here with Karan Langford.'

'No way. She's tied to Catherine Forrest's apron strings.

'I'm wearing the apron,' I said.

'What . . .!' He sprang to his feet sending a can of Coke and a magazine rack flying. His young face flushed sheepishly as a grinning Patch Hunter made the introductions.

'S-so you really are Security Division?' he stammered.

Hunter cut in with, 'Of course he is. Simon Drake is here to investigate your insatiable thirst for Coca-Cola. You're getting through a case a week, kid. Say, what are you doing with the stuff—putting it in the horses' water buckets?'

'Now look, Patch——'

'Don't talk—listen! You know it contains cocaine? Well a guy in the States got his horse disqualified for wetting its whistle with Coke. It showed in the dope tests, see. You've been doing the same. Admit it, Wade. What's a five-year ban to a young kid like you.'

'Is it true?' He looked at me for confirmation. He was shorter than Hunter, more angular and bony with slightly bowed legs in weathered Levi's.

'Perfectly true about the horse and the Coke,' I said, suppressing a grin. 'A load of bilge about the Security Division suspecting you of doing the same.'

Hunter chuckled throatily.

'Somebody oughta lock you away . . .' Wade took the joke in good part and retaliated with a few light punches to Hunter's jut of jaw.

Karan looked bewildered by all this tomfoolery. She lifted and dropped her slim shoulders and said, '*Men*' in as deprecating a manner as she could. Hunter and Wade continued to clown around as I fed a fistful of two-pence pieces into an unco-ordinated vending machine which eventually obliged by coughing out four coffees.

'I've got to have a shave and a shower,' Hunter announced shortly, ploughing fingers through his scalp and yawning. 'Today's call-sheet requires me to be changed and mounted by two p.m.'

Wade grinned from ear to ear. 'Highwayman, isn't it?'

'I should bloody-well hope so,' Hunter feigned indignance and added in an effeminate voice, 'Have I got to suffer these insults from junior jockeys? God knows I'm bending over backwards to help.'

Wade convulsed into laughter.

'Make sure you pick up the right kit this time,' Karan put in, still unamused.

'That won't happen again, my love. This is the second session of wearing. Mine will smell of sweat and horses—Julian's will smell of lavender water.'

That set Wade off again. He gurgled and coughed as he choked on a mouthful of coffee.

'How many of Miss Forrest's horses are being used?' I asked, attempting to get the conversation back on some kind of footing.

'All of them,' Hunter said. 'All of them, that is, except for My Liberty. He's too valuable an animal to risk the possibility of an accident.'

'He's won the Champion Hurdle for the last two years in succession,' Wade informed me, coming up for air. 'This year he'll make it a treble.'

'Nothing to touch him,' Hunter agreed. 'Class, sheer class.'

Karan was about to add to the exultations, but an unexpected enquiry beat her to it.

'I'm sorry to intrude,' said a liltingly soft voice, 'but has anyone seen Mr Julian Knight?'

We all turned. A small, tidy man with pale insipid eyes behind gold-rimmed glasses, stood in the doorway. He was forty-something and he was smiling. He ran a delicate hand through hair that was greying aristocratically at the temples and repeated the question.

'He's filming,' Hunter said brusquely.

'They've broken for lunch.'

Hunter shrugged.

'Karan?'

'I'm surprised you've come here Rupert,' she said tight-lipped. 'If Miss Forrest——'

'I understand she's unwell,' he picked at a spotless fingernail, still smiling. 'Nothing too distressing, I trust.'

'Are you Rupert Gibson,' I interposed, 'one time director of *Devil*?'

A small nod confirmed that he was, and I received a cold, emulsive handshake for my politeness.

'Charmed my dear fellow, absolutely charmed.' I caught the glint of a gold filling and a hint of cynicism as he added, 'Racing Adviser, eh? Well I hope you manage to stay the course, yes indeed.'

'That sounds almost premonitory,' I said.

'I can only describe it as a vague but disturbing feeling of danger. Jinxed, the crew used to say. Doomed to disaster would be a more apt prediction.'

'Go peddle your tidings of woe somewhere else,' Hunter grunted impatiently.

'I'm sorry if I'm boring you, Patrick.'

'You are.'

He shrugged in a rather affected way.

'Put your hand on the knob, turn it to the left and the door opens inwards.'

'Thank you.' Those pale eyes travelled over each one of us in turn. 'I wish you luck. All of you.'

46

With the smile still intact, he gave a graceful little flourish of his hand and left.

Karen looked a trifle embarrassed. Hunter and Wade didn't exchange any more wisecracks, and I just stared at the scum on my coffee, letting a few facts and a multitude of fancies swim disjointedly round my brain.

Doomed to disaster? A hackneyed expression all right, but coming from Gibson's lips, the words had a cold ring of truth about them. I needed to be alone and to think. My mind was alive with jocular jockeys, bosomy blondes with bows, harassed husbands, old queers and movie queens and . . . I blotted them out, groped for my cigarettes. I swore with muted fluency when I remembered where I'd left them.

Catherine Forrest made the uncompromising announcement: 'It's Rupert Gibson and Julian. They're both in it together.'

Karan and I had arrived back at Windsor. It was six p.m. and we were thawing out in front of a huge log fire, surrounded by baroque elegance and musky perfume. The lady of the house was alive, kicking, and dressed to kill in a sequin-encrusted evening gown. She paced the room like a bad-tempered thoroughbred, rattling her jewellery and expelling air through slightly flared nostrils. Every now and then she would throw back her mane of hair and whinny stepson Anthony off to his room, which only antagonized the boy. He dug in his heels and sat tight.

'Nothing would please Gibson more than an abandonment of *Devil*,' she went on bitterly. 'This would serve the double purpose of sending me down with my ship and thereby release Julian Knight from contract.'

'Would he welcome this release?'

'They can't bear to be separated. Gibson's already started work on another picture. If Julian were free he'd undoubtedly be manoeuvred into a lead part.'

'I see.'

'I hope you do, Simon. My nerves are nearly at breaking point. Gibson's barefaced arrival at the stables confirms they're planning more treachery. That mustn't be allowed to happen, do you understand?'

Her eyes told me that if I was nursing any contradictory thoughts, now was not the time to air them. 'I understand perfectly,' I said.

47

'I'm glad. Now tell me about today's filming.'

I reported our activities as accurately as I could remember them. It wasn't an informal chat, it was an interrogation. Karan was sent to make coffee and I was systematically grilled on every little detail. I had the feeling the answers would be cross-checked and Karan would be facing the same kind of questions long after I'd hit the road.

'Did you see My Liberty?' Anthony interrupted.

'A brief glimpse,' I said, glad of the diversion. 'You're right, he certainly is a beautiful horse.'

'You should see the way he jumps those hurdles. Winged Pegasus himself couldn't——'

'Will you be quiet!' Catherine sliced in scathingly.

'I was only——'

'You were only—*nothing*——' Her voice was tremulous. She took a grip on her emotions and added quietly, 'We're trying to talk business, Ant. You can see I'm distressed . . .'

'You're always distressed,' he retaliated. 'And don't call me Ant. You know how it needles me.'

'That's enough!' She raised a censorious hand. 'Go to your room.'

His jaw muscles bunched as he clenched down on his teeth. He looked briefly at me, hooked his thumbs arrogantly in his belt, and plunged out of the room. Two porcelain figurines caressed as they were caught in the slipstream from the slamming door.

'What on earth's happened to Karan? My mouth is parched. Luke's damn herbal pills I expect. God, I feel lousy . . .' The words tumbled out in a nervous rush.

'How about a drink?' I asked.

'The coffee——'

'The alcoholic kind.'

'Y-yes, of course.' She waved a hand towards an elaborately decorated corner cabinet. 'Being a teetotaller makes me a terrible hostess. Please help yourself.'

She sighed and folded languidly on to a gold-tasselled sofa. She stroked her hair with a finger, pushing a strand back behind her ear. The delicate skin, the flashing teeth, the long, graceful limbs. An armadillo hide under a flaccid exterior. Catherine Forrest, actress or woman? Or were the two so integrated they were inseparable.

I crossed to the cabinet, unhooked a glass the weight of an anvil and reached for the vodka. The telephone by my elbow seemed to jump visibly as it shrilled for attention.

'It's probably Luke or some damn newspaper reporter.' A limp hand flapped me to silence it. 'Be an angel, Simon.'

As the vodka trickled into the glass, Rhapsody in Blue trickled out of the earpiece. It was tinny and distorted and it sent thoughts darting frenetically through my mind. I had enough sense not to let these thoughts show on my face. I grunted something unintelligible and tossed the receiver back on to its rest.

'Who was it?' Catherine eyed me quizzically.

I swallowed neat vodka. 'Wrong number,' I said.

Chapter Four

MY BALLISTIC training had taught me that a ·44 Smith & Wesson Magnum revolver has a muzzle velocity of 1,570 ft per second and muzzle energy of 1,310 ft per lb. In simplified terms, it meant that the one in Catherine Forrest's left hand was close enough to leave a very nasty cleft between my eyebrows. She stood with feet slightly apart, arm stiffly extended, forefinger curled determinedly around the trigger. Her face was smooth and unlined, her lips full and petulant, her gaze intense.

The lady was in good company. Signed photographs of Ann Sheridan, Joan Crawford, Claudette Colbert, and the legendary Garbo also graced the walls of Rex Delgado's office. Cuttings from *Picture Show* and *Photoplay*, so brown you could barely read the print, were sandwiched behind glass and enclosed in neat gilt frames. Sealed for perusal and posterity. A museum of nostalgia.

I dropped down on my haunches and viewed the somewhat macabre contents of a large display cabinet. Swords, old pistols, manacles, and various items of clothing were housed within. The most gruesome was a severed head. It was realistically made of latex and bore a little card which announced: *Tales From the French Revolution, 1939.*

All the props had cards, and similarly each gave the name of the production they had appeared in. My eyes were drawn to an alabaster base with a spiked centre. The object which had once been impaled on the spike was missing. The card ran: *The House of Tyrrells, 1934.*

'Catherine's first film.' Delgado's voice broke into my thoughts. 'It dealt with the Colchester martyrs. Catherine gave a brilliant performance as Rose Allin. How are you on literary history, Mr Drake?'

I turned. 'Pretty lousy,' I admitted.

'Do you like my little collection?'

I smiled. He could take it either way.

'It's a hobby of mine. I keep a memento of all my pictures.'

'One's missing.' I indicated the base.

'I have the items cleaned periodically.' He waved me away and into a chair. His eyes sliced over me with the coldness of a surgeon's knife. He flipped open the top button of his jacket and parked himself behind his desk. 'I know all about you,' he added.

'Really,' I said.

'You're an investigator for the Security Division.'

'Freelance investigator,' I amended. 'You've been talking to Patch Hunter.'

'I've also been talking to Catherine Forrest.'

I held his gaze and trod carefully. 'What exactly . . . ?'

'Everything. She tells me you think it's Rupert Gibson.'

His answer hit me like a pile-driver. It was so direct it stung.

'Do you?' he asked quietly, adopting a confidential tone.

'It's too early,' I said just as quietly. 'Gibson's a possible front runner in a field of half a dozen or so.'

He showed me the hard furrows in his forehead.

'Don't look so offended,' I said. 'You're included in the half dozen.'

'I . . .?'

'Sure,' I jammed my elbows on the desk and leaned at him. 'You're one of the few without an apparent motive and that makes me twice as suspicious.'

He nodded, grunted. 'You're very thorough. I like that.'

'I'm also particular who I work for. A week ago the name Catherine Forrest registered distantly as a faded film actress who was big before I was born. A week from now and I'll still remember her as being big—notably her mouth.'

'Now don't be hasty——'

'The lady and I had a deal and you weren't part of it.'

'Please wait.' He caught hold of my sleeve with his left hand while his right fumbled for his tin of lozenges. 'Sam Goldwyn used to say a producer shouldn't get ulcers, he should give them. I'm unfortunate. Now let's talk this over calmly and rationally.'

'Who else knows?'

'Catherine has confided in me and only me.'

'Last night?'

'Yes.'

'Did she receive a melodic phone call after I'd left?'

51

'Several of them, in fact. At two a.m. she was in a highly charged state. She rang me because Luke was still out and because she couldn't get hold of you.'

I did a mental playback. The time checked. I'd been at Howard Grant's until the small hours sorting out the fingerprint conundrum. Two a.m. had found me gunning home along the Kingston by-pass wondering why I'd ever doubted the lab's fidelity. There weren't any may-be's. The prints on the effigy belonged unquestionably, undeniably, and irrefutably to Catherine Forrest.

Delgado was grunting worriedly about the star's mental well-being. 'She insists on working today,' he sighed. 'I've pleaded with her to rest, assured her we can shoot around her for a couple of days . . .'

'She's as safe here as anywhere,' I said. 'Just keep her away from plastic instruments that ring.'

'And you . . .?'

'My call-sheet says Kempton Park, two p.m. Somersault harness rehearsal.'

He looked at me pensively. 'You're staying?'

'My cover's in shreds and I feel vulnerable. I can't say I like you, Mr Delgado, and I can't say I'm overfond of Catherine Forrest. Instinct tells me I'm treading on very thin ice and previous experience tells me only a headcase would hang around.'

'So?'

'So insanity runs in my family.'

He breathed theatrical relief, lowering his head so I could smell the pomade on his hair. 'This evil bastard must be stopped,' he muttered. 'How much is Catherine paying you?'

'Three hundred a week plus expenses.'

'You're under-pricing yourself. You need an agent.'

'I'm doing it as a favour. Besides, money doesn't impress me.'

'Money impresses everyone. The only thing it can't buy is poverty.'

'Are you offering me some kind of alternative?'

'Better terms, Mr Drake. I'll double your fee plus a bonus for results.'

The smell of easy money wafted across the deck. It clashed with his pomade. 'I'm already hired,' I said.

'But I'm offering you——'

'I know what you're offering me. I just can't work out why you're offering it.'

'Let's say I like to be in the driving seat.'

'Well find yourself another vehicle. My upholstery would give you callouses.'

'Catherine——'

'A deal's a deal. Besides, I have a reputation for giving females a smooth ride.'

He flushed angrily. 'Very well—just keep me informed of any developments. The future of *Devil* is at stake, not to mention my reputation.'

I wasn't going to mention it. I gave him a quick bleak smile for effort and headed for the door.

'This is like strapping a pair of thirty-eight lungs into a padded bra,' Patch Hunter announced, screwing up his tanned face in an expression of agony and wheezing asthmatically. 'You'll have to slacken it off a notch, Bill. Either that or my ribs'll cave before I even reach the friggin' fence.'

The stunt arranger grinned and began loosening the leather fasteners. We stood grouped alongside the two furlong marker at Kempton, a slow unremitting drizzle scouring our faces and making life thoroughly uncomfortable. Frankie Wade, in a snazzy wind-cheater with waterproof breeches and boots, stamped his feet and blew on his hands. Unlike Hunter he wasn't going to get particularly wet. He didn't have a half-hook sticking out between his shoulder blades, and he wasn't going to be yanked from his horse in a back-somersault.

'Fine Bill, fine.' Hunter breathed rhythmically again as the leather waistcoat was adjusted. He held his hands high as an assistant slipped a sweater over his head. The half-hook appeared through a hole in the back of the garment.

'Remember to stretch the line tight,' the stunt arranger emphasized. 'Keep the tension all the way, and the instant you feel your goggles shatter push down hard on your irons and leave the rest to providence.'

'The back-flip's no problem,' Hunter said, putting a match to a cigarette. 'If I've any qualms at all, it's being blinded by that goddamn explosion.'

Bill Cooper tried to soothe his fears by indicating the tiny explosive cap built into one half of the goggles. Hunter would be wearing a precision made metal shield over his right eye, and this, the stunt arranger said, would give him maximum protection when the cap was detonated.

'At least you won't have a director yelling at you,' he added. 'Neither will you have the irritation of a fragmented blood capsule dribbling down your cheek. When they film this sequence for real, then you'll know what discomfort is.'

Rather him than me, I thought, watching as his eye was meticulously packed with cotton wool and the metal shield taped in place. Riding with only half-sight was one thing, having a hole blown through your goggles and back-somersaulting out of the saddle was quite another.

'A fiver says you'll bust your collar bone again,' Frankie Wade enthused.

'Make it a tenner and you're on,' Hunter retorted. 'I'll give it style sonny. It'll be a pleasure to steal your poppy.'

Both jockeys produced the necessary currency. As Hunter fastened his skull cap and made final goggle adjustments, I reached for my script and did a refresher on the impending action.

The scene was the highlight of the movie. Hunter, or Bob Drury in the story, was to be shot through the eye as he approached the last plain fence. His assailant would accomplish this with the aid of a high-powered rifle and by positioning himself in the commentary box. On film it would look genuine enough. In reality the shattering plastic would have been detonated by remote control, thereby simulating the effect of a striking bullet. The ensuing back-flip by Hunter would add extra impact to the spectacle.

I looked at Wade. 'Will Highwayman jump the fence without a pilot?'

'Sure he will,' he said expansively, 'I'll be alongside on Bright Babe. We'll ping over it together.'

'I'll really be motoring into that fence,' Hunter interjected. 'Highwayman'll be about two strides from take-off when I flip out of the seat. It'll all happen so fast he won't have time to run out or refuse.'

'Let's hope he doesn't tip up,' I said.

'Not a chance. This animal's a neat fluent jumper. That's why he's being used—he never puts a foot wrong.'

Several shreds of tobacco clung to his lower lip as he removed his cigarette and prised loose his top set of teeth. 'Take care of my falsies,' he said, wrapping them in a handkerchief and pushing them into my pocket. 'It wouldn't be good for my image if they popped out during the jerk.'

'He keeps 'em in race days,' Wade quipped. 'Just in case he's caught in a photo-finish.'

Bill Cooper said, 'We'll soap-up both horses on the day. Plenty of mud and sweat for these chalk jockeys too.'

Hunter took the insult in good part. He leered at Cooper, said to me, 'This is just the dummy run, see Simon—and I'm the bloody dummy. A rehearsal to make sure these T.N.T. wizards get their mixtures——' He tailed off, squinted his good eye towards the distant fence. 'Am I seeing fairies, or is that Julian Knight?'

Wade followed his gaze. 'You are seeing fairies and that is Julian Knight.'

'What the hell's he doing here? He's not listed on the call-sheet.'

'He's not shooting today,' Cooper put in. 'I guess he's just come for a gander.'

'Sweet Jesus, that's all I need! A bloody bum-bandit gawping at me from the rails.'

'There's a car parked by those dolls,' Wade pointed a finger. 'Looks like Gibson's Datsun to me.'

'Shit!' Hunter's whip cracked against his boot. 'They'll spoil my concentration.'

'Not if I sort them out,' I submitted, relishing the chance of tackling the duo.

'You mind he doesn't clobber you with his dorothy bag.'

'What time's the off?'

'Any bloody minute.'

'Say ten minutes.' Cooper consulted his wristwatch, adding slowly and coolly that the somersault harness had to be attached to the saddle and these things couldn't be rushed.

'Right, let's have 'em.' Hunter pointed to the horse manager.

Hooves rattled the metal ramp as Bright Babe and Highwayman were led from the travelling box to the turf. A bay and a chestnut. Both nice lookers and splendidly turned out. I wished Hunter luck and crossed to the studio truck.

The solitary fence, specifically erected for this sequence, stood 150 yards from the winning post. Julian Knight clad in fur jacket, fisherman's sweater and a floppy urchin-style cap, stood alongside it.

He was talking to an assistant and puffing on a cheroot with affected abandon. Every now and then he would finger the contrived tuft of hair which drooped casually over his forehead. He smiled when he saw me. Not a particularly pleasant smile. More the kind a vampire might give after transfusing a hearty meal.

'Have you seen this miracle of modern science, Drake?' He indicated the small electronic detonator in the assistant's hand. 'Remote control, terribly technical. You just flick a switch to explode Patrick's goggles—well *my* goggles really. That's me on Highwayman, you know—Bob Drury.' His clear-lacquered nails fluttered gaily as he turned to view Hunter. 'Very impressive. Don't you think I look manly?'

The assistant replied with an uninhibited belch, mumbled something about seeing the production manager and departed.

'Can we talk?' I said.

'Talk?'

'Over by the car. You, me, and Rupert Gibson.'

He studied his signet ring, said to it, 'Have we something to talk about?'

'I dare say we could work a conversation around Catherine Forrest.'

He grinned. 'My, my, what a droll sense of humour you have.'

'It's no comedy.' I nudged him gently but firmly towards the Datsun. 'Rupert looks lonely—shall we?'

'This is an unexpected pleasure.' Gibson smiled faintly as I settled myself into the rear seat. A cassette player was feeding music to the stereo speakers behind my head. Gibson leaned forward to depress the off-button.

'Mantovani?' I ventured.

'Mancini,' he said.

I tapped my temple, watching the eyes behind those thick lenses. 'Rhapsody in Blue?'

They didn't flicker. 'Theme from Limelight. Are you a music lover, Mr Drake?'

'I'm learning to appreciate it, Mr Gibson. It's amazing the way certain melodies affect certain people. How a few bars of a tune can reawaken the memory of a long-forgotten holiday, or a lost romance, or even a death.'

He looked at me unflinchingly, amusement in his eyes.

I lit a cigarette, blew smoke towards Julian's left ear. 'Music can be a very powerful instrument, Mr Knight.'

'Why are you going off on this insane tangent,' he grated. 'What the hell's all this to do with Catherine Forrest?'

'She's being mentally tortured,' I told him, smiling at the almost masculine affrontery in his voice. 'Slowly, systematically, and symphonically, she's being driven out of her mind.'

There was no immediate reaction to that. Julian daubed spittle on his cheroot in an attempt to seal up a frayed part of the leaf, while Gibson toyed absently with the steering wheel, pursing his lips as though he might have had thoughts that mattered.

I said to Julian, 'If the film was made void you'd be released from contract.'

'So?'

'So maybe that would suit you just fine.'

'That's as good as an accusation!' His thin fingers snapped the cheroot.

'You're not saying you wouldn't like to be free?'

'I can wait. A few more weeks won't harm me one way or the other.'

'But you'll miss out on Mr Gibson's picture. Don't the schedules overlap?'

His eyes narrowed instantly. 'You're very well informed for a racing adviser. Just what or who the hell are you?'

'Catherine Forrest's tutelary saint. I protect her from gay actors who might be harbouring nasty thoughts.'

'You've got a bloody——'

'Calm down Julian.' Gibson patted his hand. 'Mr Drake is trying to needle you into saying something you might regret. Something we both might regret.'

He snorted moodily and regarded me with an expression of distaste.

'Do you admire Catherine as an actress?' I asked shortly.

'I did when I was ten. Now she's like a worn-out opera singer busting a gut to sing *La Traviata*—she doesn't know when to quit.'

Gibson said, almost gently, 'She has a notorious reputation for instability. If she's being mentally tortured then it's of her own making. Nothing more than a figment of over-wrought female imagination.'

'Then it's contagious,' I said.

'You have corroborative proof?'

'I have half a dozen hat-pins, a dead dog, and a musical ear.'

'What kind of answer do you call that?' Julian growled.

'It's supposedly called voodoo, Mr Knight. Have you ever dabbled in the occult?'

'Oh, all the time,' he replied mockingly. 'My local coven and I dance around naked on Mondays and Fridays. We work ourselves into a frenzy and sacrifice things. You'd be surprised what we could do with a lock of Catherine Forrest's hair. *No*, of course I don't dabble in the bloody occult!'

Gibson kneaded his double chin and looked thoughtful.

'You have something to tell me?' I prompted.

'The last time we met I told you the picture was jinxed. I still hold that opinion. If you're looking for a material suspect then you'd be advised to question Rick Storm.'

I frowned.

'That's his stage name.'

'An actor?'

'A singer in a pop group. Amanda's husband.'

'His real name's Peter Brown,' Julian sniffed. 'He's an uncouth bum. He used to work as a scaffolding rigger at Alverton.'

'Catherine put him in the Scrubbs for twelve months,' Gibson continued. 'It was in all the papers, you must have read about it.'

Maybe I had. It wasn't worth taxing my memory. It wasn't that important. The drug-pushing boyfriend was now the husband. That was news. That was important.

'The group is called Incantation,' Gibson remarked casually. 'Storm dresses up as a witch-doctor. He wears a tribal mask plus all the trappings.' He paused, adding equably, 'It's quite an act. Almost bordering on the satanic.'

Now he was marking my card. An aniseed diversion from his camp to Storm's. I didn't give him the satisfaction of looking interested. I had a sweet tooth but an open mind.

'The flag's up.' Julian's face tightened in anticipation. He lifted binoculars to his eyes. Gibson sat forward, squinting expectantly through the windscreen. The assistant with the detonator returned the signal. Hooves resounded on the Kempton turf as Highwayman and Bright Babe started their run towards the fence.

Gibson tapped his teeth thoughtfully. 'This could be dangerous for Hunter.'

'True,' Julian agreed, 'but he's more than capable if he's sober.'

Two hundred and fifty yards.

'Does he drink?' I asked absently.

'He's a first class piss-artist.'

One hundred and fifty. A good gallop. Both jockeys riding stirrup to stirrup. Clods of earth flying in their wake.

Gibson said, 'Delgado bawled him out when Intruder finished fifth in the White Lodge. He found out Hunter had been on the booze the night before. The man's a fool to himself.'

One hundred yards.

'I'm looking good,' Julian released the binoculars from his eyes in order to show Gibson his egoistical smile. 'The public will love this sequence. It's such an athletic way to die.'

'It's only a rehearsal.'

'I know, but it's good, it's good.'

Fifty . . . forty . . . thirty . . . The assistant looked anxious, finger poised. Hunter snatched a glance towards us, then checked his mount, to adjust its pace. Wade hung slightly back. The five-foot wall of close-packed birch was only seconds away.

'Now!'

I flinched as the goggles shattered. Highwayman veered, then straightened, meeting the fence right for the take-off. Boots thrusting down on irons. Reins released. Chestnut forelegs stretching high as the big horse powered itself over the obstacle. Hunter went upwards and backwards, almost doing a headstand on the animal's rump. The half-hook disengaged. He landed feet first, wobbled slightly, then slid inelegantly on to his backside. Wade yelled gleefully as he sailed over on Bright Babe.

'Shit hot, huh!' Hunter shouted, tossing his fractured goggles high in the air and shaking his fists in triumph. He staggered to his feet and forged towards the Datsun. 'I gave it style, eh Simon? Plenty of style, yeah?'

I congratulated him and dug into my pocket for his dental work. Style he'd most certainly given it. That's more than could be said for that big toothless grin he was giving me now.

I arrived back at the studios a few minutes before six. I caught a flash of silver paintwork, heard a $5\frac{1}{2}$-litre roar from an engine. It missed me—just. A lady in one hell of a hurry.

Rex Delgado and Karan were circled in my headlight beams. They were running through the drizzle, waving, shouting, panting stertorously.

'That damn tune . . .' Delgado nearly fell onto the bonnet, his chest heaving. 'I couldn't stop her, Drake . . . She's hysterical . . . The psychic strains and stresses of late—God knows what she'll do.'

I flipped open the passenger door, told Karan to get in. Delgado leapt clear as I floored the accelerator, spun the wheel full lock, and slewed the M.G. full circle. The blast from my horn sounded a requiem for the gateman. The guy had the sense to stand clear.

Karan looked tight-lipped and pensive.

'Where's she heading?' I asked.

'I don't know—I suppose the house——' She halted rather helplessly.

'Route?'

'What?'

'What route does Catherine take?'

She pulled herself together and gave me directions. I traversed a side street and nearly up-ended some stupid sod of a cyclist with no damn back light.

'You should wear your seat-belt,' Karan said absently, indicating me to turn right. 'Here, let me help you on with it.'

As she snapped home the catch I did a forward jerk. The tongue shot out of its keeper.

'Hercules unchained,' I grinned. 'It impresses young ladies.'

'It doesn't impress me. If you know it's faulty then get it fixed.'

I grunted. I wanted to like her but she wasn't making it easy.

We headed east along the main highway. Plenty of cars to overtake but no sign of the Aston. With a top speed of a hundred and sixty I can't say I expected to be sitting on its tail. But its progress, like mine, was surely being hampered by rush hour travellers.

Karan gave a little gasp and pointed to a cumulus of flashing blue lights. I dropped the revs and eased into the nearside lane of traffic. We crawled. An ambulance and a tide of uniformed humanity loomed ahead. Tyres crunched grimly over a scattering of tiny glass chips.

'Is it . . .?' Karan began.

I depressed the dash lighter, lowered the window, and peered out on the battery of onlookers.

It wasn't fourteen thousand quidsworth of precision Lagonda. More like fifty quidsworth of ancient Mini and whatever the going rate is for illuminated bollards.

'Thank God,' Karan breathed easily again.

The lighter snapped out, I touched it to a cigarette. 'The tune,' I asked, 'where and how did it happen?'

'B stage, by phone. The switchboard girl was instructed that all incoming calls to Catherine had to be first vetted by Mr Delgado. She was supposed to put them through to his office before transferring them to the set.'

'So what went wrong?'

'The girl went sick. She's pregnant and——'

'Her replacement wasn't briefed, uh? So in her ignorance she gives us all labour pains.'

'I spoke to her immediately afterwards. She said an American voice asked for Catherine. She thought the voice . . .'

'Yes?'

'Well, she thought it sounded like Luke Taylor.'

'An obvious association.'

'You don't believe it?'

'I believe somebody wants us to believe it. There's no disputing the guy has a motive, but he's never tried to hide it. Who hasn't heard his cry of "Stop the movie—I want the star to get off".'

'I suppose he would be more subtle about it,' she admitted.

'Do you like him?' I asked shortly.

'My boss is married to him, so naturally my allegiance——'

'Do you *like* him, Karan? Like, as in personalities being on the same wavelength. Like, as in, he's sweet, he's charming, he's groovy. I want to know how you really feel about him, not hear some secretarial college's indoctrination.'

'Don't be so abrupt!' She turned away, studied the rain sheeting against the passenger window. 'I quite like him, yes.'

'Have you ever slept together?'

She whirled on me.

'A casual question,' I said, 'one that had to be asked.'

'You have a disgusting mind.'

'It was pure before I grew up and adapted it to a disgusting world

61

full of disgusting people.' I touched the brakes and turned the M.G. left. A sign announced: *Windsor 3 miles*. No overhead lighting, just bleak woodland either side. I hit the main-beam, letting the headlights cut a swathe through the bowel-darkness. 'Can you see anything in this disgusting weather?' It was a cynical remark, not a question to be answered.

'There!'

'What?'

'Catherine's car on that picnic area. Pull in, Simon, pull in!'

I felt Karan's thigh rubbing against mine. Her small white teeth worked anxiously on her lower lip as she tugged at the steering wheel.

'Take it easy!' I yelled.

The nearside tyres were scoring the kerb. I swung into the opening, braked hard, then wished I hadn't done either. The wheels locked on the greasy surface and sent us skidding towards the Aston—an Aston as empty as a freshly dug grave. Just mud-spattered paintwork and those hypnotic little wipers slapping frenziedly across the headlamps.

I could see a depression of broken asphalt ahead. The shock absorbers banged as we dipped into it. I pumped the brakes hard, felt the tyres slew for grip. We lurched, then stopped.

'That was a crazy . . .' I found I was talking to myself. The M.G. was still rocking on its suspension but Karan had vacated her seat. I could see her white leather coat charting her progress as she battled through the driving rain.

'Miss Forrest! Miss Forrest!'

'Come bloody back!' I demanded, climbing out, the wind plucking at my jacket, ravaging my hair.

'She's gone, Simon, she's gone.'

'Go back to the car!'

Rain sparkled on her cheeks as she turned to look at me. Her eyes were wide, shiny, unblinking. I grabbed her hand and pulled her a little harder than I'd meant to. Unbalanced, she clung to me, her body rubbing against mine, her eyelashes brushing my neck. Only the sheeting rain came between us. Not that I felt it. All I felt was warmth, wildness, passion. For a brief, infinitesimal moment I thought she felt it too. But then she began to struggle, her feet tangled with something and she fell heavily on to her knees. A shoe shimmered icily with silver sequins in the darkness. Catherine's.

'Oh, my God,' Karan gasped as I stooped to retrieve it. 'You don't think . . .?'

'Shut up,' I said.

'W-what?'

'Shut up and listen.'

A scream sounded from the woodland torn from a throat more adapted for delivering scripted lines in the soundproofing of a studio. A scream laced with hysteria and delirium. The kind that made your flesh creep, made you question your hearing, even question your sanity.

I looked briefly towards Karan. She'd heard it too. Her throat muscles fluttered but no words came. She squirmed protestingly as I manhandled her back to the car. The anti-theft locks made sure she stayed there.

I thought feverishly as I picked my way towards the dense knot of trees. Why had Catherine stopped at this precise spot? Why had she abandoned the Aston? Why the hell hadn't she driven straight home?

Blackness and rain. What a foul, stinking, bastard of a night. My trousers flapped wetly against my ankles, the mud hampering my progress as it gathered on my shoes. The wind was flailing at my face forcing me to view my surroundings through slitted eyes, making navigation treacherous and making the whole damn sequence seem an illusion rather than a reality.

The scream again. Loud, and coming from my left.

I altered course, caught my foot in a divot, regained my equilibrium and forged on. I bulled through some bracken, dragged my tired legs over sodden grass and found myself at a clearing. I could see fresh hoof-marks under my feet as I leaned dazedly against a tree and blinked away the rain.

Christ! There she was. Ten yards away. She was still and rigid like a corpse locked in rigor mortis, and half-covered by the undergrowth. Her red Shantung dress clung wetly, bloodily, to her body; her hair hung in lank tendrils over her face, her tights were ripped and covered in leaf mould.

'Miss Forrest, are you all right?' A stupid bloody question. I put a finger to the carotid artery below her ear, feeling for a pulse.

Her eyelids flicked open. Her lipstick twisted into a repulsive pink gash as she tried to move her mouth. 'D-don't hit her . . . don't hit her . . . don't hit her . . .'

She kept repeating the words over and over, her voice monotone, as lifeless as her eyes. A half-conscious stupor. A condition that changed dramatically as I knelt beside her. She saw me and she screamed. The adrenalin started to pump, her arms began wind-milling, and as I tried to lift her she kicked and clawed like something possessed.

It isn't in my nature to hit women, and that goes double for screen goddesses. I did it as gently as possible. With a handkerchief wrapped around my fist, I delivered a crisp, clean uppercut to that fragile jaw. I doubted if she'd ever had her mouth shut so quickly before.

The soft going was hazardous on the trek back to the car. A hundred and twelve pounds of flaccid female can weigh heavily when you're tired. So can the questions—and I was supposed to be the guy with the answers.

So far so bad.

Chapter Five

LUKE TAYLOR had just come home. He was dressed in a pale blue pin-stripe with a wide cream tie knotted loosely beneath the collar of his silk shirt. He looked dumbfounded and a little annoyed. 'With the doctor, Simon? What the hell's happened now?'

I sank into the gold-tasselled sofa, lit my first cigarette since finding Catherine, and let Karan unwrap the whole bizarre sequence. I was clad in a bathrobe, a little on the big side with 'I love Luke' embroidered on the pocket. Karan had taken a hot shower and slipped into a dry white wine. She'd also slipped into a pretty scanty excuse for a housecoat. The girl had nice legs. Legs kissed by the summer sun and sprinkled with a sheen of golden down. Legs that set my hormones twitching every time she crossed them.

I was blocking out the curves and trying to concentrate on the angles. I was on my fourth vodka, hoping the stimulant might open my mind to something I'd missed. Winding the action forward, then winding it back. Over and over. Stop start, stop start. Mental fatigue first-class. Somehow, somewhere, sometime, maybe I'd remember something that mattered. At the moment it was a nebulous blur.

'It's this goddamn movie!' Luke ranted, striding across the broadloom to the drinks cabinet. 'Catherine's health has been on the decline for some time. Delgado won't be satisfied until she's had a complete nervous breakdown.'

'The doctor says she'll be all right after a week's rest,' Karan leaned forward clasping her bare knees. 'She's suffering from the effects of a very nasty shock.'

'And who gave it her, huh? And why?'

Karan glanced at me.

'Can you elucidate, Simon?' he said. 'You saw it first hand. I'd appreciate your version.'

I hardly heard him. I was looking at his mud-encrusted shoes, the saturated trouser bottoms of his otherwise dry suit. 'Do you wear an overcoat?' I asked.

'Sure I wear an overcoat.' He summoned a grin. 'It's raining, or hadn't you noticed?'

'So what did you do—drive or paddle home?'

'The shoes? I got a goddamn flat. I had to stop at a muddy pull-off.'

'That would explain the time lag.'

'What time lag?'

'Why it took you an hour and a half to drive ten miles.'

'Simon buddy, have you been checking on my movements?'

'I phoned the Olympus,' Karan interposed. 'We weren't sure what time you'd be home.'

He gave me a troubled smile as he slopped bourbon into a glass. 'Hardly the fastest wheel change on record,' I said dryly.

He turned, every muscle tense. 'You're beginning to sound like a cop. Are you trying to make a point?'

'If the police had found her instead of me . . .'

'Sure, sure. I'm grateful. The publicity would have been bad, real bad. You're staying the night?'

'If that's O.K.'

'Of course it's O.K. I'm in your debt.'

Karan didn't appear over-enthusiastic. She fidgeted, merely offering an occasional brief smile. It was a manner which constantly promised to ease into something more settled, more cordial, and never did.

Luke looked at me earnestly and said, 'What made Catherine stop at that picnic area, and why did she abandon the car?'

I shrugged. 'Perhaps she saw somebody she knew.'

'Like?'

'Her husband.'

'Me?'

'Your alibi's not good.'

He slammed his glass down so hard that three bourbon-soaked ice cubes cavorted over the rim and slithered across the table. Karan's eyes were giving me take-it-easy messages as I tried to catch him out. Had he rung Catherine at the studio today? Did it usually take him an hour to put on the spare? Would he mind if I looked at the punctured tyre? But Taylor was either too honest or too shrewd to be netted.

'I didn't have to change the wheel. I knew the spare had a split in it—something I've never got round to fixing—so I walked to a gas-station. A half-mile walk. I bought one of those cans of compressed

air that injects sealing foam into the tyre. Ring Catherine? No I
didn't. What if I had—what the hell's going on?'

'I think someone is trying to drive your wife out of her mind,' I
said.

'And by your questioning I guess you think that that someone is
me, huh?'

I grinned awkwardly. 'I'm sorry if I'm giving you a rough time,
but at the moment, as you Americans say, you're the only game in
town.'

His dark eyes looked slightly hostile as they jerked from me to the
door. The doctor threaded his way in.

'Catherine's asking for you, Mr Taylor,' he said.

'How is she?'

'She's under sedation.'

Luke checked his appearance in the mirror. He fiddled with his tie
for a few seconds then made a brisk exit.

Karan quizzed the doctor on Catherine's well-being.

'Physically she's in very good shape. Mentally . . .?' he paused,
sucked in his breath. 'Well, that's quite another story.'

'Has she spoken of what happened?' I asked.

'A few broken sentences, the odd incoherent word.'

'Can you be more specific?'

'I really . . .' He consulted his pocket-watch.

'It's important,' I coaxed.

'She said something about music. The car was alive with music, I
think those were her words.'

Karan and I exchanged glances.

'That's why she stopped,' I said.

He frowned.

'To get away from the music.'

'The music was inside her head, Mr Drake, not the car. She's been
under a great deal of pressure and this is the mind's way of rebelling
against it. A course of psychotherapy might——'

'I doubt it. Did she mention anything else—names for instance?'

'Gibbon or Gibson, something like that. The rest was unco-
ordinated. Delusional ravings about a horse and a woman with blood
on her hair. Now if you'll excuse me, I do have——'

'Other fee-paying clients, of course. You've been most helpful.'

He gave me a straight-lipped smile and followed Karan to the door.

I spent two or three minutes walking aimlessly around the room, meditating, working hard at untangling the cloying chaotic thoughts which crowded into my lagging brain. A patchwork piecing together of the facts as I now knew them. The tune was being used as a manipulator. Predictably, it had sent Catherine fleeing from the studio. Confused, emotionally volatile, she'd taken her usual route home along a dark country road with a picnic pull-in. On cue the tune had been triggered again. I didn't know how, I only knew it had produced the desired effect—escape. Catherine had stopped exactly where it had been planned for her to stop.

The ensuing part of the nightmare was complete supposition. I saw it as a horrific reconstruction of some past event. A carefully staged playlet. A horse, a girl with blood on her hair, Catherine's cries of: Don't hit her . . . don't hit her . . . It was all part of a fear technique to unbalance the actress.

Who was responsible? Thinking back to the doctor's recital it should have seemed a patently stupid and self-evident question. But Gibson just didn't gel. Most homosexuals abhorred violence. Not every horse runs according to the book, but the dramatics of a few hours ago just didn't seem his style.

Karan padded back into the room. I reached for the vodka and tried vainly to ponder on a few other suspects. Vainly, because my erotic imagination had decided it much preferred to ponder on the fleshly delights that lay hidden beneath a cotton voile housecoat. I could feel my mouth begin to dry up and it had nothing to do with the liquor.

'Rhapsody in Blue was playing inside the car. How, Simon?' Karan settled on the sofa, pulled her knees up to her chin, and peeked at me.

'Several possibilities,' I said.

'Give me a simple one to start with.'

'A simple one . . .' I feigned concentration. 'How about Julian in the back seat playing with his harmonica?'

'I don't think that's funny.'

I didn't think it was very funny either. But when a girl sits on a sofa apparently oblivious to the fact that she's showing more leg than a foal during 'presentation' then my double entendre's are never at their best.

I altered my viewpoint. 'A hidden tape-recorder or receiver might work,' I submitted, sliding casually next to her, letting my arm hang over the back of the sofa and then bringing it slowly . . .

She moved faster than a rector caught in a red-light raid. 'T-the tape-recorder would have to be fitted with a time-switch,' she said quickly.

I was too stupefied to feel indignant. I let my hand slide gracefully on to my knee. 'Yes,' I said. 'Yes, I suppose it would.'

'Not very likely, though,' she went on, groping for words. 'It couldn't rely on traffic conditions, so it couldn't possibly guarantee accuracy.'

'No,' I said. 'No, I suppose it couldn't.'

'Although I dare say a sophisticated piece of equipment——'

'Karan, baby.' I nestled against the soft resiliency of her breasts, looked deep into her eyes. Dark chestnut eyes flecked with amber. 'Circumstances have placed us in a sex situation. We're half nude, both feeling turned on, and we both want it—so stop trying to talk your way out of the inevitable.'

Her lashes fluttered and she blushed. 'Y-you're quite wrong,' she stammered. 'If I've given you the impression——'

'Stop apologizing. Modesty went out the day people started sending each other smutty birthday cards. There's been a sexual revolution, or haven't you heard?'

She put her hands over her ears, turned her face to the wall.

I caught hold of her chin and gave her a reasonably chaste kiss. I could feel her firm-nippled breasts heaving against my chest as she squirmed to break free.

'That was awful of you,' she breathed raggedly.

'Awful, awful,' I said.

'Y-you forced yourself on me.'

'Don't tell me it didn't give you a kick because I could feel your pulse racing.'

'You're horrible.'

'You're desirable.'

'I wish to get up.'

I said nothing.

'You're sitting on my hand.'

I sighed and shifted position. 'What's the matter, Karan? Am I jumping off too early? Are you going to report me to the stewards for interference? Or are you just immunized against sex?'

'I don't—I mean—well, men just don't kiss me like that.'

The second time around I aimed for quality—an intimate exploration that kisses are made of. French ones.

'God . . . you're unbelievable!' Her tone indicated it wasn't a compliment.

'O.K., so wipe the sensation from your mind. Kill it stone dead, or else savour it and look forward to the next time.'

'You're brash, conceited . . .'

'And you loved every lip-clinging second of it.'

'I hate you, Simon Drake!'

I was about to reply that I was rapidly falling out of love with her too, but the telephone bell beat me to it.

'The bedroom extension?' I queried.

'It's switched off.'

'Something you and it have in common.'

'Oh, shut up.' She looked confused. 'Shall I . . .?'

'Why not. If it's musical—hang up, if it's a heavy breather—tell him I sympathize.'

It was Rex Delgado and Karan was going to make full use of the diversion. Her nose went high in the air as she stroked her fingers lovingly along the flex. She looked as if she would be there for the duration. I said hallelujah and pulled up my sticks. The virtuous-little-girl act she was giving me was getting under my skin. I had another body to look over. One just as aggressive and with just as many curves, only this one wouldn't bite when handled.

'You're wearing my dad's raincoat and loafers,' a voice announced as I snapped open the Aston's driving door.

A heavily macintoshed figure sat hunched in the passenger seat. I'd have recognized those eyes and that curious lopsided grin anywhere. Anthony Taylor was the kind of kid who left an indelible impression.

'She goes mad if she sees me with a cigarette,' he said, pulling on the butt and feathering smoke at the windscreen.

'The "she" being your stepmother?'

'She's crazy. She throws fits and all sorts.

'You'll have to make allowances. She's unwell.'

'She's a psycho. You haven't heard her screaming at night, ranting

70

about the walls closing in on her. She has visions that put people in strait-jackets.'

I remembered Grant telling me much the same. I gave it a few seconds' thought, then kicked it out of my mind. Extraneous complications I could well do without. If I started believing that Catherine was really cuckoo then I might as well quit with a week's pay, a new suit, and my sanity in extenso.

'How long have you been out here?' I asked, pulling a flash from my pocket and snicking it on.

'Ten minutes, give or take.'

'Smoking, huh?'

'Yep.'

'You're very wet.'

'I spent the day at Berkeley stables. Chuck Busby's been schooling My Liberty.'

'Good jockey.' I began probing under the dash.

'He's better than good—he's the maestro. The best freelance . . . Hey, what are you doing?'

'Looking for the lost chord,' I said.

'The what . . . ?'

'Never mind. You were telling me about Busby, how good he is, why your stepmother uses him instead of Patch Hunter.'

'I didn't mention Patch Hunter.'

'My mistake. Tell me anyway.'

As he talked, I scrutinized, worming my way under the passenger side of the dash. Hunter was used regularly at one time, the boy said, until his drinking got out of hand. Now he was only offered the 'scrubbers' in the Forrest string while Busby straddled the cream.

'He can't be too pleased——' I stopped abruptly as four shining metal thread marks glinted in my torch beam. Screw holes made by self-tappers. About the right spacing to have anchored a cassette player, I reckoned. I came up for air, flexing benumbed fingers.

'Found something?' Anthony looked intrigued.

I gave my nose a couple of taps.

'Well it is my dad's car. I have a right——'

'It's Catherine's car. If you think I'm trespassing then go tell her. She might be glad to know you care.'

'No way.' He folded mutinous arms.

I shrugged and went for a further inspection. To the rear of the

71

screw holes I could feel the sticky residue left by pieces of adhesive tape. The track led me to the top of the steering column. I trained the torch beam into the indicator/headlight flasher exit hole, and there she was. A half-inch of red wire. Copper filaments clubbed by a hasty snip job. A haste that betrayed how the music had been triggered.

Feeling very smug, very self-satisfied, I switched on the lights and toyed with the multi-purpose lever. On flicking the stalk to main beam the ingenuity of the scheme became as clear as the beautifully land-scaped garden I'd illuminated. Catherine had done exactly that on the route home. There was only one section of road that required full headlights and the brains behind the charade had capitalized on the fact. They'd rigged a recording of Rhapsody in Blue to the main beam switch knowing the precise spot it would be activated. Clever—and damn bloody fast. Only a few hours had elapsed and already the tape or whatever had been dismantled.

'Something bothering you?' Anthony leered at me and stubbed out his cigarette.

'When you arrived—did you see anybody hanging around?'

'Nope.'

'Anybody near the car?'

'Nope.'

'Anything unusual?'

'Nope.'

'Don't overwork your vocabulary. You might rupture a jaw muscle.'

'What's going on?'

'Somebody is playing nasty little games on your stepmother. He glanced at me uneasily. 'With wax and pins and things?'

'Hell's teeth!' I said the words louder than I meant to. Anthony Taylor recoiled. His eyes widened and he stared. 'Who told you about the effigy?' I demanded.

'Nobody told me.' He groped between his legs and pulled a box from a rather tatty duffle bag. 'I found this a few minutes before you arrived.'

My stomach lurched as I peeled back the lid. No pink ribbons—this one was equine not canine. The perfectly shaped image of a horse. A chestnut with white markings.

'It's near foreleg's been broken,' the boy pointed out. 'I think it's supposed to be Highwayman. See the white blaze and white pastern?'

My eyes were riveted to the thin strand of cotton which separated the fetlock joint from the cannon bone. It made the broken limb wobble grotesquely whenever the box was jogged.

'This was where?' I queried.

'On the back seat.'

'In the duffle bag?'

'No, the bag's mine. I was taking the box in to show dad.'

I wondered how long it had been there. When and where it had been planted. I'd driven the Aston back to Windsor while Karan had followed in the M.G. I hadn't seen the box. When you had a be-draggled actress who you'd just rendered unconscious, snoring in the passenger seat, even the nodding dog on the parcel shelf went unnoticed.

'Did you take it out of the box?' I asked.

'Nope.'

'So you haven't handled it?'

'Nope.'

The Yankeefied locution was beginning to strangle the conversa-tion. 'I'll take the box,' I said. 'I want your word that you won't mention its contents to anyone.'

'What about dad?'

'Especially not dad.'

He straightened his back, reached for the door handle.

'I want your word,' I repeated.

'Big deal.' He shrugged, 'O.K., so you've got it.'

'Thanks.'

'I'll see you around then?'

'Yes,' I said. 'Around.'

'Will you be at Newbury for the Schweppes?'

I looked at him a little blankly. The question hadn't really pene-trated.

'February the eighth—next Saturday. You'll be there to see my stepmother collect the trophy?'

'That could be wishful thinking,' I murmured.

'Do you mean My Liberty? He'll romp home.'

'No, your stepmother collecting the trophy,' I said.

Howard Grant had one of those little spy-holes embedded into his door. On lighter occasions I'd have either planted my thumb firmly over the lens or attempted to adopt a menacing pose. Tonight I was too tired and dispirited to play games. I leaned on the bell-push and offered my unsmiling image for inspection. Over a brandy I verbalized the evening's odyssey and showed him the effigy.

'Has she seen it?'

'I haven't asked. I brought it straight here.'

'You'll have to talk to her, Simon,' he advised in that suave, dominant tone of his. 'It's unquestionably Highwayman. Catherine will have to decide if she wants any protective measures introduced. It's not going to be easy.'

'It's going to be bloody impossible,' I said.

'We can try to eliminate some of the risks.'

'But for how long? The horse has got to be exercised. She can't keep it wrapped in cotton wool for the rest of its natural.'

'They'll have to postpone the film stunt. Either that or use another animal.'

'Surely you're just delaying the inevitable. If you believe voodoo really works then Highwayman is going to bust that near-fore, protective measures or not.'

'Maybe, maybe.' He pulled at his ear, looked thoughtful. 'Leaving sorcery aside, how would you go about doing it?'

'Break a horse's leg—make it look like an accident?'

'Precisely.'

'Pure fiction. I remember a novel where they put trip-wires across a fence. It read well, but in reality——'

'Detectable and unreliable. This would have to look convincing, totally convincing.'

'I'd say it was impossible.'

'So would I.' The lines around his eyes bunched humorously. 'Back to the occult, eh Simon?'

Luke Taylor paced the lounge like a man with trouble on his mind. He'd been giving the bourbon plenty of stick. 'Catherine wants to see you,' he murmured.

I groaned, said it was late, that I was tired, and that Catherine needed all the rest she could get. Tomorrow we'd all be more receptive.

'It's not my idea,' he retorted, 'she was most emphatic. She refuses to tell me anything. My being married to her carries very little weight. I'm treated like an outsider while you and Rupert Gibson appear to have *carte blanche*.'

'Rupert Gibson?'

'Sure Rupert Gibson. That guy's name has cropped up so many times it's unhealthy. Is he behind all this?'

'All what?'

'Don't act dumb, Simon, you're no more a racing adviser than I am. You're from a detective agency—right?'

'Wrong,' I said truthfully.

'C'mon pal, I can smell a private cop a mile off.'

'Then get your nose fixed—I smell of horses. Ask me the year Darius won the Eclipse and I'll tell you. Ask me to tack up a racer and I'll show you. Give me an animal with girth galls and I'll treat it. Get me to count in tic-tac jargon and I'd lose you somewhere between a stripe and a cockle. I don't carry a Beretta, Mr Taylor. I carry a penknife with an attachment for getting stones out of horses' hooves.'

He fixed me with a steely glare. 'Quite the boy scout, aren't you. What have you been doing for the past two hours—practising with your knots?'

'Untangling a few,' I said.

'I'm gonna check into your background, buddy.'

'Let's hope you find it as interesting as I'm sure I'm going to find yours.'

As I motioned towards the door he showed me he had a good set of teeth, but there were no further questions. I'd given him five-star bullshit and he'd accepted it. He didn't believe me but he'd accepted it. I breathed relief and grinned a little. For the life of me I couldn't remember the year Darius won the Eclipse.

Catherine looked worse than I'd expected. The only colour to break up the ashen complexion was the red tracery of a few scratch marks running across her nose. She dragged back her lashes and made a conscious effort to smile. I waited placidly for her to speak.

'Gibson, Simon . . . It was Rupert Gibson . . .' She could barely enunciate the words. She groped for my hand, clutched it tightly.

'What happened?' I asked.

'Screaming . . . I heard this screaming. Is she dead? Oh God . . . yes, yes, of course she must be dead.' I felt her nails bite into my palms as she shuddered. She took a ragged breath and added, 'He

75

kept hitting her with this spade . . . over and over and over . . .
The blood—her hair was covered in blood . . .'

'Whose hair?'

'I—I couldn't see her face . . . she was a blonde on horseback. He
just kept hitting and hitting and hitting . . .'

Saliva was beginning to bubble at the corner of her mouth. I
gripped her shoulders, made her face me. 'Listen,' I said, 'it was
phoney—contrived—a pre-arranged stunt. Somebody is trying to
unbalance your mind. If we hadn't found you they would have
succeeded—so take it easy.'

'Gibson . . .?'

'You're sure it was Gibson?'

'Yes.'

'How near were you?'

'I can't remember.'

'Try.'

'T-twenty yards, maybe less.'

'In those weather conditions, without a moon, it would have to be
less. A hell of a lot less.'

'I saw the grey hair, the glasses. I *know* it was him!' She managed to
summon enough strength to sound affronted.

I didn't push her any further. I wanted a yes or a no to a rather
delicate question. 'Did you notice anything on the rear seat of your
car?'

A lift from her eyebrows confirmed that she hadn't.

'Nothing important,' I said awkwardly. 'It'll wait until morning.'

'Not another . . .?'

'It'll wait,' I repeated.

She levered herself up. Her lips quivered. '*T-tell me.*' The voice was
weak but it was a definite command.

I told her.

'Oh, God . . .' Her mouth sagged.

'We'll take precautions——'

'Futile, Simon. You can't prevent supernatural forces, the powers
of evil.'

'You're an intelligent woman. You don't believe mumbo jumbo
like that, surely?'

She closed her eyes and launched into a shaky piece of narrative
about a West Indian dresser whom she'd known in the thirties. 'The

76

girl was young, pretty, and highly intelligent until a jilted lover made her a present of a braided horsehair effigy. She changed overnight, Simon. She lost weight and aged dramatically. Within a week she was dead.' She paused, sighed, 'An experience like that remains with you. You can't ignore——'

'You can and you must. That girl believed she was going to die, told herself she was going to die, lived with the fear of dying twenty-four hours a day. Eventually that fear killed her—not the effigy, but fear.'

'And Fiona?'

I shook my head. 'I don't know,' I said.

'Highwayman *will* break that leg.'

'If he does, it'll have nothing to do with the occult.'

She fumbled two capsules into her mouth, gagged a little as she swallowed water. 'What am I going to do, Simon? I'm so confused . . . Oh, God in heaven . . .'

'You're going to rest and get stronger and carry on with the movie. The public are demanding another Catherine Forrest picture, remember?' I gave her the most confident smile I could muster.

'You believe that, don't you?'

'Of course I believe it.'

'S-sure you do—I'll be back in a few days—mustn't hold up the production—you and Luke can carry me on to the set in a sedan chair. I'd like that. They did it for Gloria Swanson . . . *Sunset Boulevard* . . . Wonderful film . . .'

The drugs were making her ramble, slurring her words.

'Close your eyes,' I said. 'Rest and sleep.'

'You used to be in pictures. You used to be big . . . I am big—it's the pictures that got small . . . Wonderful dialogue . . . *Sunset Boul* . . .'

I left her with yesterday's memories and tiptoed out of the room.

I thought it might have been Karan.

I thought she might have changed her mind.

I was in bed, half-way between sleep and consciousness, groaning pleasurably as fingers brushed my cheek.

Stupid, blind, bloody male vanity. Instead of tasting fornication I was suddenly tasting suffocation and not liking it one bit. My lungs pumped, desperately craving air. My legs and arms thrashed in an attempt to dislodge the heavily calloused hand that had clamped itself over my mouth. A stiletto shimmied dangerously in front of my eyes.

'Play dead!' a voice rasped. 'Keep your crack shut or I'll cut your deformed breather back to the bone.'

I felt my nostrils go rigid as the threat became a distinct probability. The cold tip of steel scythed a few hairs from its path as it channelled an inner journey to the bridge of my nose. I blinked back saline and lay rooted, looking into a face as craggy as a lunar landscape.

'Get dressed!' the face ordered. The stiletto was reversed and retracted. My bedding was thrown back.

I heard a snigger from across the room, as mother-naked I groped for my clothes. 'It looks like the knotted end of an Italian salami,' a voice mocked.

I pulled on my briefs, zipped up my slacks. 'Go screw yourself,' I muttered.

'What'd you say?' Stiletto whirled.

'You look like a guy with a frigid wife,' I said, buttoning my shirt. 'If it's healed over I was offering you an alternative.'

The blade was just a blur as it flashed forward and snicked a sliver of flesh from my earlobe. I didn't feel pain. I didn't have time. I saw a dribble of blood fleck my collar just as a meaty forearm curled itself round my throat. The stiff leather sheath of a shoulder holster was pressing against my spine. The hardware it housed wasn't far away either. Its muzzle hugged my ribs with the gentleness and affection of a rapist prior to a score.

'Get his jacket and shoes,' the mouth by my ear ordered. 'It's got to look as if he's just upped and gone.'

Stiletto obeyed. He was playing with a new toy. A hypo. A thin stream of clear fluid ejaculated ceilingwards as he depressed the plunger. He decided to sterilize the needle by wiping it on his cuff.

I fought against it. Futilely.

I tried to hold back the giddiness. Vainly.

My fingers clawed as the needle was pushed ever more firmly into a vein. My arm began to burn up as the injection scattered into the bloodstream. Nausea syphoned queasily up from my stomach. The more I retched, the more the throat hold tightened. The metal links of a wristwatch strap were butchering my neck. I wriggled enough to glimpse the luminous dial of a Rolex. It was two-thirty precisely as the earth fell gently away and I crashed into oblivion.

Chapter Six

I AWOKE to feel polythene sheeting sticking clammily to my cheek. An oxygen tent was my first conscious thought, a hospital.

I should be so lucky.

The optical haze cleared slowly. My body felt as though it had taken a tumble at Becher's, my head as though half a dozen siren-wailing squad cars were using it as a skid-pan. As I tried to move, my wrists and ankles screamed defiance.

I was trussed up by rope so tight I couldn't feel my fingers.

I moaned. I lay still and I moaned. My inner thighs felt wet and cold with discomfort. The acidy smell of urine plucked at my nostrils. Suddenly the polythene's usage became sickeningly apparent. From the state of my trousers I'd been here for days.

At the rim of my vision was a small window. Emulsion paint had rendered it opaque but the brightness behind the glass was enough to tell me it was daylight. Awkwardly and painfully I shifted my position and took stock of my surroundings.

A garage was my first impression. I could see a work bench, tins of varnish, a jar full of dirty brushes and a spray gun and compressor. Plywood off-cuts and wood shavings littered the floor. Something jarred. I did a double-take. The plywood had a reddish tinge—the marine variety. Boats? The thought leapt out of my brain and smacked me between the eyes.

Things began to crystallize as I viewed the other wall. A can labelled 2-stroke-mixture sat close to an object covered with a dust sheet. The bulbous top, the way it tapered in at the base didn't take much imagination to figure it as an outboard motor.

The floor was wooden not concrete. I could feel the spring in the boards as I did a sideways shuffle. I scanned for something with a cutting edge, something to free me of my bonds. The effort to move was strenuous. I drew and expelled air in hot, rancid little hisses. I strained, I ached, and I cursed the thoroughness of my antagonists.

There was no broken mirror or bottle glass for me to conveniently find. No heroine bound and gagged with a nail file in her handbag. No fire smouldering in the grate so that I could offer my fettered wrists to the flames. Not that it would have mattered. The will might have been there, but I doubted whether I had the strength or the ability to behave like a latter-day Flynn.

Spurred on by desperation, I wriggled to the bench and levered myself into a sitting position. This brought relief of sorts. As the dull foggy ache in my head began to recede I coaxed saliva over my leathery tongue and took inventory of myself.

Feeling and smelling like a street-arab went without saying. My sheepskin jacket was a write-off and my trousers defied description. I reckoned I'd been dragged not carried. My watch glass was smashed, the backs of my hands were scratched, and my elbows felt raw. It took several minutes and a lot of sweat before I'd rucked up my right sleeve enough to view the half dozen puncture marks in my forearm. I felt hungry, thirsty, and would have willingly traded my shoes for a cigarette.

Several hours passed. The glare behind the emulsioned window darkened. My morale hit an all time low. My thought processes wallowed in self-pity. Eventually I dozed. A few dreams and then a weird sensation of a dim radiance penetrated my closed eyelids. I looked up at a bulb dangling on a frayed wire. Somebody leant over me, eclipsing the light.

My bonds were severed. I almost cried out as blood surged warmly into my fingers and toes.

Stiletto grinned showing chipped teeth. His sidekick applied a steely grip to my biceps and hauled me to my feet. I lolled feebly and silently against the bench, gazing at my own reflection in a pair of dark glasses.

'You smell,' Stiletto growled. 'Get yourself cleaned up, you're going to have a visitor.'

He began unpacking the contents of a carrier bag. A vacuum flask, towel, soap, shaving tackle and a mirror. His sidekick snapped open a valise. A selection of my clothes tumbled on to the bench.

'Yeah,' he said, crinkling up his rawboned face. 'We've been to your flat. I hope they're to your liking.'

I stiffened.

'Shave!' A safety razor was jabbed at my face. Stiletto unscrewed the vacuum, poured hot water into a bowl.

80

I didn't try to resist. I felt a kind of philosophical acceptance of the situation. That, coupled with the fact that I couldn't have punched my way out of a carton of eggs.

'How long have I been here?' I asked shakily.

'A couple of hours.'

'Were you born a liar or did you just grow up to be one?'

'Just wash!'

I plied shaving soap to about five days growth of beard. The face which stared at me from the mirror looked pretty grim. Skin the colour of oiled putty, dry chapped lips, and baggy dark-rimmed eyes. I hacked away the bristles and raked a comb through matted hair. Clothes maketh the man, they say, and I guess I managed to resemble something akin to humanity in sports jacket, shirt, and slacks.

'You look hungry,' Stiletto observed.

'I feel hungry,' I said.

'Fight it. We only supply accommodation.'

'Without riverside views.' I gestured to the blanked out window. 'What's out there, the Thames?'

His mouth twitched. 'Are you trying to be smart?'

'I'd have to be deaf not to have heard the cries of the rowing eights. We're in a boat-house, not a backstreet bed-sit.'

'You *are* smart, Drake. Give your brain and your backside a rest— Siddown!'

An upright wooden chair was propelled in my direction. It skidded across the floor, up-ended itself and ricocheted off the wall. A box filled with old newspapers teetered off a shelf. A small ornamental lifebelt half covered in dirt and spray-dust rolled past my feet. I glimpsed the word *Bella* just before Stiletto's hand halted its progression.

'Truss him up!'

The sidekick approached me, righted the chair and pushed me into it. I got a close up view of that long narrow face, the sparse hair, the slight quirk on those thin lips as he shackled my wrists to the wooden slats. His voice, although hostile, was laced with mock servility. 'Try to relax, Mr Drake,' he said. 'We don't want to resort to unnecessary violence.'

'You're lucky to be alive,' Stiletto added, putting a match to a cigarette. 'Just keep your cool and you'll stay that way.'

'All part of the plan, uh?'

'Plan?'

'Well you haven't ponced me up just to impress the mortician.'

'How right you are.' He waved the smoke away so I could get an unobstructed view of his malformed smile. 'We could cause you considerable pain, of course. A few mutilations might even add to the effect.'

'A frame,' I said tonelessly.

'I prefer to call it a partnership. One active, one sleeping. Be patient, Mr Drake, don't dampen the team spirit.'

An icy ripple of sweat meandered down my spine as he extracted a hypodermic, a box of ampoules, and a bottle of Scotch from the carrier bag.

'You have two choices,' he advised, breaking the seal on the whisky. 'My colleague here—let's call him Bernard—can either hold this to your lips while you swallow naturally, voluntarily and without hassle, or you can struggle against it and compel me to use the needle.' He paused, pinged the bottle neck with a fingernail. 'I'm bound to tell you that choice number two isn't advisable. Bernard would force the alcohol down your throat while you were unconscious and there's every possibility of it getting sucked into the lungs. That causes aspiration pneumonia—tut, tut, very unpleasant.'

'My sympathies lie with Bernard,' I said sourly. 'When a bottle of Scotch hits my empty gut he'll be swimming in vomit.'

'A third of a bottle will suffice. Keep it down or the process will be repeated.'

'So you get me drunk, then what?'

'A journey. You won't be harmed.'

'Just set up, huh?'

'Your presence is agitating certain people. You have to be stopped.'

'Send me an effigy—maybe I'll wither away.'

A grin flittered across his jowly cratered face. 'I prefer to be practical. Now is it to be with or without your co-operation?'

My thinking was becoming difficult and complicated. Although weakened I knew I had to do something. I was being kept alive for a reason so maybe I could afford to sail a little close to the wind. At the worst I'd be risking a hiding. I didn't weigh up the odds. My malaise was begging off. 'The easy way,' I said.

'Good.' Stiletto snapped his fingers.

Bernard approached, clutching the whisky. His overcoat was held only by a top button. It flapped open giving me a panoramic view of sharply pressed slacks. I gathered what energy I could, kicked out hard, and felt a solid satisfying jab as my toe cap connected with his genitals. He let out a shriek of pain, then crumpled gripping his crotch. The bottle bounced across the wooden floor, jettisoning its contents in all directions.

Stiletto was quick to react and my co-ordination wasn't good. He had an antidote ready the instant I launched myself at him. With a chair harnessing my wrists I couldn't help but telegraph my intentions. Bernard's fleshy rump provided a spring-board and I had plenty of height and momentum when we collided. The angle was such that the chair edge sliced a red weal across his temple, but it didn't halt his fist. He sunk it so hard into my mouth that for a moment I thought half my teeth had gone.

Blackness washed over me.

I tried to summon resistance.

The siren-wailing police cars returned to my head.

I tried to bar them entry.

I held back the incipient pain until the gates buckled and the full cauterising mass burst into my skull. Red flecked spittle dribbled involuntarily over my lips. I toppled backwards, crushing my hands with my own bodyweight as the chair keeled over.

'What have I got to do to convince you, Drake?' Stiletto straddled me, teased my busted top lip from my teeth with the front sight of a Webley & Scott. 'What have I got to do? Pull a trigger!'

I went to return an obscenity, then thought better of it. Blood was spilling down my chin. I could feel it eddying around my Adam's apple, idling into my shirt collar. The sight of Bernard, standing now with legs crossed and looking as though he needed a visit to the little boys' room lessened my own pain. He took three awkward steps and retrieved what was left of the whisky. I saw that same bloody Rolex on his wrist as he forced the bottle neck into my mouth. The hands and date-square swam into focus. Eight-forty on the 7th.

Alcohol was seering pitilessly into my raw lip. Resistance would have sent it flooding into my eyes. I swallowed and kept on swallowing. I gulped, I retched, and choked the bottle dry.

'What was left?' Stiletto barked.

'Just over half a pint—he's drained the lot.'

'Get him up. Get that shirt off him and stop the bleeding.'

Bernard ripped it off my back and indicated that I should use it as a swab. As it was one of my best I applied it almost sacrilegiously to my throbbing lip. A hesitant exploration with my tongue revealed torn flesh, but my teeth felt good. A little loose perhaps, but good.

'There's a polo neck in the valise. Get it on the bastard.' Stiletto's fingers wandered to the graze on his temple. He winced, then added, 'Make sure he stays in that chair—I'm gonna use the pricker.'

With the amount of Scotch I had careering around my brain he needn't have worried. Him, the room, the whole goddamn world, was beginning to rotate crazily before my eyes.

He took a grab at my forearm but a knuckle-rap on the door forestalled the movement. The hypo was postponed. Bernard made a hissing sound in his teeth as he clapped a band of adhesive-tape over my eyes.

'Your visitor,' he announced. 'Just to show we care.'

'Get the door,' Stiletto hustled.

I sat with head back, hands tied, shirt draped loosely across my mouth. The wetness was subsiding, replaced by coagulation and stickiness. I heard a key turn, a latch lift, a light tread of feet on the boards.

Stiletto said, 'I know he looks bad. The guy's a suicide pilot, he brought it on himself.'

There was an angry expelling of breath.

'Is everything set?' Stiletto barked. 'Good. A couple of c.c.'s should be enough to send him on his way.'

I didn't flinch as the needle went in. I was past flinching. Over the hill and far away, my endurance tottering on the edge-rail of unconsciousness. I breathed deeply, almost contentedly. A trace of expensive after-shave wreathed around my nostrils, or maybe it was perfume. I was too far gone to notice subtleties. Numbed by the drug and high on the alcohol, the click-stops functioned smoothly and effectively as the aperture which governed my comprehension closed down.

I came out of it slowly.

Voices and the stench of petrol. I felt my pupils dilate as a torch beam lanced painfully at my eyes. I didn't know where I was, and I didn't care.

'Get his other arm, Les. The tank's split. If the vapour finds its way to the exhaust——'

'He'll fry. No more than he deserves—drunken bastard.'

'Over the limit, you reckon?'

'Reckon? Jesus, this speed merchant's legless.'

I moistened my swollen lips. 'Set up,' I mumbled.

'Hear that, Les?'

'Hear what?'

'He spoke. Set 'em up, he said. He wants you to get the next round.'

'The pub's closed mate.' A young face loomed close, gave me a cold little smile. A face wearing a blue peaked cap. The badge and chequered band told me it wasn't the Salvation Army. 'You're pissed, my old son. Brahms and bloody Liszt—and you're in big trouble.'

'I didn't—' I began.

'Oh, but you did. A blood-test is going to confirm it.'

'What speed were you doing, eh?' asked the other voice. 'Sixty . . . seventy? This hot rod of yours is scrap metal.'

'A b-boat house,' I stumbled over the words. 'Bella . . . the name, Bella.'

'Who's she, a hostess? Doing the clubs were you?'

'I was forced——

'Sure you were. These hostesses can be very persuasive. Only trouble is mate—she wasn't driving.'

I sighed feebly. My assignment that was to have been Catherine's path back to sanity had suddenly become my own personal nightmare. The torn filaments of time came together as my seat-belt was released and I was lifted clear of the wreckage.

The M.G. was a twisted gleaming mass of ruptured metal. Mechanical entrails hung from its gutted belly, its nose buckled and broken and buried deep into the trunk of a tree. The front suspension had collapsed, the windscreen had starred into opacity, and the severed radiator hissed and gurgled as it released steam into the cold night air. A uniformed policeman retrieved the front number plate from a neighbouring bush, tossed it into the boot of a white Triumph and began erecting an accident warning sign. Flashing lights started to rotate, pulsing a ghostly blue radiance over the awesome scene. Cars cruised slowly past, gawping faces pressing against misty side windows, necks craning to catch a glimpse of someone else's misery. Mine.

It was all I could do to stand. Like a boxer who'd just made the count of nine, I wobbled unsteadily, my legs feeling and acting like rubber hoses. I tried to suppress the dull ache in my head, tried to blink away the distortion as my eyes traced the path where the M.G. had left the road and slashed its way into the woodland. Branches and pieces of bracken were strewn across the crumpled bonnet. An expanding patch of oil seeped around my shoes as it ebbed from the fractured sump. A headlight bulb, still functioning, dangled limply from a broken reflector. Cold sweat moistened my palms as I saw a splash of redness glistening on an overrider.

A voice said, 'His skull was laid open to the bone. Death must have been instantaneous.'

I suddenly felt very sick. I turned and stared. Hazel eyes stared coolly back. He was fiftyish, wide in the shoulders, and a little paunchy about the middle. The metallic décor on his uniform told me he'd risen higher than constable. He held a spaniel on a leash.

'Found this little fellow in the woods,' he went on casually. 'Probably belonged to the dead man. Was he walking a dog when you hit him?'

'I didn't hit anyone,' I said.

'Perhaps the dog caused the accident. He ran in front of the car, you swerved and that's when——'

'I didn't hit anyone,' I repeated.

'I'm afraid you did, Mr Drake. It is Simon Drake, isn't it?'

I nodded listlessly.

'Inspector Ryan, Alverton traffic division.' He drummed up a weak smile, pulled my wallet from his pocket and consulted my T.S.D. warranty card. 'It says here that you're a racing investigator?'

'Is that a question or a statement?'

'A question.'

'Then it's a rhetorical one,' I grunted. 'You're looking at my bloody photograph.'

'It's not a good likeness. You look paler, slightly more gaunt in the flesh.'

'That's because I've had a rough time. I haven't eaten since God knows when.'

'Been on a bender have we?'

'No we haven't.' I lifted unsteady fingers to my bruised mouth. 'It's tritely known as "a long story". Have you got a cigarette?'

'Of course—but first I'd like you to turn some crystals green. I take it you have no objection?'

I shook my head despondently, resigned to the inevitability of the situation. My mouth, my clothes, my stinking guts reeked of whisky. Breathalyser, blood-sample—those excess milligrams were going to hang a death by dangerous driving charge round my neck. A sour-faced sergeant called Harris produced the necessary little bag and I blew into it. I didn't have to look. Ryan's smug, 'Oh dear, oh dear,' confirmed the worst.

Harris faced me and rattled out a lot of copy-book spiel. I guessed I was being arrested and cautioned—I hardly heard him. A covered body was loaded into an ambulance. The stark white vehicle was caught briefly in the overspill from a police photographer's flash gun. Uniformed officers began dispersing a crowd of curious onlookers. Others armed with torches and tapemeasures swarmed around the M.G. like flies around a trash can. They worked silently and methodically, all looking as if they wanted a pound of my flesh. As the impact of the thing slammed home, I began to shiver uncontrollably. Gratefully, I reached for the cigarette in Ryan's outstretched hand.

'Have you identified the victim?' he asked Harris.

'Not yet sir. We're checking the address on the dog's disc now.'

'Cherryburton Towers. Aren't they luxury apartments?'

'Sixty quid a week jobs, sir. About a quarter of a mile down the road.'

Ryan nodded, looked thoughtful. 'Any witnesses?'

'A few of the locals heard the crash, but nobody actually saw it.'

Nobody would, I thought grimly. This little frame had been sewn up tighter than a gelding's scrotum. The law would throw the book at me and I'd pick up the form. Drunk and incapable, killer of innocent pedestrians; the prosecution would ride me into the ground. I breathed a lungful of soothing smoke, not wishing to dwell on the outcome. Ryan escorted me to a waiting squad car.

'What speed were you travelling?' he asked, pulling open a rear door and gesturing me inside.

'I wasn't driving,' I said, 'I was framed.'

'Framed?' His tone was cold, careful. 'By whom?'

'I don't know.'

'For what reason?'

'I don't know that either. I suppose somebody wanted me struck off.'

'Pretty badly too. They killed a man to achieve it.'

'It doesn't make sense.'

'Now there I'm in agreement,' he murmured thickly.

'Listen, Inspector!' I snapped the words out so quickly that I felt the scab on my lip part. 'I've been through too much to listen to your cushy sarcasm. I've been drugged, roughed up, held against . . .' I tailed off and coughed as a glut of blood invaded my throat. Little specks of crimson stippled Ryan's blue serge as I kept right on coughing.

'Use this.' His voice conveyed disgust as he dangled a handkerchief in front of me. 'Your injuries are in keeping with those received during a fist fight. Such a fist fight was reported earlier this evening by the landlord of an Alverton public house. A man fitting your description was involved. He was also seen leaving in a blue M.G.C.'

I mopped my lip, managed a mirthless smile. 'They've given you a watertight case,' I said, pulling back my sleeve and showing him the needle marks on my forearm. 'How do these fit into the saga?'

'Don't make it worse for yourself, Mr Drake. The drug squad is overworked as it is.'

I sighed weakly. 'Are you saying I'm a junkie?'

'I'm saying you killed a man while driving under the influence of alcohol. At the moment that's all I'm concerned with.'

I could see the sour-faced sergeant striding in our direction. Ryan wound down the side window. His wristwatch glinted at me and jogged my memory.

'What's the time and date?' I asked.

'Eleven-thirty on the 7th.' He looked at me obliquely. 'Why?'

'Three hours ago I was trussed up in a riverside boat-house. Two goons were pouring whisky down my——'

'Are you saying these two men then resorted to murder just to put you in a tight corner?'

'Yes. It's crazy, but yes.'

'Heavies were they? Gangster types?'

'Well they weren't Pinky and Perky,' I grated.

'They weren't very professional either. If they meant to kill somebody then why not kill you? All this preparation to get you on a death by dangerous driving charge? You have an admirable imagination, Mr Drake, but I'd be obliged if you'd contain it within the realms of the probable.'

He was right and I knew it. It *was* crazy. Utterly bloody crazy. Why involve an innocent dog-walker? Why not just take me out of circulation—permanently.

Harris put his elbows on the sill, raised his palms in a gesture of prayer and leaned at me. 'You ran down quite a big shot,' he said. 'A film director, name of Gibson. Rupert Gibson.'

Suddenly it meshed like the greased gears of an intricate machine. Two birds with one bloody stone—that's why. 'Oh, Christ,' I groaned.

Chapter Seven

I LAY on the hard clinical mattress and woefully surveyed my new environment. It was daylight and I'd spent the last seven hours under the hospitable roof of the Alverton Constabulary. It was only a question of time before they discovered my connection with Gibson. Only time before I'd be facing a possible murder rap. *Time.* A commodity I suddenly had on my hands. Time to think, to brood, to waste. Each confining second seemed a minute, each minute an hour. Even sleep refused me asylum. It came in spasmodic little drifts. It had me tossing and turning as a nightmare of fragmented pictures haunted my thoughts. A police cell, I discovered, wasn't the best place to doss down if you wanted sweet dreams.

No word from Howard Grant. I'd phoned him around midnight asking him to pull strings to clear my name. His reply had lacked the conviction I'd expected. The shellac-coated words of comfort sounded stale and thin. As he'd replaced the receiver, the hopelessness of my predicament filtered through. The message was simple: Complications took time, miracles took for ever.

I swung my legs off the bunk and sat with my head in my hands. I could still smell the liquor on my shirt as I stroked my scabbed lips across the material. What an unholy bloody mess. They'd wrecked my bastard car and now they were trying to wreck my bastard life. I stood up and vented my frustrated emotions at the graffiti-etched door. My fist thudded into a rather applicable phrase. *If you had it last night—be grateful. If you didn't—get used to it.* Somebody had scrawled an obscene reply. Their sentiments echoed my own exactly.

I lay back on the bunk and tried to doze. A couple of hours passed before the sound of keys in the lock snapped me out of my reverie. A fresh-faced constable escorted me to the Detention Room.

'Simon—my God you look bad.'

'Howard . . .' I tried to smile but my lip told me not to. 'Christ you're a sight for sore bloody eyes.'

Ryan stood with his back to a radiator, studying me with a cool, dispassionate stare. He'd changed his uniform. The blue serge looked sharp and unsullied. Another guy in plain clothes, hair slicked back to follow the contours of his skull, gave me a bleak smile and waved me into a chair. 'Chief Inspector Clarke,' he announced. 'That's Clarke with an "e".'

Sod the 'e', I thought. Plain clothes meant C.I.D. Was this the beginning of the end? I sat, mentally bracing myself for a steady build up of loaded questions.

'We're not taking any further action against you,' Ryan said.

I gaped. It hurt, but I gaped just the same.

'The case has been taken over by Mr Clarke. Premeditated murder isn't my province.'

'The drunken driving charge?'

'You're innocent, aren't you?' Clarke's brows arched.

'Virgin white,' I said.

'Then there won't be any charge. You're held in very high regard, Mr Drake,' there was a faint undertone of resentment in his voice. 'The Commissioner of Police knows all about you. Commissioner Sir Desmond Fox—I believe he owns three racehorses?'

'Two,' Grant corrected through an embarrassed little cough.

'Thank Christ for sporting Commissioners,' I breathed.

'Sir Desmond was able to vouch for your good character, Simon—nothing more. You've been cleared because new evidence categorically proves you weren't driving.'

'Evidence that *we* would have found,' Clarke interjected.

'That's always assuming Inspector Ryan had requested C.I.D. assistance,' I stated bluntly. 'Always assuming my story had been believed.'

Ryan listened without any apparent emotion. He warmed his palms on the radiator and studied the floor.

'Well that's academic,' Clarke continued, 'in the final analysis it wasn't Captain Grant or the Commissioner who wiped your slate clean, but a Miss . . .' He flicked through a fistful of statements. 'A Miss Karan Langford.'

'Karan?'

'We did pursue the boat-house line of enquiry but that proved fruitless. There are several craft named Bella registered with the Thames Water Authority but none——'

'Karan,' I broke in. 'How the hell . . .?'

'You weren't marked.'

'What?'

'The windscreen shattered on impact, but you didn't go through it.'

'Your seat-belt saved you,' Ryan summed up. 'It did, yet it didn't, if you follow my meaning.'

Suddenly I very much followed his meaning. I cursed my own stupidity, my own witless naïveté as the explanation presented itself with blinding clarity.

'Miss Langford told us about the malfunction so we ran some tests on the tongue and keeper. That belt wouldn't have held a hernia in place.'

Grant put his fingers together in an attitude of meditation. 'It's not too difficult to reconstruct,' he advanced. 'Gibson was jumped while walking the dog, taken to a pre-arranged "accident" site, and laid out. The M.G. was driven over him, the driver leaping clear——'

'Not over him,' Clarke shook his head. 'Into him would be more technically correct. The nature of his injuries indicate he was vertical when struck by Mr Drake's car.'

'They went to a lot of trouble to make it look right,' Ryan said. 'Score marks on an overhanging branch suggest they used a block and tackle, some kind of lifting harness to hoist Gibson into a standing position.'

I was receiving not too pleasant mental pictures of the film director hanging there like a dummy, a suspended target for the speeding M.G. It wasn't difficult to imagine how the hoist had been released on impact, how the driver had deserted his seat sending Gibson and the car plummeting into the tree. All that remained was to manoeuvre me into the driving seat, perhaps douse my clothing with a little whisky, and make sure my seat-belt was securely fastened. A few weeks of freedom before the trial and then a full stop and new paragraph for Simon Drake. Probably two years in Pentonville or its equivalent.

'Of course the doors buckled and jammed,' Clarke was saying, 'but they'd calculated for that. The hood was down—that's how they got you in so easily.'

Grant unlatched his fingers and gave a relieved sigh. 'The seat-belt was the one fissure in an otherwise perfect plan.'

'So what was their motive, Mr Drake?' Clarke asked. 'It must have been a bloody big one to involve such elaborate planning.'

I shrugged, gave Grant a pass-the-buck glance.

'I—I really don't know, Chief Inspector . . .' he blew out his cheeks, floundered a little. 'Our organization exists to combat horse-racing crime, so naturally all types of villains pass through our hands. I can only tell you that our men aren't protected by rank and are therefore susceptible——'

'Spare me the speech, Captain. I'm interested in one man—Mr Drake here. Is he currently engaged on T.S.D. business?'

'No he's not,' Grant said truthfully.

'But he did know the dead man?'

'I believe they'd met once or twice.'

Clarke's eyes swivelled to me. 'Can you elaborate?'

I fingered my scabbed lip as if elaboration was going to be a painful experience.

'Does it hurt?'

'Only when I laugh.'

'Highly amusing,' he grated. 'You might be laughing on the other side of your face if we do you for withholding evidence.'

Grant said, 'You have Mr Drake's statement, Chief Inspector, and you know where he can be contacted should the need arise. I'm afraid I must insist that medical attention takes priority——'

'I'm not a green D.C.,' Clarke flashed. 'You both know far more than you're letting on and in so doing you're obstructing a murder enquiry. You have friends in high places—very well—I know when to bow out.' He leaned forward and breathed at me. 'I understand you're a man of some prowess, but you're not immortal Mr Drake. Don't do anything foolish.'

'Foolish?'

'Like conducting a one-man investigation. We're dealing with ruthless people. Don't add to the shortage of National Health beds.'

I assured him that I had no desire to break up the long-suffering prostatectomy queue. I took a pen from his outstretched hand and signed for the envelope containing my personal effects.

Back in my flat, after a therapeutic hot shower and a change of clothing, I sat on the couch and listened numbly as Grant filled in the gaps.

'Catherine's prints were on the second effigy . . .' His voice ebbed and flowed. 'Highwayman snapped its fetlock joint during the stunt . . . Luke Taylor has an intriguing past . . .'

'Either she's crazy or else she's sending them to herself,' I stated.

'Does she deny handling it?'

I thought back. 'She even denied seeing it.'

'Odd,' he said in an undertone. 'Very odd.'

I wouldn't have put it quite so mildly; farcical seemed a more apt description. I shifted the topic to Highwayman.

'So the supernatural scored again, huh?'

'It happened as predicted, yes. Apparently the horse hit the top of the fence and somersaulted. He had to be destroyed.'

'Did you see it?'

He shook his head. 'I assumed you had it in hand. Nobody realized you'd gone absent until yesterday. Karan thought you were with me, and I thought . . .' He sighed apologetically.

It's nice to be missed, I thought sourly, cursing misguided assumptions. Highwayman had tipped-up as forecast, but nobody had bothered to cover the bloody event. Our chance of affirming or exploding the voodoo myth had died right along with the horse.

'Have they got it on film?'

'Mm, from several angles, I understand.'

'And the carcass?'

'No trace.'

'Butchered at the knackery, huh?'

'As far as we can ascertain the animal never reached a knackery.'

I looked at him obliquely.

'There are two disturbing factors surrounding the incident, Simon. We can't find either the vet who applied the humane killer, or the van that carried away the carcass.'

My head jerked up. 'You've lost 15 cwt of horsemeat?'

'I'm afraid so.' He kneaded the flesh of his forehead, rubbed his jaw. 'Obviously, the vet and the meat wagon were hired for the occasion. Nobody was meant to get a close-up look at that fracture.'

One of the reasons I'd been taken out of service, I reflected grimly, standing up and pacing, hoping the exercise might stimulate my thinking process. My body ached with every stride, launching its protest against a week of ill-treatment. Common sense told me to go to bed, to consider number one, to forget the stream of oddities that were sliding chillingly into my bloodstream. Grant had similar ideas.

'Luke Taylor's history,' he unbuckled his briefcase and handed me a manilla folder. 'Have a browse through it tomorrow. I suggest you devote the rest of the day to recuperation.'

I slipped into my jacket. 'My own company drives me mad,' I said.

'Simon?' He looked anxious.

'I'll need transport. Where are you heading?'

'Newbury. Today's Saturday—the Schweppes Gold Trophy, remember?'

'Who'll be there?'

'Most of Lapwing films. My Liberty and Intruder both run.'

'Then that settles it, I'm going.'

'A crowded race meeting is hardly the best place for you to convalesce . . .'

'Stop worrying. Just tell me who knows what about my part in the Gibson business.'

'Only Karan,' he murmured mildly, 'so if you just appear out of the blue you'll have to be pretty inventive in countering the inquisitive questions.'

'Is Catherine well enough to attend?'

'Yes she is,' he looked at my mouth and grimaced, 'but you most certainly are not. Reconsider, Simon, for your own sake.'

I ran an exploratory finger over the puffy ridge of flesh. 'I'll just keep a stiff upper lip,' I said, and headed for the door.

'Simon darling!' Catherine Forrest put her arms around my neck and hugged me with maternal warmth. She was hidden behind wrap-round dark glasses and clad in a swirling cape-coat with a big furry Dr Zhivago hat. She smelled quietly of rose petals, the kind that cost a fortune when liquidized and put into a *Patou* bottle.

Friends and admirers clustered nearby. The same old faces, the ones I'd seen a few weeks earlier at Grant's dinner party. Hangers-on, social climbers, people who spend money they haven't yet earned, on things they can't really afford, trying to impress people they certainly don't like. A large bosomed woman with bluish hair and a pampered face waved gaily from the paddock rails, and in a voice meant to be heard by all, shrilled, 'Liberty looks absolutely riveting sweetie!

The big race atmosphere was beginning to build. The magnetic attraction of the parade ring had drawn a seam-bursting mass of keen-eyed punters who clamoured and jostled in an effort to catch that all-important last glimpse of the twenty-seven runners. Minds were made up, then changed, then made up again. An impatient swish of a tail, a slight showing of sweat between the hind legs, eyes, ears, gait—all the factors were mentally weighed and catalogued. Selections were finalized, racecards were marked, the units on the tote indicator board shifted and changed as the money began to flow.

'*Will jockeys get mounted please.*' The public-address system clicked on.

I watched the probing eye of a television camera as it roamed over the multitude of highly-tuned horseflesh. The sun made an on-cue appearance, adding warmth to the occasion as it lit up the vivid jigsaw of racing colours. Legs were hoisted into saddles, girths were tightened. Fifteen minutes to the off. The multi-deep ringside spectators began peeling away to the stands.

Chuck Busby, lean face, dark humorous eyes, straddled My Liberty and adjusted his jerks. He offered Catherine a smile that would have charmed the birds off the trees and touched his cap. 'I'll have to go the wrong way to get beaten,' he said confidently.

Catherine laughed, a little forced, but good to hear just the same.

'See you in the winners' enclosure,' he added, gathering the reins, his heels tapping the big grey horse forward for its final circuit of the ring. He sat as tight as a limpet, looking cool, supremely capable, and worthy of all the superlatives lavished upon him by the sporting press.

Patch Hunter followed on Intruder. He caught my eye and grimaced. His mount looked sluggish, a little as though he wished he was back in the travelling box and on his way home. At odds of 33–1 the betting public seemed in agreement.

The clusters of owners and trainers began to disperse. I could see a not too happy Rex Delgado forging in our direction. As the distance between us closed, his stride seemed to falter, almost as if he'd been struck by the sudden realization of who I was.

'Good grief man,' he blinked at me, frowning in astonishment.

'Where have you been for the past week? What on earth have you done to your face?'

'I had an accident,' I said.

'That's patently obvious. Were you so incapacitated you couldn't reach for a phone, or was it just lack of courtesy on your part?'

'Don't bully Simon,' Catherine countered protectively. 'I expect he'll tell us what happened in his own good time. He's safe and well, that's all that matters.'

'He owes the company an explanation. I know he's racing adviser in name only but——'

'I've been in a hospital bed,' I lied blandly. 'The morning after Catherine's woodland episode I drove back to the area hoping to have a daylight look around. I didn't reach the spot because I had a shunt—a bad one. The M.G.'s breaker's yard fodder.'

'You crashed?' His eyes narrowed circumspectly.

'That's the general nature of the message.'

'Was anyone hurt?'

I ran my tongue over my swollen lip. 'Well I haven't just been mugged at the turnstiles.'

'I meant apart from you.'

I shook my head. 'A cat lost one of its lives and I demolished a council wall. The only thing that's going to suffer is my wallet.'

'Poor Simon.' Catherine kissed her fingertip and touched it gently to my cheek.

'You've heard the news, I suppose?' Delgado asked bluntly.

I assumed he was referring to Gibson. I nodded.

'This morning's papers are full of it. Very few facts, just the usual biographical crap. Apparently a man is helping police with their enquiries.'

Was helping, I thought, but I said, 'Nasty business. How's Julian taking it?'

'Badly.' The inflection in his voice spelled frustration. It prompted him to reach for a lozenge. 'I brought him to Newbury hoping the diversion might neutralize the shock. It hasn't. He's in one of the bars working himself towards a hangover.'

'No self-discipline,' Catherine snapped. 'Let him wallow in his grief. I for one won't be mourning for Rupert Gibson. My mental torment is over, thank God. What happened was retributive justice.'

'There was never any proof——' I began.

97

'It's over, Simon,' she repeated, lidding her eyes, shuddering as cruel memories stabbed. 'That man was responsible for the death of Fiona and Highwayman. His ultimate goal was to destroy me. Now his own mortality has prevented him from achieving that objective.'

I didn't comment. I knew damned well that it wasn't so cut and dried, so black and white; I'd been fitted up good—and not by a corpse. I didn't like admitting it, but the fusion of illogical events even had me doubting Catherine's innocence. If Gibson had sent the effigies, then the actress more than anyone had the best bloody motive in the world for wanting him eliminated.

'The film you shot of Highwayman,' I turned to Delgado, 'I'd like to see it.'

'The stunt with the goggles?'

'Right.'

He fingered a mole on his chin and studied me critically. 'I can arrange for you to view it, of course, but what possible good will it do?'

'Satisfy my scepticism, maybe.'

'That's a rather vague answer.'

'I'll try to be more specific after the screening.'

'Stop fishing, Drake,' a ripple of annoyance disturbed his impassive features. 'The trail stopped at Gibson. Learn to accept that fact and let the motion picture business get on with its job. We're weeks behind schedule.'

'Don't be so pernickety, Rex,' Catherine intervened, in between flashing a smile at a passing course executive. 'If Simon wants to see the film, then let him see it.'

'But I assumed you'd be dispensing with his services. Is he still on the pay-roll?'

'Yes, until I say otherwise.'

'I see.' He nodded with strained composure, turned full face and looked at me steadily. 'Be at the studio tomorrow morning at ten. I'll meet you at theatre seven.'

'*As the runners and riders canter slowly past the stands,*' the course commentator's voice boomed out, '*we can see the top-weight My Liberty in the royal blue and white quartered colours . . .*'

'See you in the grandstand, Simon,' Catherine squeezed my hand.

I watched Delgado usher the actress clear of the paddock and vanish into the dense knot of spectators. I did likewise, heading for the members' bar. My thoughts were interrupted as I ran briefly into Sidney Newton-Smith and the young Anthony Taylor. The boy was brandishing a tenner and bursting with enthusiasm for his stepmother's horse.

The members' bar was practically empty. The air that only moments before had pulsed with the aroma of cigars, snorters, snifters, chasers, and freshly minted money was given a brief remission before the next thirty-minute session of celebration or sorrow drowning.

Luke Taylor and Amanda Stewart appeared to be taking advantage of the interlude. They sat drinking and talking at the far end of the counter, backs turned and well away from the solitary figure of Julian Knight. The actor, flawlessly dressed in a fashionable white suit, mauve frilly shirt and matching bow-tie toyed with a cocktail cherry impaled on a plastic sword. His skin looked taut and yellowy, his mouth curved downwards, and his voice, when it came, had a decidedly bitter edge.

'Well, if it isn't Catherine Forrest's tutelary saint. Been playing truant, dear?'

I displayed my tolerant smile and ordered a vodka.

'Lovely shade of scabbed lip you're wearing.'

'They're easily acquired,' I said dryly.

'Stick on?'

'Knuckles.'

'How vulgar.' He winced.

A little billow of laughter echoed from the far end of the bar. Luke and Amanda were obviously enjoying each other's company.

'Promiscuous bitch,' Julian muttered.

I swallowed alcohol and said nothing.

'It's common knowledge that I'm not overfond of the female sex,' he went on, taking a delicate bite of the cherry, 'but I positively loathe tarts.'

'Amanda?'

'Not so you'd notice, dear. She's choosy—what I'd term a slag with a Harrod's price tag.' His bloodshot eyes drifted to Taylor. 'I don't blame the cowboy for showing an interest. Catherine's bait is hardly as fresh as it was.'

'Rupert Gibson wasn't exactly youth personified either,' I grated.

'And just what is that meant to imply?'

'Nothing in particular. Just a statement of fact.'

'Rupert's dead,' he breathed dramatically.

'I know. That's why I used the past tense.'

'Then why bring it up!' There was a distinct tremor in his tapered fingers as he caressed his hair. His voice was tight, almost tearful. 'I was half-way to forgetting the tragedy and then you . . . you . . . damn tactless, insensitive bastard——'

'Where were you when it happened?' I challenged him.

'That's none of your damn business.'

'How about a few hours before—say eight-forty?'

His face twitched in a spasm of anger. 'I think you're a little touched, Drake. What was it last time—music and the bloody occult? Foreskin of toad, blood of viper, and all that rubbish. Get away from me.' He flapped a dismissive hand. 'I've decided I don't like you one iota.'

'Hi there, stranger!' a voice bubbled excitedly against my neck, 'Who's been absent without leave? Naughty, naughty, Simon.'

I turned and looked into Amanda's blue eyes. They widened, frosty eyeshadow shimmering behind rapidly blinking lashes.

'Your poor, poor lips, whatever . . .?'

'Some guy slug you?' Luke Taylor arrived to pose the question.

'I ran into a little static,' I said.

'More than a little, buddy. Your face looks a helluva mess.'

'It looks lived-in and I like it,' Amanda stated emphatically. 'Look at the size of those irises.' She turned to Taylor. 'He has Brando's eyes, wouldn't you say?'

'He has Cagney's big mouth,' Julian muttered through an inebriated snarl.

Amanda ignored him. Ice cubes jostled amid pink bubbles as she toasted my health. I liked her tweed knickerbocker suit, the scarf tied peasant style around her forehead, hugging her blonde curls. Tarty? A little perhaps, but delectable just the same.

'Another?' I suggested.

'Perhaps just a teensy one.'

'We haven't time.' Taylor jabbed a finger at the television monitor above our heads. Most of the runners had arrived at the start. 'I take it you're here to watch the race, Drake. Or do you intend to go missing again?'

'Are you concerned, Mr Taylor?'

'No, but the Security Division might be.'

'You checked, huh?'

'I checked.'

'And learned precisely nothing. I was hired as racing adviser because my T.S.D. background lent itself to the picture. There's no cloak and dagger—my paycheck comes from Lapwing Films.'

'Horseshit.'

'Check the books.

'Too many damn questions,' Julian cut in, putting a match to a cheroot. 'I knew there was something phoney, I knew it.'

'Just my curious mind,' I bluffed, in what I hoped was a casual tone. 'I have difficulty switching off.'

Taylor said, 'You've been switched off for the past week, buddy, and missed a huge slice of the drama—namely Highwayman and Gibson. Rather like your namesake, uh, Drake? Playing bowls instead of being in with the action.'

Before I could counter he turned on his heel and whisked Amanda towards the exit.

'I've put fifty pounds on My Liberty,' she was saying, 'and five pounds each-way on Intruder.'

'Intruder isn't gonna race, honey,' Taylor drawled. 'He's gonna sit in the stands.'

She laughed. It was a stimulating laugh, sexual, ultra-feminine, as sparkling as vintage champagne. And the kittenish walk—Jesus, that was something else. The movement just oozed blatant allure. It was the best thing I'd seen for a very long time.

All eyes were on the start as the white flag was raised. All eyes except mine, that is. Karan Langford had attached herself affectionately to my arm and I was getting the right vibrations. I hoped I wasn't mistaking aeffction for sympathy.

'I'm glad you're back,' she said warmly, putting a hand to my face and touching the tender parts.

'Ditto,' I said.

'You're looking pretty grotty.'

'I'd kiss you, only the scabs might get in the way.'

A ghost of redness coloured her cheeks.

'As a gesture of appreciation,' I added hastily. 'It's a little more personal and a little less corny than delivering a line that would make a greeting card blush.'

'It's unnecessary.'

'The kiss or the poem of thanks.'

'Either.'

I was about to reply, but the tape beat me to it. The patchy twenty-seven horse line-up bounded forward. The public-address belched out the familiar '*They're off*'. Tote windows were lowered, chalked odds were wiped from bookmaker's slates. Jockeys steadied their mounts, settling into position for the run to the first flight of hurdles. Several thousand pairs of 7×50s tracked the serried kaleidoscope of colour. Ears hung on to the commentator's every word. Two miles to race and ten thousand quid to the first horse past the lollypop.

'What do you think, Simon?' Karan clung a little tighter.

'I was wrong,' I admitted, looking at her hair and liking the cute way she'd coiled it at the nape of her neck. 'I'm usually a pretty good judge of women, but Catherine was right, you're not the wham, bam . . .' I tailed off. 'You're just not that sort of girl. I realize that now.'

'I was talking about My Liberty.'

'Sod My Liberty, I'm talking about you.'

'*And as the field swings out into the country . . .*'

'Damn these bloody loudspeakers,' I cursed, 'how the hell can we talk——'

'Shouldn't we be watching the race?'

'I want to get a few things straight before Catherine snatches you away.'

'She doesn't snatch.'

'She covets you like a mother hen.'

'Her intentions are good.'

'And the road to hell is paved with them, I know.'

'Sim——'

I ventured a lips-to-cheek kiss and she didn't recoil. 'I used the wrong approach last time,' I admitted, 'and I'm sorry.'

'You didn't use any approach,' she said amusedly.

'Dressing gowns and couches tend to be very direct. In a different setting I can be very romantic. Take Grant's dinner party—now there I could have given you the treatment. I'd have found out your favourite drink; sent it with the compliments of the guy with the broken nose; our eyes would have locked—across a crowded room and all that . . .'

'Then you would have taken me home and we'd have ended up on the couch just the same.'

I smothered a grin. Her observation was unerringly accurate. 'That's unfair,' I said quickly. 'Stop speculating and watch the race.'

'*And as they jump the cross hurdle it's Lofty Major and Tribal Crest, these two just clear of Albany Alley who's making very good progress on the inside, then comes My Liberty, Jezail, Intruder . . .*'

Karan gave a little gasp as Intruder came into the hurdle half a stride out. Gorse splintered as the animal's forelegs clipped the top of the flight. Patch Hunter, with an incredible display of jockeyship held on to his seat and literally picked the horse up off the deck. The guy behind wasn't so lucky. His mount bulled into Intruder's hind-quarters, tipped, and sent him catapulting from the saddle. Karan's teeth worked nervously on her underlip as she watched the little splash of colour roll then lay prostrate. He'd wrapped his arms instinctively around his head. A skull cap and backpad is hardly armour-plating, and with a score of horses left to jump he looked pathetically vulnerable. I found myself feeling every jar and jab as he twitched like a marionette, his body caught in the barrage of onrushing hooves.

'That was horrible.' Karan shuddered, pushing her face into my shoulder.

'A bad one,' I agreed.

The race went on. The ambulance following the runners stopped briefly at the cross hurdle to offer assistance to the now vertical, but badly limping, jockey.

'And to think,' I said, 'last night I would have willingly traded places with that guy.'

'Were you treated badly?'

I showed her the needle marks in my forearm and explained what had happened.

'Who were the two men?'

'A couple of heavies hired to stitch me up. I'm not interested in the brute strength and ignorance, I'm after the draughtsman. The grey-matter behind all this. The person or persons unknown who drew up an intricate scheme to get rid of Gibson and get me in bad with the boys in the big helmets.'

She let her breath out raggedly. 'And I thought Gibson . . .'

'Everyone thought Gibson. Truth was, we never had a scintilla of evidence against him.'

'Catherine saw him—that night in the woods.'

'Beating some blonde to death with a spade? Who was this blonde —Julian in drag?'

'She wouldn't lie——'

'Just a little mixed up maybe. Like the effigies—both were covered with her fingerprints, yet she denies touching them.'

'Are you saying she sent those things to herself?'

'I'm not saying. I just don't bloody know.'

'But what about the phone calls, Simon?'

I shrugged, bewildered. 'O.K., let's suppose Gibson was the guilty party. Who had the best motive for wanting him dead?'

'Someone who wanted an end to Catherine's mental torment, I suppose.'

'And in my book that whittles the candidates down to Delgado and Taylor. I thought me showing up might be a jolt to their composure, but it wasn't. Delgado looked stunned, but with anger rather than guilt, and as for Taylor . . .'

'Coolly arrogant?' she ventured.

'Right.'

'Simon?' Those brown eyes widened. 'If Gibson didn't send the effigies, then that would put a whole new slant on things, wouldn't it?'

'Very definitely,' I said. 'That would mean he was either murdered for something he didn't do, or for something he did do only we don't know what that something was.'

'That sounds very complicated.'

'Not complicated, baby, just mass confusion. Rather like trying to pick a winner in a field of three-year-old maidens.'

'That's difficult?'

'A punter's nightmare.'

'I see.'

The commentator's voice rose in pitch punctuating our conversation. Three furlongs to run. The suppressed excitement felt by even the most staid of racegoers was beginning to bubble.

'*And as they jump the second last, it's Tribal Crest being pressed by My Liberty with Jezail coming very strongly on the outside . . . Front Page is well there, so is Albany Alley . . . Antarctic's a faller at that one, so's Lofty Major . . .*'

There was a brief gasp from the crowd as the two horses crashed cumbrously into the hacked turf. One righted itself, avoided the groping hands of its unshipped rider and galloped blindly off to hamper the leaders. Throats tightened, screams of excitement erupted from vocal chords as Tribal Crest and My Liberty, stride for stride, came into the last. Perhaps a few eyes still lingered on the fallen horse that tried bravely to climb to its feet, only to stumble and collapse, its chest heaving. Irreparable damage. Flesh and bone. Rugged, athletic, durable up to a point, but not unbreakable. Perhaps a few hearts were touched by the way the jockey knelt by his quivering mount, stroking the thoroughbred's steaming neck. One could almost hear the whispered, 'Take it easy, boy . . . take it easy,' as he waited for the vet, the screens, and the inevitable. This was racing. All part of the spectacle. All part of the game.

'My Liberty's over safely!' Karan broke into my thoughts.

Three horses touched down simultaneously. Tribal Crest on the near side, Jezail on the far side, and My Liberty in the centre. The pressure was on. The roof of the grandstand seemed to lift visibly, a crescendo of noise swelling and engulfing the course as they raced into the final 150 yards.

'He's going to win, Simon!' Karan exclaimed, nearly wrenching my arm from its socket. 'He's going to win!'

Certainly the big grey didn't seem to be labouring under his handicap of twelve-five. Jezail was beginning to weaken and hang to the right, and although Tribal Crest was responding to his jockey's lashing whip, he was no match for Liberty's rhythmic stride. Chuck Busby had the race in his pocket and he knew it. Using hands and heels he triggered the power and swamped his two rivals, setting Newbury alight with a blistering display of supremacy.

Karan was bobbing up and down with delight as Catherine's horse glided past the post. I was looking back at the straggling finishers, trying to spot Delgado's colours, but Karan's breasts moving amply against her sweater were causing me considerable distraction.

'Intruder's seventh,' I said, summoning concentration.

'Another fried egg.'

'Duck-egg,' I corrected, grinning.

We cleaved our way to the winners' enclosure. My Liberty, led in by the young Anthony Taylor was receiving a gigantic reception from the spectators. Catherine Forrest, surrounded by a crowd of clamorous photographers stood with arms outstretched, smiling ecstatically, and slightly overplaying the part of the elated owner. Shutters clicked, flashbulbs popped as she hugged and kissed the horse's muzzle.

'He'll win the Champion Hurdle,' she prophesied as a couple of microphones were thrust towards the pretentious display.

My Liberty appeared unperturbed. He stood quietly swanking his tail as Busby dismounted and removed the saddle. The jockey, his silks smeared by mud and sweat, exchanged a few words with the actress and then made his exit to the weighing-room. A cooler was thrown over the horse and once again there was an outbreak of cheers.

Luke Taylor had now joined Catherine in the enclosure, Newton-Smith stood talking to a lozenge-sucking Delgado, Frankie Wade was sharing a joke with the luscious Amanda, and Julian Knight rested rather lamentably against the rails, a cheroot dangling from his lips.

I turned to Karan. 'What's a collective noun for film people?'

'A gaggle?' she suggested.

'Very applicable,' I agreed.

She laughed.

'Where's Amanda's pop-playing husband? Storm or Brown or whatever he calls himself.'

'At a gig, I suppose. He usually is on a Saturday.' She paused, frowned. 'Why do you ask?'

'Gibson mentioned him once. I thought it was a red herring, but now . . .'

'Yes?'

I shrugged. 'Perhaps I'm tending to concentrate too much on the favourites and not enough on the outsiders. The draughtsman paid me a visit yesterday at precisely eight-forty p.m. Everyone here plus Storm had better have bloody good alibis.'

'Most of them have. Sidney was shooting an exterior, a night scene, it went on till eleven at least.'

'Anyone missing?'

'Only Amanda.'

'So the rest are on celluloid.'

'Apart from those behind the camera like Rex and Sidney—and of course Luke wasn't there.'

Another piece of film to view. I made a mental note. 'One last question,' I said. 'It's a horrible pun, but does the name Bella ring a bell?'

She thought about it then shook her head.

'A boat, maybe?' I coaxed.

Again the shake. 'Sorry, Simon.'

'Forget it. Let's head for the bar.'

'What about the trophy? We'll miss the presentation.'

'That's right,' I said.

'Catherine will expect . . .'

'So disappoint her.'

'I . . .'

'You'd prefer to disappoint me?'

'You're making it very difficult, Simon.'

'That's the general idea,' I agreed, reaching for her hand and guiding her out of sight and earshot of the Disneyland spectacular.

Once the presentation ceremony was over, Catherine and her entourage would head for the members' bar behind the grandstand. It would be 'Congrats dahling—Champers all round', and I was in no mood for alcoholically induced gaiety.

The course offered a selection of bars and the one furthest from the unsaddling enclosure suited my purpose just fine. No film faces, just a cluster of punters and us. As we talked I realized I'd been very wrong about Karan Langford, and her puritanical feelings about sex. I'd previously categorized her as a sheltered little virgin who thought copulation was an unnatural act and I'd been wrong on both counts.

Her story wasn't unique. She'd left secretarial college bubbling with big job enthusiasm but finding only harsh reality in the big-city-single-girl-syndrome. She'd suffered a broken engagement and rebounded into a string of unsuccessful affairs. Men had abused and exploited her to the point where she wanted no further part in physical love. Her protective barrier had been strengthened the day she'd taken her typewriter and inhibitions to Catherine. The actress's world might be cardboard but it was safe and secure. The outside world held only callous males and bitter memories.

I was glad she had told me. I was also glad she'd cared enough to step out of her world and spend half the night at the Alverton nick making a statement about a callous male and a faulty seat-belt.

'Time we weren't here,' I commented, taking hold of her hand and glancing at her wristwatch. 'Grant'll wonder where the hell I've been hiding.'

She pulled back the sleeve of my jacket and looked at the tell-tale white circle left by my own missing timepiece.

'Like my lips,' I grinned, 'it got a little bruised.'

'Bruised lips heal, Simon,' she breathed.

Was that a plain statement, or was she offering me hope? Bruised feelings heal, too, I told myself. I noticed for the first time the way her left cheek dimpled when she smiled. After the way I'd behaved, I was damn lucky to be getting that. I gave my ego a mental kick for presupposing I'd be getting anything else and gestured her towards the exit.

'Mr Simon Drake?' The voice was clipped but cultured; the face rugged, moustached, and one I felt I knew but couldn't place. 'May I see your T.S.D. warranty card, sir?'

'Who's asking?' I said, slightly at a loss.

'Baker, sir. Newbury security.'

'Have we met? I seem to know——'

'That's highly probable, Mr Drake. We *are* in the same line of business—*aren't we*?' He thrust his left hand at me palm uppermost. 'The identification, sir.'

I handed it to him. He studied it briefly, then handed it back.

'Now what?' I asked.

'Now this is your sole responsibility,' he replied, transferring a black leather case from his right hand to mine. 'The Schweppes Gold Trophy, sir. I suggest you take it straight to the car.'

'Isn't this rather unorthodox?' I frowned slightly as he gave me the key.

'Very, sir, but then Miss Forrest is hardly an orthodox lady. We've tried to reason with her, insist on the usual security precautions, but she has a very persistent nature. Her instructions were most emphatic. Find Simon Drake and let him take charge of the trophy.'

'I see.'

'Do you want me to escort you to the car?'

I shook my head.

'It has been stolen once before,' he reminded me.

'Not from my hands,' I said.

'True enough, Mr Drake, then I'll bid you good day.' He nodded, lifted his trilby to Karan and departed.

We set course for the owners' car park. I took a firm hold on the leather handle and told Karan to keep talking and smiling as we tried to stroll unconcernedly through the milling spectators. Faces came and went. I felt myself stiffen every time a thigh or arm brushed unconsciously past the case. People with racecards in their hands but thievery in their hearts? Who could tell. Solid gold trophies gave me the jitters. The security machinery was available and it was meant to be used. Catherine had to be a little loose in the brainbox to shoulder me with the responsibility.

CF 2. I was never so glad to see a registration plate in my life. As Karan unlocked the driving door I caught a flicker of movement at the corner of my vision and turned my head.

'So there you both are,' Catherine walked gracefully towards us, her eyes pinned on the case, her expression a curious medley of surprise and bewilderment. Luke Taylor followed in her wake.

'Is that the trophy?' he drawled slowly.

I nodded. 'Can I leave it in your capable hands?'

'Has there been some change of plan? I understood the course supplied security men who took charge of delivery.'

Karan looked baffled. She said to Catherine, 'Didn't you delegate that duty to Simon?'

'Burden Simon?' She looked aghast. 'Of course not, dear. I leave matters of security to the experts . . .' Her voice straggled away as she saw me clench down on my teeth. 'Oh, God!' The two syllables emerged falsetto. 'You don't think . . .?'

My thoughts were austere as I pushed the key into the lock. I was back-tracking to Baker or whatever he'd called himself. Take away the moustache, the neat suit and the accent; cover his eyes with a pair of dark cheaters—put a stiletto in his hand . . . Christ, I'd even noticed the mark on his forehead as he'd lifted his trilby to Karan. It hadn't registered at the time, but now . . . Shit! I hadn't been taken once, I'd been taken bloody twice.

Catherine gasped as the leather lid dropped back on its hinges. A bay horse with three white stockings and a pin through its chest stood mounted on an onyx base. It was a hideous replica of the genuine article, bearing Catherine's name and the sick inscription: *Gold Cadaver Trophy*.

Only Taylor grinned. 'That's Captain Marvel,' he said. 'Is this someone's idea of a gag?'

'Captain who?' I queried.

'Captain Marvel—one of Catherine's horses. They're using him in the movie.'

I could see the cords tightening in Catherine's neck, every muscle stretched to the limit, the elegance suddenly gone from her body. She drew in a long breath and let it out tremulously. 'But G-Gibson's dead.' Her voice began rising in pitch. 'He's dead I tell you! Dead . . . dead . . . *dead* . . .!'

Chapter Eight

It's NICE to be proved right. There's that brief, luxurious moment when you know that your unconscious skill called instinct hasn't let you down. This morning I was good-humoured, amiable Simon Drake, the world's best friend.

I had three reasons for feeling pleased. First, my improved relationship with Karan, second, I'd been made a gift of a new set of wheels, and third, and this is where the instinct comes in, I'd been proved right about Luke Taylor having a colourful past. That guy had 'lived' in every sense of the word.

I laced up my seat belt and coaxed the red E-type 2 + 2 away from my apartment. A classy machine. Taxed, insured, a tankful of fuel and a little label hanging from the ignition key which ran: *Don't take a powder on me. I need you. Love, Catherine.* A generous lady. Generous to the point that she had me doubting her motives. Not that I'd return the car. The doubts would have to be a hell of a lot stronger before I'd look a gift horse in the mouth and demand a saliva test.

I headed for Alverton. My eyes were on the road ahead but my thoughts were on the facts contained in Grant's dossier. Thirty-nine years ago Luke Taylor was the youngest of a family of six in a Brooklyn slum. He'd run away from home when he was twelve, lived rough, and ridden the freight cars to Oklahoma. He'd spent six months at a stud farm before moving on to an auto factory in Toledo, Ohio. Then Louisiana, Mississippi, Georgia—by the time he was twenty-one he'd covered a lot of mileage and was learning to use his physique and good looks to advantage. Summer of '57 found him fame as a quarter-back in a football team. It also found him sharing a luxury suite at a Miami Beach hotel with the daughter of a wealthy industrialist; a woman called Jennifer Main who was later to become his wife. They married in the fall of '58, daddy made them a present of a 200 acre farm on the eastern shore of Maryland and son Anthony was born six months later.

It wasn't a happy-ever-after parable. Taylor had come too far too quickly to be contented with his lot. The inevitable affairs followed. Age and looks weren't important, the only criterion was money. In 1964 the United Press news agency released a story of how Taylor had been involved in a fight with the second and then present husband of Catherine Forrest. Taylor had had a broken bottle pushed in his face, hence the scar, and had retaliated in kind. The husband lost an eye, Taylor claimed self-defence, and the district attorney's office decided that the facts gathered by the police didn't warrant a prosecution.

Wherever Taylor went he made headlines. His very presence seemed to precipitate violence. So did his absence. In June of '66, Jennifer Main was found by her young son draped over the bath, blood leaking from her slashed wrists. She died a few hours later. Taylor was at an hotel in Palm Beach, Florida, when he heard the news. He'd had to climb out of Catherine Forrest's bed to answer the hospital call. A nice neat suicide. Money in the bank and his freedom. Was he going for a win double? Was Catherine Forrest number two on his slip? The questions prompted uneasy feelings as I barrelled the Jag through the studio entrance, found the theatre block and dragged on the handbrake.

'Going up in the world, eh, Drake?' Delgado braced his shoulders and tried to look like a film producer who was never short of problems, and I was only adding to the burden.

'It's transport,' I· replied matter-of-factly. 'A present from Catherine.'

'Catherine?' His brows lifted. 'Does this mean you've solved the mystery of the battered blonde and the music, or is she just being extravagant again?'

'The latter,' I admitted.

'So you're hanging on for what you can get.'

It was an under-the-breath remark and one he tried to nullify with a parody of a smile as he waved me towards theatre seven. I reminded myself that today I was good-humoured, that he had an ulcer, and that film moguls weren't the best people to deal with if they thought their authority was being eroded. I told him about the gold cadaver trophy as he pushed open the soundproof door.

There was no immediate reaction, just a momentary stiffening as he clasped his hands behind his back, and walked funereally towards a row of seats. He didn't even reach for a lozenge. 'Who is it, Drake?' he asked finally. 'I—We were all convinced it was Gibson, but obviously——'

'Obviously,' I said, adding, 'I don't have the answers. I have a few vague shadows of suspicion, nothing more.'

'Would you care to expound?'

'Not particularly, I'd rather see the film.'

'Now look, Drake——'

'No, *you* look, Mr Delgado—preferably at that screen. Let's see some moving pictures of Highwayman's fall. I'm interested in evidence, not conjecture, and that film might just provide it.'

'I will not be dictated——'

'I'm merely the piper,' I put in quickly. 'Catherine Forrest calls the tune.'

'A fact I'm only too aware of.' He sighed, massaged his temples. 'How is she? We're filming tomorrow.'

'Her condition's satisfactory.'

'That sounds like an hospital bulletin.'

'I'm not a consultant.'

'You're not Sam Spade, either, so don't provoke me with your Bogart phraseology.' He glowered at me, lowered himself into a plushly upholstered seat and barked instructions into the projectionist link-up phone by his elbow. The interior lights dimmed. There was a psychedelic splutter of colour as the screen came alive. 'What you are about to see is unedited. This sequence was filmed simultaneously from three camera set-ups—long shot, medium shot, and close-up. You'll view each one in turn.'

I nodded and settled back in my seat. The long shot had captured the incident from a camera mounted high on the roof of the grandstand. As Hunter propelled himself from the saddle, Highwayman appeared to plough right through the top of the fence. He met it squarely; there was no apparent reason why he shouldn't have cleared it with inches to spare, but he hit it and hit it bloody hard. A hurdle might have given way under the pressure, but as this was a fence it did not.

It was a spectacular fall. Spectacular in the sense that if you enjoy watching half-a-ton of racehorse travelling at 30 m.p.h. hit an obstacle and do a nose-dive, then you would have loved this one. Certainly cinema audiences would lap it up. Special effects they'd say. Horses in films don't really hurt themselves. It's trick photography. Bravo! I knew differently and winced at the sight of the big chestnut's legs thrashing to get a grip on the Kempton turf. Three legs. The fourth, the near foreleg, was just a dangling piece of smashed bone, hanging together by skin and ligament. Wade cleared the fence easily on Bright Babe, and Highwayman's misery was left behind as the camera panned to the winning post. The screen went blank.

Delgado stuck his lower lip out reflectively. 'Very unfortunate,' he said. 'Tragedy on one hand, yet by a curious twist of fate, it will undoubtedly enhance the picture. Life is full of compensations.'

I lit a cigarette, kept my eyes on the screen. The projector was beaming the same sequence but from the medium shot angle. Clearer, bigger, more detail. Delgado was spouting out a lot of technical stuff about undercranking the camera so that the projected image was faster than the real life event, but I wasn't listening. There was something about the footage which had captured my attention, something which sparked off a nagging sensation in the back of my mind. I saw the goggles explode, saw the phoney blood spatter Hunter's face and helmet, saw him leave the seat a milli-second before Highwayman's forelegs crashed . . .

I whirled on Delgado. 'You didn't detonate until after the horse had left the ground. It was two strides from the fence at rehearsal, not mid-bloody-jump.'

'We thought it would be more realistic that way.'

'It was. The horse died.'

'Patch Hunter's suggestion, Drake. You weren't around to be consulted so I gave the O.K.'

I savoured smoke and reflected. Why would Hunter stick his neck out? The stunt was doubly dangerous to the jockey if done while the horse was in mid-air. It rankled all right. It reeked of conspiracy and slammed Hunter's name up with the prime suspects.

'Patch Hunter.' The words emerged involuntarily from my lips as I turned my attentions back to the screen.

'What?'

'Sorry,' I said. 'Just thinking aloud.'

'Is something troubling you? Something about Hunter?'

I let the question ride. The close-up was passing in front of my eyes. The goggles were shattering, the redness was streaking across the B.D. initials on Hunter's skull cap, and Highwayman's near-fore seemed to jerk and drop, unbalancing the animal as he piled into the fence. Hunter went and the horse capsized; forelegs spreading, knees collapsing, a horrible entanglement of unco-ordinated limbs battling against gravity; a disgusting mockery of a vibrant thoroughbred whose powerful haunches had driven him to disaster.

'Re-run it,' I faced Delgado. 'Slow down the projection speed and freeze the frame at——'

'Here,' his hand flipped towards the phone in a quick little gesture. 'Just voice your instructions into this.'

I did. The film crept slowly up to the point of detonation and was halted the instant the goggles fractured. I studied the still frame with methodical diligence. A full minute must have passed before Delgado began drumming impatient fingers on the arm-rest.

'Look at that near-foreleg,' I said shortly, 'look closely and tell me what you see.'

'I see a foreleg, Drake,' he replied through a frustrated sigh. 'A foreleg protected by a buckle-up gaiter or whatever you call them.'

'So do I,' I agreed. 'A jumper wearing leather boots, nothing wrong in that, a perfectly normal piece of equipment to prevent damage to legs and tendons.'

'Well what——'

'How many buckles do you see?'

'Three.'

'There are four on the other leg. Notice the way the boot has expanded, those leather thongs are stretched to breaking point.'

Delgado kept his face impassive, but there was a disconcerting stare in his eyes. I asked the projectionist to re-start the film at the rate of one frame-per-second, and then I told Delgado to watch for a little blurred speck moving from the boot to the right hand corner of the screen.

'The buckle?' His forehead ridged as he followed the speck's progression. 'It became detached in some way?'

'By the same method that smashed Hunter's goggles.'

'Explosive? That's ridiculous.'

'Look at the way that near-fore's beginning to drop. You can even see a faint trace of smoke coming from the boot. That leg's been broken on take-off—long before the horse hits the fence.'

'Sabotage?'

'Call it what you like. When your special effects man threw that switch he shattered more than a pair of goggles—he also shattered Highwayman's cannon bone.'

'But the vet said the horse had snapped a fetlock.'

'Another enigma. The vet can't be traced, neither can the knacker's van.'

Delgado digested this in silence. Only the sudden sweat glistening on his upper lip told me it was giving his stomach dyspepsia. He cleared his throat. 'If an explosive cap linked to the remote control detonator was used in the way you suggest, then why didn't it blow the boot to smithereens?'

'Why didn't Hunter lose an eye?' I countered.

'Because a metal shield . . .'

'Exactly—only this worked in reverse. It protected the boot and thereby contained the explosion.'

'These are serious allegations,' he muttered, twisting his signet ring until the diamond came uppermost. 'You're intimating that Patch Hunter deliberately engineered the leg break.'

'Not quite. Let's say I'm fairly confident that he knew it was going to happen.'

'Well surely that's the same thing. Hunter tacked up the horse so the buck stops there.'

'I doubt it.'

'Which means?'

'Too many loose ends.'

'You'll question the jockey?'

'In my own way, yes.'

'But why would he do it, Drake? I can't see the logic of the situation.'

I helped his logic along by explaining how Anthony had found the effigy in the car.

'Why the hell wasn't I told?' he growled, suddenly going on the offensive. 'Why wasn't I informed?'

'Because unlike English law, I work on the premise that everyone's guilty until proven innocent—and in your case that still applies.'

'I see.' He interlaced the fingers of his hands over his right knee, sighed heavily, and closed his eyes.

'You've run out of questions?'

'One final one. Why tell me now?'

'Because of the gold cadaver trophy. The horse is Captain Marvel.'

He collected his memories, then said, 'The horse we're using in the fire sequence. He arrives at the studios tomorrow. He'll be on the premises for a couple of weeks.'

'Treat him as you would a Ming vase. Your leading lady is convinced he'll die. If that happens she'll probably have another mental breakdown and your ulcer will end up with more perforations than the stubs in your cheque-book.'

'A sobering thought, Drake. And the ultimate purpose behind all this?'

'The destruction of Catherine Forrest. When they're good and ready they'll probably send her an effigy of herself.'

'Which would produce . . .' He halted mid-flow.

'A crack-up job, a total bust,' I provided.

'Yes, yes.' He lifted his hands, not wanting me to elaborate.

'What time did you commence shooting on Friday night?' I asked, pulling a notebook and pencil from my pocket. 'I want to see the results.'

'Six—er—no, eight-thirty.'

'You don't sound very sure.'

'We wanted darkness, so we planned to shoot the exterior at six. We'd just started the first take when the heaven's opened. The sequence had to be postponed for a couple of hours until the rain petered out.'

The projector flickered into life.

I watched the clapperboard jump and fall out of shot to reveal Catherine and Julian standing by the loose-boxes at Berkeley Stables. They started to argue, he hit her across the face and she fell untidily to the ground. He left her there, pulled a fully tacked horse from one of the boxes and prepared to mount. The girths must have been ridiculously slack. I found myself grinning as Julian, left hand on pommel, right hand on cantle, wrestled vainly with the loose saddle. Finally he gave up in disgust, as the pressure of his foot in a stirrup prompted the leatherware to slip under the animal's belly. He stood with hands on hips swearing at the camera. The film jammed momentarily, the images flickering, then settling as Delgado rushed into shot. He waved a script at the camera. The screen blacked out.

'Damn fiasco,' the breath from a strangled sigh caressed my ear.

The screen brightened, again the clapperboard, same scene third take. The phone by Delgado's hand buzzed noisily. He snatched it up, uttered a few moody consonants to a guy called Taffy and dropped it back on its cradle. 'The projectionist apologizes for the film flicker,' he said tightly. 'Blames it on a broken sprocket hole—probably his own negligence for failing to clean the gate.'

I nodded, only partially hearing him. The third take had gone well. Julian had hoisted himself into the saddle quite smartly and guided the horse out of shot. The ensuing sequence of horse and rider jumping a brick wall and galloping off into infinity couldn't be credited to the actor's equestrian talents.

'Patch Hunter,' Delgado remarked.

'At what time?' I asked.

'Around nine-thirty.'

'Was he there when the saddle slipped?'

'Yes, he was.'

'And that was what—eight-thirty, eight-forty five?'

'I suppose so.' His expression was a blend of anger and irritation. 'You seem to have a preoccupation for time. Is there something you haven't told me?'

A little matter of a hypo, a Rolex, and a visit from the effigy sender, I thought wryly. 'You've been most helpful,' I wound up. 'Next stop Amanda Stewart. Just give me her address and I'll be out of your hair.'

'You're not levelling with me, Drake,' he growled, scribbling it down.

I motioned towards the door. 'Just remember what I said about Captain Marvel.'

'Like a Ming vase—yes I know. I watch the horse and somebody watches me, is that the idea?'

'You're in the clear,' I stated.

'Just like that?'

'Just like that.'

A tense, nervous smile glinted briefly.

'Intruder ran well yesterday,' I said, deciding to lift his ego. 'There's obviously room for improvement, but he seems a good sort.'

'He wasn't disgraced. I'm expecting a far better performance in the Champion Hurdle.'

'He's entered?' I was a little surprised.

'Back him ante-post and you'll get odds of 30–1.'

'I never gamble,' I told him. 'The only thing I back with any degree of certainty is my judgement.'

His eyes never left the screen. 'Some people can't tell the difference between sugar and saccharin,' he muttered obscurely.

I caught Luke Taylor off base. Hollywood Mansions, Weybridge. His tie was askew and he had a pearly pink smear of lipstick on his chin. Our eyes locked as he stepped out of the elevator and he couldn't have looked more guilty than if he'd just fallen out of a knocking shop window clutching his trousers and a leafless nymphet.

My disarming smile caused him to scratch nervously at a sideburn, tug at his collar, and arrange his lips into something between a sheepish grin and a sneer. The combination wasn't attractive. The narrowing gap of the elevator panel saved him from further embarrassment.

Amanda Stewart's flat door was ajar. I tapped lightly, entered, and was immediately confronted by a garish piece of erotica hanging on an opposing wall. A large complex mural of intertwined bodies draped across motorbike saddles. A fusion of limbs, loins, and exhaust pipes. Resisting an urge to pause and reflect, I moved quietly forward, looking for the bedworthy blonde with an affection for cowboys.

Kitchen, bathroom, single bedroom, all empty. At the end of the hall, a spacious studio—tribal masks, spears, skins on the walls; huge posters of Storm in witchdoctor garb; a marble pedestal that looked remarkably like an altar with its cosmopolitan trappings of African idols, Chinese joss-sticks, and Woolworth candles. Amplification equipment and an electric guitar rested nearby.

'You left it on the dressing-table, honey.' Amanda Stewart's voice wafted out from behind a pop-poster of Storm. Closer inspection showed it to be a door. The handle was cleverly disguised to correspond with the tremolo arm of the guitar. I flicked it down.

Stunned was my immediate reaction. I'd seen wall-to-wall carpeting before but never a wall-to-wall bed. It was circular and pink. Everything was pink. Pink furniture, pink drapes, even the floor was tessellated in pink tiles. The mirrored ceiling reflected Amanda lying on a pink quilt, in a pink negligee, idly thumbing through a copy of *Harpers*. It was quite a view.

'It's on the dressing-table,' she said again, without looking up.

She was right, it was. Taylor's wallet by the look of it. It had to be that. The colour of pigskin just didn't blend in with the surroundings.

'I'll see he gets it,' I promised, slipping it into my back pocket.

'S-Simon . . . ?' The *Harpers* slipped showing classically formed nipples pressing against the translucent negligee. 'I thought you were——'

'Luke? Yes, I know. I used his elevator. I hope you don't mind.'

'Of course not.' Her laugh was nervous. She stroked the eider-down affectionately. 'Come and sit, and don't be so silly. You make it sound as though he uses it to the exclusion of anyone else.'

'No, I imagine your husband has the odd ride.'

A flutter from her lashes told me she followed the double meaning, but she decided to play it silent and coy, in a sulky, sexy sort of way. Certainly the pose she'd adopted was openly provocative. She moved closer, legs slightly akimbo.

'Where's Rick?' I asked.

'Windsor Great Park. There's a pop concert there today, surely you've seen the advertisements?'

'I'm a little out of touch,' I said.

'Not from me,' she breathed, wrapping soft cool arms around my neck.

'I want to ask him some questions.'

'How dull.'

'Important questions.'

'Even duller.'

'Amanda . . .' I unwrapped the arms. 'Just how far are you prepared to go before you scream rape?'

'Rape?' Her voice rippled with amusement. 'Oh, Simon, you are funny. I've never screamed rape in my life.'

'So what's the angle? You're not exactly suffering from sex-starvation and I'm hardly the world's most physical guy . . .'

'Don't you like my body?' She kneeled in front of me and abandoned her last tenuous link to modesty by peeling off the negligee. Her fingers rippled over the contours in self-loving appreciation. I could see a scattering of tiny red marks on the otherwise flawless torso. Love bites. Taylor's handiwork, I mused sourly, watching as she kissed a finger and daubed it on each one in turn. No wistful innocence now, just the cheap brazenness of a calendar nude. 'Touch me, Simon,' she whispered disturbingly. 'Touch my body.'

My face was being pushed gently into the soft cushion of her breasts. She began moaning, whimpering, clinging, working the buckle of my belt loose and clawing anxiously at my zipper. Her hands were everywhere, chest, navel, thighs, groin . . . *wallet*!

'Smart little lady!' I snared the wrist. 'What incredibly nimble fingers you have.'

'You're h-hurting me, Simon!'

'Put it back.'

'It's Luke's.'

'I'll see he gets it—now put it back!'

She did. She eeled out of my grip, swore with vicious fluency, and flung herself on the bed.

My eyes wandered over the curvaceous expanse of naked skin pressed hard into the eider-down; lingered momentarily on the filmy nothingness of her panties, strayed on the visible dark hair which fanned from the moist cleft of her thighs and finished a few inches short of her navel.

'Simon . . .' There were alligator tears in her eyes. No need for theatrical blobs of glycerine, she'd learned how to manufacture the real stuff at will. 'I-I'm sorry. Y-you wanted to talk about Rick?'

Suddenly Rick was the last thing on my mind. She'd aroused me far beyond the point of no return. My heartbeat had accelerated and the urgency was beginning to build. Effigies, melodies and dead directors seemed to have no place in my thoughts as I caressed her swollen nipples, running my tongue around the hard, pink stems. My arm muscles knotted as she struggled. She wriggled a hand free and began slapping my cheeks. She bared her teeth and began working her jaw as if she was about to spit in my face. I took hold of her hair, and pushed the wet hardness of my tongue against hers. Her body heaved unwillingly as I dragged her pants over the smooth flesh of her buttocks, her protests now coming by way of an almost imperceptible quivering of her mouth against mine. 'No, Simon . . . please . . . *Oh, God* . . .' It was a murmur of submission.

Her thighs parted and I went down on her, warmly, eagerly, relentlessly pursuing the sensual trigger spots. A shimmer of pink toenails were scraping down my calf, frenzied fingers biting into my shoulder-blades, hips moving in a rhythmic circular motion, little passionate moans breaking through teeth. The shuddering eruption of a climax. Two bodies spasming and soaked in perspiration. Panting, trembling, clinging from exhaustion. Contented and drained.

Ten minutes passed. We lay in companionable silence recovering our strength and our senses, letting ecstasy wane and the harshness of reality filter back.

'Was Taylor's wallet *that* important?' I asked shortly.

The warm flesh beside me stirred. 'I'm a member of Equity, Simon, not the Festival of Light.'

'Is that a yes or a no?'

'Luke's not too sure who you are. He thinks you're working for Catherine and he thinks you're dangerous.'

'He'll get his property back.'

'By way of Catherine?'

'By way of me, tomorrow at the Olympus.'

She swung her legs off the bed and lit a cigarette on her walk to the dressing-table. She ran a brush through the gloss of gold hair and began dressing as though nothing untoward had occurred.

'I didn't come here meaning to bed you,' I said.

She blew out smoke, eyed me via the mirror. 'Cherish the memory, there won't be any seconds.'

'How about some coffee?'

'There's a launderette two hundred yards down the road. You put five pence in a vending machine.'

'Thanks.' I pulled on my slacks. 'I'll turn over the welcome mat on my way out.'

'Do that. And next time you get the urge to gather information for divorce proceedings, try knocking first.'

I drummed up a weak smile. 'You've got hold of the wrong script, baby. Divorce is a game. I don't play games.'

'You were hired by Catherine to spy on Luke and me.'

'Wrong.'

'You'll use that wallet as evidence.'

I shook my head. 'Who sleeps where and with whom doesn't interest me. Tell me Taylor spent Friday evening here in your apartment and you'll be doing him a favour.'

'You must think me pretty stupid.'

'Was he here?'

'Get lost.' She began brushing her hair again, this time with sudden intensity.

'What about Rick?'

'Rick?'

'Your husband—was he around on Friday night?'

'He was at a gig in Putney.'

'So what time did Taylor arrive?'

She banged a tiny fist on the glass surface of the dressing-table and eyed me coldly. 'I think you'd better get out!'

I stared at her reflection and began buttoning my shirt-front. She avoided my gaze and busied herself applying mascara to her lashes. Suddenly she stopped mid-stroke and turned to look at me. Her face had blanched and her eyes weren't cold any more. They were unblinking, almost expressionless, the kind that conceals what goes on behind them.

'You're infatuated with me!' she shrieked suddenly. 'You pester me at the studios and then you force your way into my apartment. How dare you make filthy suggestions!'

I stood dumbfounded, shaken by her flow of invective.

'I'm not that sort of girl,' she went on unceasingly. 'If you undo one more button of your shirt I'll call the police. Men like you are a menace to society . . .'

I caught the brief flicker of movement in the mirror, heard the faint rustle of cloth against taut muscles. I stiffened. This bloody garbage wasn't for me—she was playing to the gallery.

'But you told me you loved me,' I murmured through clenched teeth, joining her at her own game. I didn't turn around. Her eyes would tell me the moment. 'Bed and breakfast a speciality, you said. Satisfaction guaranteed.'

'I said what!'

I smiled sourly.

Her eyes narrowed and flicked left.

The hard blade of my right hand went seering towards the optical location. I'd figured it as Taylor and mentally judged the height and angle so as to connect with his throat. But this guy was shorter. Instead of finding flesh, the backhanded chop found his forehead and the impact of bone against bone sent a sharp current of pain seething up to my shoulder.

'Ricky!' Amanda screamed as the blow took him backwards, breath bursting from his lips in a tortured gasp. 'You bastard!' She turned on me and began raining little punches into the small of my back. Nuisance value really, until they started to bloody hurt. I threw her on to the bed, leaned against the dressing-table and began flexing life into my numbed fingers.

Storm was holding his head and groaning. His face was gaunt, dominated by high cheekbones and a large lipless mouth. I'd seen healthier complexions in an intensive care unit. His long fair hair was held in place by a beaded Indian band, and his voice when it came held the gentle phrasing that only a truly cultured background can provide.

'Who is this ponce?' he grated. 'Which vomit box did he crawl out of?'

'His name's Drake,' Amanda told him, manufacturing tears again. 'He's racing adviser on *Devil*.'

'But getting his oats elsewhere, uh?'

'Even cowboys indulge in a little horseplay,' I replied, looking at Amanda.

A nerve fluttered in her cheek. 'Simon,' she said, acting it sweet and reasonable now. 'You're heated . . . we all are. I don't want any more violence, so just go, yes?'

I didn't object but Storm had other ideas. He'd recovered his faculties and moved swiftly to the door, blocking my exit. His physique wasn't anything to write home about but I didn't under-estimate his destructive abilities. He had big, bony hands and the look in his eyes told me he could more than cope if given the provocation—and certainly I'd given him that. I'd been caught in his woman's bedroom and he'd have to get back his self-respect. All I'd left him with was a bruise on his forehead and a little semen on his pretty pink sheets.

'I got this phone call,' he growled. 'The guy told me I'd find you here, said you were the type that couldn't keep his mind above his flies.'

'What guy?'

'Just a guy, Drake, somebody who knew you fancied my wife. Dragging me back here has cocked up a rehearsal. You ain't jus' walking out.'

Amanda did a circuit of the bed and took refuge by a wardrobe, as though expecting, and secretly welcoming, trouble.

I said to Storm, 'You're going to get yourself hurt and that won't do the image any good.'

'I'll worry about the image, you worry about that lip of yours.'

I was watching him closely. He stood clenching and unclenching his hands, his knuckles bloodless as his fingers bored into his palms. He wanted me to come at him and I wasn't going to oblige. He'd braced himself against the door, his right leg bent slightly and taut with

124

anticipation. He was getting ideas about sinking his platform boot into my groin. I was getting ideas about quashing them.

'I don't know whether you're lucky or unlucky,' I goaded him, 'but your wife has the sexual thirst of a mare in season.'

His reaction was swift. He threw himself at me, his fist arching through the air, seeking my face but finding his own reflection as it crashed solidly into the hinged wing of the dressing-table. There was a burst of mirrored splinters and a sob of frustration in Storm's voice as he realized how easily I'd blocked the blow. A calculated flick from my fingers had sent the wing into his path like a protective shield, and his hand was now suffering the consequences. His mouth gaped as blood seeped thick and shiny from glass encrusted knuckles.

'Oh, bloody Christ!' he whimpered and then I hit him.

I didn't have to, but violence begets violence, and I wasn't in a very charitable mood. There was a strident crack as my fist took him to the floor. He lay there, staining the carpet, wheezing and making a few unintelligible noises. I reckoned I'd broken a tooth, possibly split his tongue, perhaps even fractured his jaw. I didn't stop to think about it, just flicked a glance at Amanda. She was still huddled by the wardrobe, muttering something about me being a vicious bastard, but making no attempt to aid Storm.

I didn't know Queensberry rules, only dirty ones. I dried my fist on my shirt and checked out.

Chapter Nine

'DON'T LOOK a bad sort of an 'orse,' Len Potter declared, scratching absently in the region of his left buttock and casting a scrutinous eye over Captain Marvel. 'Gonna go sick y'say? Might die y'say? Can't see it meself, but then o'course I aint no kind of expert.'

Len Potter wasn't any kind of anything. To label him as a stable lad would be to label an assassin as a delinquent. He was an unseemly, unethical, uncouth little yob who was made use of when it suited the Division's purpose and whom I only tolerated because I had to. The mere sight of him upset my system. Oily acne-pitted skin, sloping shoulders, scuffed shoes worn down at the heels, and a manner as cocky as an inside leg measurement.

'You're quite sure you understand what you have to do?' Grant's tone was dry.

'Sure I'm sure. I keeps me eyes on Marvel at all times, makes sure nobody nobbles the bleeder.'

'You feed him, exercise him, sleep with him if necessary. That animal is out of bounds to everyone except you and the horse manager.'

'Is the horse manager to be trusted?' I asked.

'His background is flawless—besides, without his consent we would never have got Potter in.'

''E's gained a nephew.' Potter drilled his ear with a forefinger and chuckled, 'Now aint 'e a lucky feller.'

Grant lifted his eyes to me but said nothing.

'You bloody behave,' I growled. 'If anything happens to that horse due to your negligence you won't be wearing a grin, you'll be wearing a truss.'

'Keep yer cool, Drakey, Marvel's as safe as 'ouses.' He slammed the box door shut and secured it with a padlock. 'Now if yer don't mind I think I'll point percy at the porcelain and splash me boots.'

'You'll what?' Grant frowned.

'Go to the lav's. Where are they?'

126

'E stage,' I said.

'Ta.' He showed me the yellow film on his teeth and swaggered off.

'Did you have to?' I muttered.

'I didn't want to,' Grant replied apologetically, 'but the mere fact that he's obtrusive makes him unobtrusive, if you see what I mean.'

We strolled away from the studio stable block and paused at the huge artificial lake. Another production in the making. Mediterranean blue water lapped the keels of a couple of speedboats as they bobbed contentedly against a backcloth of canvas and scaffolding and plaster-of-Paris cliffs. A scattering of plastic olive trees adorned the horizon and the scenic department was busily erecting coded sections of what appeared to be a jetty. We could have been in Algiers, Tunis, or even Barcelona. It was only the damp chill in the air that told us it was February, Alverton, and England.

Grant cleared his throat. 'What I find so damn mystifying, Simon, are these fingerprints. There was a perfect right-handed set on the cadaver trophy.'

'Catherine's?'

He inclined his head. 'Three effigies and each one——'

'Did you say right-handed?' I cut in.

'Yes, all the effigies have carried prints from Catherine's right hand.'

'Then it's a very clever blind. Clever but stupid.'

'I don't follow you.'

'She's left-handed.'

'You're sure?'

I had this indelible picture of Catherine pointing a Smith & Wesson Magnum at me from the wall of Delgado's office. The revolver was in her left hand. 'I'm sure,' I said.

'So what does it tell us?'

I lifted and dropped my shoulders. It had to tell us something; there had to be a credible reason why only right-handed prints were being found. It helped to ward off any last doubts I might have been having about Catherine's innocence in all this, but it created other problems to nurture, greater complexities to brood over.

'A very effective hoax,' Grant was saying. 'Getting you to believe you had the real trophy while all along the solid gold article was protected by stringent security arrangements.'

'The perfect patsy,' I said, cringing at the memory.

He flipped open a cigarette case, offered me a line up of Rothmans. 'We've been working with the police on this boat business. Every vessel called Bella, owners present and past, have been thoroughly vetted. Dead end I'm afraid.'

'What about Storm?'

'The Putney alibi checked out. He was performing at the Plaza from eight until ten.' He frowned suddenly. 'When you phoned last night you said something about him smashing his own image. What exactly . . .?'

'The literal interpretation. He took a swing at himself and discovered he had glass knuckles. It'll be weeks before he can hold a plectrum.'

'You saw this happen?'

'Ringside. Amanda's bedroom.'

The flame from his lighter hovered a few inches from his cigarette, his I'm-not-sure-I'm-going-to-approve-of-this expression very much in evidence.

'Taylor's wallet,' I said, producing it and steering his thoughts from salacity to surprise, 'found on Amanda's dressing-table and full of the sort of letters that make the *Kama Sutra* read like an exercise in modesty.'

'I see.'

'She thinks I'm a divorce specialist hired by Catherine.'

'And Taylor?'

'Likewise. I think he tipped-off Storm, hoping he'd put the boot in.'

'But you're not sure.'

'If you'd known your wallet was sitting on the dressing-table would you tip off the husband?'

'Perhaps he didn't discover the loss until afterwards.

'It has to figure that way to make sense,' I agreed.

'Luke Taylor and Amanda Stewart,' he mulled over the names, a new interest infiltrating his voice. 'It's a fascinating combination but totally out of character from what we know of Taylor's past.'

'I don't think it's the marriage stakes, but he could be stringing her along, using her. Divorce would put him on the losing end and Taylor's never on the losing end. Last time it was suicide—so now perhaps he's trying for insanity or even death.'

'Do you plan to tell Catherine about the letters?'

'I wasn't hired to bust up a marriage.'

'But if Taylor——'

'He needs more rope, Howard. We'll let him marinate, force his hand.'

Grant pursed his lips and strolled leisurely towards his waiting Daimler. The driver snapped open the rear door and the security chief climbed inside.

'You're right, Simon,' he convinced himself, 'but it's a delicate situation. Caution is the order of the day.'

'I'll follow the rules. I've no desire to go back to GO and start all over.'

'How are you enjoying your venture into the world of cinema?'

'It's a stimulating change.'

'It's idyllic,' he remarked, casting a glance back to the lake. 'Just the whir of cameras and the smell of greasepaint. Not a bent jockey in sight.'

I could have shaken the smile he was now giving me by fitting Patch Hunter into the 'bent' category. I could have made his jaw sag a little with a few revelations about Highwayman, a leg boot, and a substance that goes bang. Grant's driver looked anxious. He was standing stiff-shouldered, leather-clad fingers twitching on the door handle, eyes wandering from his wristwatch to me and offering the same kind of endearing smile as one offers to the proverbial spare at a wedding. A brief nod and a farewell lift of my hand despatched the car, driver and Grant towards the exit gates.

There was nothing idyllic about B stage. The smell of greasepaint wasn't apparent to my broken nostrils and there was no whirring of cameras, just a kind of awed silence. It was supposed to be a party yet it looked like a wake. Extras and bit-players stood strategically spaced around a tastefully furnished lounge that was large enough to hold a masonic dinner. Their faces, like the atmosphere, were anything but relaxed.

Sidney Newton-Smith was breathing heavily. He stood with an arm draped over the camera, his face displaying a harassed expression as he studied the script. 'Felix is right Catherine, and you are wrong,' he submitted, his voice sounding strangely vibrant in the strained, almost sacred, hush of the studio. 'You haven't been well, my pet. You have every excuse for not being word perfect.'

I saw Catherine's face pucker as if she was about to cry, but she controlled herself well. 'I learn the lines I am given,' she replied with considerable vehemence. 'How dare you suggest that my dialogue is anything less than consummate.'

'Your delivery is excellent, Catherine . . .' he faltered, glanced again at the script as if to make doubly sure, and to his obvious embarrassment added, 'It's just that the lines written down here in no way correspond with the ones coming out of your mouth.'

Julian Knight sniggered at that. He was sitting on a large squashy settee, hands on knees, middle fingers neatly in line with the creases of his trousers. 'I think she's flipped,' he said. 'She's been learning lines that just don't exist. It's farcical. Bloody farcical.'

'Give me that script!' Catherine launched herself at the camera, hands outstretched, the heel of her shoe catching the hem of her gown and causing her to stumble slightly, much to Julian's delight.

'Love the mode, darling. Do you think it will ever come back?'

'Don't be so damn cynical!' She threw him a piercing glance, head lifted high, neck elongated, lips tight stretched. 'Your chance of playing the male lead in any other picture died along with Rupert Gibson. Nurse the part you have because any kid from props could match your acting ability.'

'You cow!' He stood up, his face contorting in anger. 'You damn bloody cow! If *Devil*'s released in India they ought to make you sacred!'

'That will do!' Delgado roared, climbing from his canvas chair. Julian huffed moodily but it stopped him. Delgado went down a couple of decibels. 'Is it impossible for us to work together as a team? Am I asking too much by requesting that personal differences should be left outside the studio gates? Let me remind everyone that we're trying to make a grade A movie—not a spaghetti episode in a third-rate TV series.'

'They're conspiring against me!' Catherine said sharply, her hands trembling as she flipped through the script. 'All of them! It's a conspiracy, Rex, they're trying to make out I'm mad. I know my lines. Tell them I'm always word perfect.' She tossed her hair off her face and I saw the taut webbing of wrinkles around her mouth and something in her eyes—they were large, glazed, almost pleading. 'Tell them, Rex. Please t-tell them.'

'Of course, my dear, of course. Now calm yourself. There's obviously been a mistake—some kind of typing error, perhaps.' He plucked at his lower lip, ran his eyes briefly over a copy of the script and told Felix Mancroft, a mild, dapper little man with a head of superbly tended silvery hair to pick up the line.

'I'm sorry about this,' his voice was constricted as he looked towards Catherine. 'I do so hate unpleasantness and I'm sure——'

'Hold it, Felix,' Delgado interjected. 'What line are you on?'

He hesitated, then said meekly, 'None, I was simply apologising.'

'For crying out loud,' Julian voiced his impatience. 'Talk about confusing the issue!'

'Catherine is a very fine actress. I admire her tremendously and it grieves me to find myself the direct cause of this upset.'

'Thank you, Felix,' Catherine said.

'Damn crawler,' Julian muttered.

'Don't get so bloody uptight!' Amanda snapped.

Delgado purpled and bared his teeth. 'The line, Felix, *if you please.*'

The line was said and Catherine, unaided by a script, duly replied. Another line, another reply, with Felix stammering over his words and Delgado looking stricken. I followed Karan's forefinger as it traced the typewritten dialogue. We exchanged puzzled glances. Catherine's delivery was as crisp and as fluent as ever, but not a single word of it tallied with the script.

'Enough!' Delgado called a halt as some of the bit-players started to giggle. He guided Catherine to the sidelines and instructed Newton-Smith to shoot around the actress by jumping a couple of scenes.

Karan looked uneasy as her eyes lifted from the script to me. 'I don't understand, Simon. It's almost as if she's been learning the lines from another production.'

'We're supposed to believe she's going crazy,' I said, marshalling my thoughts into some semblance of order. 'This is just one more way of hammering that fact well home.'

'But the dialogue . . .?'

'Easy. Just get hold of a spare script and re-write a section of Catherine's lines. You're aiming for maximum effect, so you want a sequence with a lot of extras around—this sequence. What could be better than a party full of people.'

'Somebody switched scripts? That's impossible, Catherine's copy never leaves the house.'

'Where is it now?'

'On her bedside table. She doesn't have to bring it to the studio because . . .' She faltered, then plunged on, 'because she's always word perfect.'

'And of course Luke would know that, wouldn't he?'

'Luke?'

'That she has this thing about being word perfect. That she wouldn't bring the script to the studio and therefore couldn't prove that the lines existed. He's switched them back again by now. We won't be able to prove a damn thing.'

'You honestly believe . . .'

'Who else. You said yourself the script never leaves the house. I bet he was watching her memorize her lines in bed last night, secretly smiling while——'

'No, you're wrong. Last night was a terrible night.'

'Terrible?'

'Paranoid hallucinations, Luke calls them. We had to hold Catherine down. She was thrashing about and screaming—it was awful. It took hours to calm her.'

'Did you call the doctor?'

She shook her head. 'I thought we should have done—they have been getting progressively worse, but Luke . . .' She tailed off, sighed.

'Suggested otherwise, and Luke knows best, uh?'

'He wants to treat the illness in his own way, Simon. Nature's way he says, which reminds me . . .' She pulled a little bottle of pills from her shoulder bag. 'I have to make sure Catherine takes one of these every four hours.'

'Taylor's herbal cure, no doubt.' I unscrewed the top and teased a couple of brown tablets on to my palm. 'Buy a box of Smarties and give her those instead. She won't know the difference and they'll probably do her more good.'

'You really think . . .?'

My thinking mechanism had packed up the day events started overlapping events, and bits of Catherine Forrest's sanity began flying off in all directions. 'I can offer a logical argument, instinct, and enough circumstantial evidence on Taylor to make a very big hole. An analyst's report on these tablets might just be enough to bury him in it.'

Karan looked at me pensively but said nothing. Newton-Smith was preparing for a take. 'Are we ready, mes enfants? This is supposed to be a party, so for God's sake look as if you're enjoying yourselves. Plenty of bright party talk. The hand-held camera will weave amongst you capturing the close-ups, so let's have plenty of spontaneous laughter. The dolly-mounted camera will concentrate on Julian and Amanda. Are you chewing gum, Lloyd? Well get rid of it boy. O.K., places everyone.'

I found myself staring at Amanda. She stared implacably back, patting her lacquered curls and nibbling at a wafer-thin mint. The gold, figure-hugging dress, cut deep and low at the cleavage was giving the mike-boom operator plenty of visual amplification. It wasn't doing much for Julian. He just yawned, manoeuvred himself into some kind of clinch and began mechanically kissing and stroking her hair.

'Think sex, Julian. Think happy everyone.' Newton-Smith's eyes did a last scrutinizing sweep, then, 'Action!'

It was just after midday when I arrived at the Olympus. The sky was clotted with clouds and it was beginning to drizzle. Threading my way through the parking lot was like thumbing through a current Motor Show catalogue. Virgin paintwork, vast acres of chrome, and personalized number plates. Nothing here went *phut phut* it all went *brmm brmm*. I docked alongside a Ferrari and headed for reception.

Muted elegance was my first impression. Walls covered in a plush velvety fabric with a display of diplomas, hide-leather furniture, a huge bronze statue of Apollo, and a decorative little blonde who sat behind a variegation of telephones, sandpapering crimson nails.

'Have you an appointment?' she asked, affecting a smile.

'No, I haven't,' I said.

'We're very busy,' she tutted. 'You're too late for a maxi, the midi's have already started and the mini's don't begin until two.' Her eyes flicked briefly from her nails to an appointment book. 'Do you want me to fit you in?'

'For what?'

'A two p.m. mini.'

'I don't think so.'

'They're very good value. The treatment costs eighteen pounds and includes physical culture exercises, steam bath, foam bath, Swedish massage, ultra-violet lamp, *and* traxator therapy.'

'The traxator's a big plus, huh?'

'Very definitely.'

It sounded akin to the rack. 'I'd set my heart on a maxi,' I said.

'Out of the question. You have to book weeks in advance.'

'Just tell Mr Taylor I'm here. The name's Drake, Simon Drake.'

'Really,' she said, consumed with indifference.

I waited. She continued to buff her nails, pausing from time to time to blow away the debris and cross her eyes as she studied her handiwork. I put the flats of my hands on the desk and leaned forward. 'I don't think you heard me,' I grated. 'I asked you to tell——'

She released her breath violently. 'He doesn't see anyone without an appointment.'

'He'll see *me*.'

'Oh, yes,' she murmured, using the same tone of indifference as before.

'Yes.' I took hold of the cardboard file, snapped it once, snapped it twice, and dropped the pieces on to the blotter.

'How dare you!'

'Do I get to see Taylor now?'

'I c–can't disturb him, he's on his back in the solarium.'

'I don't care if he's on his knees in confession—get him out here!'

She flushed angrily, snatched up a receiver and tapped out a combination on the digit panel. I took a complimentary book of matches from a dispenser, lit a Chesterfield, and tried to keep my face deadpan as she complained bitterly about this horrible man in reception.

'Been upshetting the staff, Shimon?' I turned to face a foolishly grinning Patch Hunter and a somewhat sombre Frankie Wade. 'Chatting it up are you?' Hunter put a hand on my shoulder letting his breath wrap me in an alcoholic miasma. 'A piece of advish, Shimon. A piece of advish, ye–esh?'

I looked at Wade.

'Smashed,' he said simply. 'And this cowboy's supposed to be riding in the third at Windsor.' He turned to the girl. 'Key to sauna two, please Sally.'

'Do you use the Olympus regularly?' I queried.

'All the time. Best sweat-boxes for miles.'

'Advish, Shimon,' Hunter gave a lecherous wink and leered blearily. 'You need what the French call shavoir . . . shavoir . . . fff . . . Ish known as tact. You have to be gifted—*I*, Shimon, have that gift.'

'Really.'

'I'll s-show you.' He wobbled towards the desk. 'Shally, Shally, sweetie. Howse about some rudies? Let's gy-gyrate together—my place or yoursh?'

'You're pissed, Patch Hunter,' she snapped, tossing the key to Wade. 'You're pissed and you're a bum.'

'Eh?' He looked affronted. 'Lemme tell you I've straddled more fillies than you've had hot dinnersh.'

'I only eat salads.'

'She only eats shalads.' His eyes drifted lazily to me. 'Shesh trying to be smart. P'haps ish the wrong day in the month. Maybe she has cystitish or maybe ish bricked up. Who knowsh. If rumoursh are right then ish like going through a three minute car wash anyway.' He paused, belched. 'Christ, I feel shitty.'

'C'mon Don Juan.' Wade coaxed him away from the desk. 'I'm gonna try and get you sober.'

They made their way along a corridor, Wade doing his best to keep Hunter on a straight course and not doing it very successfully. I decided to lend a hand. I told the girl I'd be in sauna two, proffered my best smile, and left her making cutting observations on the verbiage of jockeys.

Hunter was having hysterics. Tears rolled down his cheeks as he pointed to a fat woman in a black leotard. She sat on the edge of the swimming pool, a leg dangling either side of a marble dolphin which spouted water from its mouth. I had to admit to seeing the funny side. Wade wasn't smiling, neither was the instructress taking a class at the far end of the pool. Old men in open-neck shirts and shorts and elderly women in tights looked aghast as Hunter joined the instructress in a unisonal, 'Exshale! Inhale! Exshale! . . .'

'You're a bloody menace,' Wade croaked, wrestling Hunter into the sauna. 'Whoever sent you that case of booze oughta be pole-axed.'

'One of my f-fansh.' Hunter teetered precariously on the balls of his feet as he struggled out of his trousers. 'Harmlush. No kick. Only had a couple of fingersh.'

'Couple of hands, more like.' Wade looked at me, smiled crookedly. 'Scotch, neat.'

'He . . . he can't hold his liquor, Shimon,' Hunter whispered, leaning on me. 'He's jealoush. Three splashes of water and a wine gum and he's anybodish.'

135

Wade drew a pained breath. 'Do you want your underpants on or off?'

'Is Julian Knight around?'

'No he isn't.'

'I'm shafe?'

'Perfectly.'

'Becaush the onush is on the anush, Frankie.'

He stood with one hand on hip, the other held limply out in front of him. Wade removed the underpants and guided him to the bench. He wilted. He gave a long, lazy smile, dropped his eyelids and snorted contentedly.

Wade relaxed. He loosened his tie, unbuttoned his collar, and studied the temperature gauge. 'He can roast for an hour and a half. I'll drag him out from time to time for a cold shower—if that doesn't sober the sod up nothing will.'

We backtracked to the pool. Wade threw himself on a lounger and lit a cigarette. He looked beat. His pale skin was drawn taut across his angular features and I could see sweat glistening through the stubble on his chin. He released smoke at the ceiling, watching it unfurl in the warm still air.

'People usually drink for a reason,' I said shortly. 'What's Hunter's reason?'

His shoulders went up a quarter of an inch and down again. 'Perhaps it has something to do with failure. The effect of two broken marriages, a run of bad luck, and a body that's taken so many falls it's held together by scar tissue and surgical steel. Maybe he's losing his nerve, Simon, who knows.'

'Had he been drinking the day Highwayman tipped-up?'

'The stunt?' He shook his head very positively. 'He's not crazy.'

'So what happened?'

'You'd better ask Patch.'

'I'd prefer the non-alcoholic version.'

He looked uncomfortable. 'You're not doing me a favour, Simon.'

'I'm after the truth, Frankie. A first hand account of what took place.'

'Am I talking to Simon Drake, racing adviser, or Simon Drake of the T.S.D.?'

'The former, unless . . .'

'Yeah, it could be "unless". I don't know. I guess I'm kind of mixed up.'

I told him I'd seen a frame by frame re-run of Highwayman's fall and how I thought it had been achieved.

He sat upright, threw his cigarette away half-smoked. 'An explosion? The poor bastard. Patch must have known—he must have. I thought there was something odd about that bloody vet.'

'Do you know who he was?'

'That's just it—he appeared from nowhere. When the accident happened Delgado asked me to find the clerk of the course and telephone for assistance. I was on my way to his office when I ran into this guy. Can you direct me to the isolation block, he says. A case of strangles, he says, and I'm a vet. Well I didn't question it at the time —I was more concerned about getting him and his little black bag to Highwayman. But afterwards I got to thinking. Strangles? Bloody hell, that's a contagious fever. The horse must have been there since Saturday's meeting and this guy didn't know where the isolation block was.'

'He was planted,' I told him. 'The isolation block patter was just an easy way of introducing himself.'

'I don't get it.'

'When you've got a free weekend I'll enlighten you.'

'It's that complicated, huh?'

'A ouija board without a glass.'

His tongue crept out to lick his lips. 'The vet or whoever he was wouldn't let me near Highwayman. I was with Delgado. We watched from a distance as he applied the humane killer. Broken fetlock, he shouted out, and Patch who was holding the horse nodded in agreement.'

'Mr Hunter's a liar,' I said. 'What was his version of the fall?'

'He blamed himself and the somersault harness. He was aiming for a spectacular back-flip, so he really kicked down on those irons. The reins were released a little too late and Highwayman got a jerk in the gob. It unbalanced him.'

The word 'unbalanced' was becoming all too familiar. Actresses and horses. The nuance was different, but the end looked predictably similar. I said, 'What else do you know?'

He opened his mouth, changed his mind, and shut it again.

'Frankie?'

He looked suspicious. 'Did you come here to pump me?'

'I came to see Taylor. I didn't even know you used the Olympus.'

'You've stuck the knife in Patch, now you want me to give it a sadistic twist.'

'I'll try and help him but only——'

'No way. The you'll-be-doing-him-a-favour routine doesn't cut any ice. It's too easy to forget you're T.S.D.'

I'd pushed a little too hard and the affability of a few minutes ago had gone. He'd remembered that Hunter was a fellow jock, that they were buddies, and that my overt questioning could only bring trouble to Berkeley stables. It left him looking worried. It left me with a sense of frustration.

'It's nothing . . . nothing to do with Highwayman,' he added after a lengthy silence. He looked past me, relief suddenly eclipsing the harrowed features. 'Hello, Mr Taylor. How's it going? Boy, you sure look well.'

I turned.

Six feet two inches of muscle and sinew looked down at me. The eyes were hostile, the lips unsmiling. A knot of tanned biceps flexed as big hands pumped at an isometric exerciser, effortlessly collapsing the chrome tube to half its extended size. He said nothing. This was a display of power. I watched his chest expand with each breath, his stomach contract with each exhalation. A pair of white stretch trunks sat low on his hips emphasizing the hard ridge of abdominal muscle, the sturdy thighs. Eight, nine, ten. Pump, pump. Sweat beaded his forehead like moisture on a glass of chilled lager. Twenty . . . one . . . two . . . three. Blood surged through enlarged veins as the exerciser moved with ever-increasing intensity. Suddenly he stopped. Silence.

Wade gave a nervous little cough and stood up. 'Better check on Patch,' he said. 'Get him in the shower.'

'Is he stoned again?' Taylor's lips barely moved.

'Stoned?' Wade forced a note of incredulousness into his voice. 'No, I wouldn't say he was stoned. A little merry, that's all.'

'Merry my ass. Sally said he was canned.'

Wade made a few noises which could have meant something or nothing and weaved his way around us.

'He cracked a pane of glass last time,' Taylor said flatly. 'You tell him he'll pay for any breakages.'

The corners of Wade's mouth tensed. 'I'll tell him,' he muttered, and retreated out of sight.

Taylor pumped the exerciser a few more times then tossed it on to the lounger. He studied me coldly as he fiddled with the sweat bands on his wrists. 'For a racing adviser you sure get around,' he said.

I smiled mechanically. 'I try to combine business with pleasure.'

'That can't be easy.'

'I work hard at it.'

'Yeah, I know,' he snapped the fingers of his right hand. 'O.K., give.'

'Sorry?'

'The wallet. I said give.'

'Yes, I heard—I thought you might have said please.

'Don't get cute, Drake!' The fingers snapped a little louder.

I gave. He rifled through the contents, satisfied himself nothing was missing and jammed the wallet into the front of his trunks.

'Passionate stuff,' I said through a whistle. 'If I hadn't been blessed with a pure mind I might . . . well . . . who knows.'

'Amanda says it isn't divorce, so what are you, a lousy black-mailer?'

'No, just lousy.'

'And you're gonna make trouble, huh?'

'I don't make it, I prevent it. If I had a malicious nature, I'd have wasted no time in telling Catherine about your love nest. You took a chance tipping off Storm. What were you hoping for—an hospital job? A few busted ribs and a stitched up mouth? Well, it backfired, Taylor. Three out of ten and a try harder note in the margin.'

He moved stealthily forward, hands balled into fists. 'If I'd wanted you worked over I'd have done it personally, not get a boob like Storm to do it for me. That way you *would* have been a hospital job—believe it, buddy.'

The hair on the nape of my neck believed it. My nerve wasn't exactly disputing the fact and the bulk of those biceps didn't call him a liar either. It was only a streak of stubbornness which made me stand my ground and press on. 'Answer a couple of questions,' I said, 'and your concern for my health might seem a little more sincere.'

'Such as?'

'Did you murder Rupert Gibson?'

139

'N-no!' He almost stumbled over the denial. 'Are you outta your head?'

'Where were you Friday night?'

'That's none of your goddamn business.'

'Amanda Stewart's?'

'Well maybe I was. Why don't you level with me—what's the beef?'

'Your wife's disturbed pattern of behaviour. Somebody's winding her up by playing mind-games. People are getting killed, horses are getting shot, I'm getting knocked around, and all the time the spring is getting tighter and tighter. Who's turning the key, Taylor—you?'

He didn't oblige me with a direct answer. He just clenched his fists a little more firmly and growled, 'You're pitching it a bit strong, Drake!'

'Politeness isn't one of my virtues.'

'Well get one thing straight—I love my wife.'

'So who's Amanda, a stable companion?'

'I've been known to have the odd affair. It's no great secret. Catherine accepts that there's a twenty-year gap in our ages . . . Look, why the hell am I telling you all this?'

'Because I'm doing the paperback psychology and you're trying to convince me you're as honest as the day is long.'

'I'm not a penny-ante hood,' he stated.

I smiled sourly. 'No, you've come along way. The rich way. You were making love while Jennifer Main was slashing her wrists. You were the instigator yet they called that suicide. I once knew a trainer who filled a horse so full of amphetamines that it ran amok killing three spectators and its jockey. They destroyed the horse and took the trainer's licence away. They called that justice.'

His dark eyes didn't flicker. They were strangely impassive. No menace, no hostility, nothing. It was only the blur of his fist connecting with the skin of my cheek which slammed home his anger.

The punch took me backwards. I'd dodged enough to avoid the full impact and I suppose what landed could only be termed a glancing blow. Nevertheless it stung badly. It felt as if I'd been smacked in the face by a batsman's six and the power behind it rocked me in a slow ungainly way towards the edge of the pool. My heel clipped the ceramic lip and I was suddenly floundering like a demented turtle in twelve feet of chlorinated water. Dizziness swept over me, shuffling my thoughts like lottery tickets in a drum. I surfaced, coughed and gulped air, easing the agonizing constriction in my lungs, trying to recover my senses. My head was pounding and I felt nauseated. I trod water, waited for the distortion to clear, and focused on the steps. Somebody was kneeling, extending a hand. I kicked towards it and grabbed. It was Wade. His whole body was trembling and he was shouting something hoarse, incoherent. I managed to retch out an 'I'm O.K.,' but it wasn't me he was worried about. His bottom lip was bleached white from the pressure of his teeth and his eyes were wild, frightened. He gripped my lapels in a stranglehold and began shaking me. Suddenly, alarmingly, my head cleared and a broken sentence seeped through to my waterlogged brain.

'The shower, Simon,' he croaked. 'Hunter . . . the sh-shower.'

I was too dazed to grasp the full significance of the words. I looked briefly around for Taylor but he wasn't in sight. Wade began pulling me towards the sauna. I stumbled, hampered by my wet clothing. My movements were sluggish, unwilling to accept my mental commands. I swayed through the open door, groped my way to the shower cubicle.

'I-I've phoned for an ambulance,' Wade stammered, and then I saw Hunter. He was huddled in a foetus-like bundle on the porcelain floor, a black, sticky stain of blood pulsing from a wound on the side of his head; a four inch gash that gaped symmetrically like a melon slice.

'Have you moved him?' I asked.

'Only to release the water. He was lying f-face down, his body blocking the drain-hole. The spray was full on . . . Christ, if I'd been a few seconds later he . . . he would've drowned.'

I took a towel, made a compress and tried vainly to stop the bleeding. His eyes flicked open only to stare blankly out of their sockets. The lips were moving in the crimson-streaked face, his broken plate of false teeth wobbling hideously as saliva dribbled over his lips. He was breathing, but only just.

The wail of an ambulance siren percolated the stillness. Shakily Wade turned away. He fumbled for a cigarette, inhaled deeply, holding the smoke long in his lungs before expelling it. His face had drained and his chest began to heave against a surfacing sickness. He put a hand to his mouth and said predictably, 'I've gotta get the fuck out of here.'

Chapter Ten

THINGS GRADUALLY slipped back to normal. I resumed my duties as racing adviser and a fortnight passed without anything untoward happening.

Patch Hunter remained on the critical list. Fractured skull, cerebral haemorrhage, possible brain damage, no visitors. They said he'd been lucky. They said that jockeys who took showers while under the influence of alcohol should be grateful to sober jockeys who arrive in time to save them from drowning. It was an accident, they said. Hunter had slipped and caused his own injuries. Knowing all about convenient accidents, I remained sceptical. I dare say hundreds of people slip on hundreds of bars of Lux every day of the week—perhaps even a few split their heads open in the process. But Hunter? Exploding leg boots and wax effigies provided more than enough doubt. The jockey was too ill to even know he was ill, and even if he pulled through, the odds were stacked against him remembering what had happened. So that left me with an educated guess. Names, like Taylor, Bernard, Stiletto. Hunter was a pawn in an intricate game. A pawn who liked his liquor, and was therefore unreliable. The game couldn't continue with any degree of safety just so long as he had a hole in his face. That hole had been effectively plugged.

This morning Delgado looked happy; a phenomenon I credited to two reasons. Fourteen days of uninterrupted filming and Intruder winning the Princess Royal Hurdle at Doncaster on Monday. The relatively inexperienced Frankie Wade had ridden a flyer of a race and piloted the horse to an easy three lengths victory. He hadn't been up against My Liberty but he'd flattened some very impressive opposition just the same. Delgado had ordered champagne for everyone and immediately announced that Intruder would now be a definite runner in the Champion Hurdle. Glasses clinked and Julian actually said something nice to Catherine. Life was full of surprises.

I'd been keeping a watchful eye on Captain Marvel. Every morning and evening I would take a stroll to the stable area and exchange a few enquiring words for a mouthful of cockney lip from Len Potter. This morning I hadn't broken that routine. I'd strolled, asked after the animal's health and received the usual reply, 'Course 'e's O.K.—bin running round like a blue-arsed fly to keep 'im that way, ain't I. By the way, Drakey, who's the bird with the big norks?'

It was a limited description but I assumed he was referring to Amanda Stewart. I told him passion personified, to which he replied, 'Passion who? Never 'eard of 'er. This film ain't got nuffin. I've seen better casts on a busted leg.'

The cast, lousy or not, were all gathered at Berkeley stables. Technicians manhandled equipment from trucks as I wrestled with the temperamental tack-room pay-phone in order to contact Howard Grant. I was after the analyst's report on Taylor's tablets, a report I would have had ten days ago had I not overbalanced into the pool. The aquatic mishap had loosened the screw cap, water had seeped in, and I'd ended up with a bottle of chlorinated brown mush. It was back to square one and a lengthy time-lapse before Karan had been able to obtain a fresh supply.

'I have the report.' Grant's voice came grudgingly down the line after accepting the call transfer charge.

'Good news or bad?'

'That depends whose side you're on.'

I held my breath as words like 'potassium molybdate', 'inositol', 'pyridoxine', 'ascorbic acid' echoed from the earpiece.

'Sounds lethal,' I said.

'Absolutely harmless,' he replied.

'Harmless? Isn't there anything among that lot that could cause her to throw fits?'

'Nothing.'

I was stunned. 'What about abscorbic acid, surely that's——'

'Vitamin C, Simon. You're on the wrong tack. Those tablets can do her nothing but good.'

I managed a dispirited thank you and rang off. I stared out of the tack-room window, my thoughts orderless. Julian and Amanda were behind the camera talking to young Anthony Taylor. Newton-Smith and the assistant director were huddled in conference on the steps of Catherine's caravan, with Delgado near at hand as always. Could I be wrong about Luke Taylor? The question blotted out the scenery like a safety curtain during an interval. Intuition told me I wasn't wrong, but I couldn't set intuition against facts. The pills were as wholesome as sugar candy kisses and that was an end to it.

On my way out I ran into Wade. He'd been deliberately elusive since that morning at the Olympus, and now we were face to face he looked decidedly apprehensive. He held a saddle and bridle in one hand and a can of Coke in the other. Sweat glistened along his hairline as he removed his skull cap. 'Just back from the gallops,' he announced in a strained voice. There was a sharp hiss as he pulled off the strip tab and punctured the Coke. He gulped greedily at the contents, belched, and wiped foam from his lips with fingers that wouldn't have built the first tier in a house of cards competition.

'You seem a little nervy,' I said. 'Do I bother you, Frankie? Why the wide berth treatment of late?'

He coughed awkwardly. 'W-wide berth treatment?'

'Something's weighing heavily on your mind. Why not release the tension.'

'I-I don't know what you mean. I've got to take a shower.'

'Hunter did that and look where he ended up.'

'Leave it out, Simon.'

'I can't leave it out, Frankie. We were both there, remember?'

He said nothing.

'I'm going to keep probing, Frankie.'

Still nothing.

'You're not helping Patch by clamming up.'

'I told you before—it hasn't anything to do with the Highwayman stunt.'

I made a big show of sighing heavily. Hunter's touch and go condition was my highest card, so I played it and lied a little. 'If Hunter pulls through, and that's a bloody big *if*, then he'll only be a shadow of his former self. Sure, he *might* recover in time—but he hasn't got any time. He's the wrong side of thirty-five and as a jump jockey he's finished. If he's lucky he'll get an annuity from the Injured Jockeys' Fund and part-time employment chalking up odds in a betting shop.'

'All right!' He hurled the saddle and bridle on to the tack-room floor in a kind of impotent fury. 'Perhaps he didn't slip in the shower. Perhaps somebody did fix him, I don't know. Maybe I don't bloody care. I've kept quiet up to now to protect him, but if I'm gonna get this martyr bit rammed continually down my throat then . . .'

'Yes?'

'Then you oughta know how bent he is.

'And how bent is he?'

'He's been strangling Intruder.'

'Intru . . .?' I began, then halted, astonishment robbing me of further speech.

'He's been stopping it every race, pulling the back teeth out of the bastard.'

'You're sure?'

He nodded heavily. 'That horse moves faster than shit off a shovel—yesterday I proved it. I've known for months that it was a good animal but I've never been allowed to get a leg either side of it. Patch might've fobbed Delgado off with his phoney excuses—he even had me fooled at first, but you can't fool all of the people all of the time. I knew it in my gut. Call it jock's instinct if you like.'

I did like. I wasn't sure if it had any bearing on my present commission, but it was certainly my line of country and very much T.S.D. business. I wanted to hear some of the excuses.

'First it was the hurdles. French hurdles are box hurdles, Patch used to say. Intruder's not used to the British ones, he's trying to go through the top of 'em and he keeps rapping himself badly. Then he dredged up the old one about the horse going short on him—you know, not striding out. His action went scratchy so he eased him because he thought he was feeling a bad leg. He was worried, he said, about doing further damage in case the animal broke down. All crap. All lies. He had Intruder's head screwed round to his bloody boot.'

I pushed a cigarette between my lips and he produced a box of matches from a pocket in his jodhpurs and gave me a light, the match shaking in his cupped hands. I said, 'The only time I've seen Intruder in action was during the Schweppes. He looked about as impressive as a drugged tortoise.'

'You only saw half a horse that day.'

'Meaning?'

'Read between the lines, Simon.'

'Dope?'

'I think so. I've never seen Intruder so listless.'

'Hunter must be crazy,' I murmured, breathing smoke. 'You'd have to be crazy to deliberately tranquillize a horse and then jump hurdles with it.'

'You'd have to have one hell of a good reason,' he agreed.

I reflected. 'You systematically strangle a horse to get the price up and the weight down. You do it because you're corruptible or because you're under pressure from the owner or trainer or both and you don't want to lose your job. If you're really ambitious, you use the guile God gave you, keep the owner and trainer out of it, and make a private killing. Which way was Hunter playing it, Frankie?'

He gave a vexed sigh and parried with a question of his own. 'More to the point, Simon, which race?'

'A big one with a nice fat ante-post book.'

'The Champion Hurdle?'

'You're reading my thoughts.'

'Do you think the money's already been spread?'

'I reckon it has to be. The ante-post odds on Intruder must have taken a tumble since that win of yours.'

An intensity came into his voice. 'But in the Champion Hurdle they all carry fixed weights. As good as Intruder is, I can't see him beating My Liberty.'

'Neither can I, Frankie, unless . . .'

'Unless what?'

'Unless Liberty's scratched.'

He grinned. 'Fat chance of that. Why on earth would Catherine Forrest withdraw a horse that's won the race for the last two years in succession.'

'Why indeed.'

'Is that supposed to mean something?'

'Just an observation.'

He grunted with sour amusement. 'Busby without a ride—ha, that's a laugh.'

'Frankie Wade without a ride isn't quite so funny, huh?'

'Me? I ride Intruder.'

'Wrong. If Liberty's scratched you'd ride sweet eff-all. You'd be jocked off because Delgado would put Busby up. It's all part of a plan to justify Intruder's improvement. You unwittingly played a key role by winning Monday's race. That performance must reflect on Hunter. He'll be seen as a has-been lush and Intruder will be seen to be settling into English racing. When Intruder wins the Champion Hurdle, Delgado will pass it off as brilliant jockeyship on the part of Chuck Busby.'

'You mean *if* Intruder wins.' A flash of annoyance rippled across his face. 'This is hypothetical rubbish, Simon and you know it. Give me one reason why My Liberty should be scratched?'

'Highwayman's leg boot.'

'That's a reason?'

'I don't expect you to understand, Frankie. I'm only just beginning to understand myself.'

He drained the Coke, his mouth loosening from anger into a reluctant grin. 'Yeah, I remember, a ouija board without a bloody glass.'

'You've just provided the glass.'

'Are we getting a message?'

'How about some people can't tell the difference between sugar and saccharine.'

'Eh?' He nibbled on his lower lip. 'I think you lost me somewhere.'

'Rex Delgado,' I murmured, feeling my skin tighten with a sudden chilling awareness as the name flowed in on the slip-stream of my thoughts. 'He said that to me about Intruder—even told me to get on while the odds were high. The bastard spelled out the plan in a sentence and I thought he was nothing more than a dreamer.'

'Sugar and saccharine?' He mulled over the words. 'Is that what you call a synonym?'

'No, Frankie,' I grunted, 'that's what you call confidence.'

I spent the rest of the morning avoiding people. I wanted to be alone and to think things through in a calm and rational manner. Not easy, not now. Not with Delgado smiling sweetly at Catherine and prancing about like a head prefect on Open Day.

My mind spun wildly, like a disengaged cog-wheel.

Tell him you know, one half of it said. Wipe that big china-white smile from his face with a question about the fourth and final effigy. It's My Liberty isn't it Rex? Of course it is, the wax is grey. And something's broken—his leg, neck, back . . . Can't run him now. Not in the Champion Hurdle. Far too risky. Poor, poor, Catherine. Chuck hasn't got a ride? Put him on Intruder—Wade hasn't the experience and Hunter's half dead. He did it? He won? A horse that at one time seemed destined for the glue factory?

No . . . ! I took a calming breath. The other half, the tenable half, said nail him with evidence. Unscramble your brains, you've got time to collect it. Tenability won, by a very short head.

The lunch wagon arrived at one-thirty and I was forced to socialize. I joined the queue, took a plastic tray, and filled it with a random selection of plastic pots containing an obscure selection of plastic food. I steered Karan away from the assembly and opted for straw upholstery in the seclusion of the barn.

'Not eating won't solve anything.' She advanced, curling a strip of smoked salmon around a fork and teasing it into my mouth. 'You're beginning to look peaky and undernourished.'

'All work and no play,' I said.

'You're not getting enough.'

'I know. I need a good woman.'

She fluttered those richly-lashed eyes. 'I'm talking about food.'

'Boiled beef and carrots.'

'What?'

'I haven't had that for years. I need a housekeeper, old and homely with a good line in boiled beef and carrots.'

She looked at me, evaluating my expression, a little unsure. She transmitted a mysticism, a purity, an aura of total femininity. It smothered my uncouthness, inverted everything I'd learned about sex being a game of skill, and almost turned my lascivious urges into something akin to love. I held her gaze while the seconds passed, then said, 'Good, housekeepers are hard to find. Maybe I'll just settle for a course of Luke Taylor's pills.'

She lifted an eyebrow. 'Has Captain Grant——'

'He has and Taylor's clean. They contain an alphabet of vitamins plus herbs and amino acids. Take one with a nut cutlet for a healthy, more rewarding life.'

'They have no ill-effects?'

'None whatsoever. I've had to file right-handed fingerprints and paranoid hallucinations under "Pending". But, all is far from lost—as one door closes another door——'

'Please, Simon!' She cut me off with a quick little gesture. 'I don't like it when you're flippant. Something has made you angry and you're trying to neutralize it by making fun of yourself.'

'That's an astute observation, Miss Langford.'

'Do you want to talk about it?'

I talked.

'Rex . . .?' There was a fixed, agonized disbelief in her eyes. 'You're sure—I mean you're absolutely sure?'

I rubbed my neck a few times. 'It's not like a ship in a bottle. Wade provided the string but it doesn't all come together when pulled. Delgado sent the effigies—of that much I'm sure.'

'But t–that's horrible. He's been a friend of Catherine's for years.'

'Time can have the effect of an impenetrable set of blinkers, and that's where he's scored. Did Catherine ever tell you about a West Indian dresser who died after being sent a voodoo doll?'

'That happened more than forty years ago.'

'Catherine never forgot it and, if my guess is right, neither did Delgado. He remembered the shattering effect it had on her, so he built his whole scheme around it. An evolution of effigies which would culminate in the withdrawal of My Liberty from the Champion Hurdle.'

Karan looked perplexed. 'Why not just slow Catherine's horse down with drugs? If Rex had Patch Hunter on the inside, wouldn't that have been easier?'

'Much, but drugs have a habit of showing up in tests and red hot favourites that run badly don't get overlooked by the stewards. No, Delgado's plan is foolproof. Use My Liberty to prop up Intruder's ante-post price, disperse a large sum of money in discreet quantities throughout every betting medium in the British Isles and then kick away the prop with effigy number four. No risks. Catherine's been properly programmed. If that effigy arrives, then nothing on earth will stop her from pulling My Liberty out.'

The vapour dissipated as she blew on her coffee. 'I can't believe it, Simon,' she said softly. 'Rex wouldn't . . . he couldn't . . . not torture Catherine's mind to the point of insanity. What about the film? He has everything to lose.'

'He has nothing to lose,' I reminded her, 'it's Catherine's money that's backing the production. I think he set the movie up solely because he needed a platform from which to operate. He bought the screen rights on a racing novel because that provided a workable format. I'm not saying he wants the film to be a flop, but with the kind of money he's going to make from the betting coup I don't expect he gives a damn either way.'

She jerked her head away looking dazed. 'So the accidents on the set, the music, the switching of scripts——'

'Isn't the work of Delgado.'

'Isn't?' she gaped.

'The effigies are effective enough on their own. Delgado wouldn't want to completely unbalance her mind. Have Luke Taylor take over her responsibilities? No chance. Risk the fact that she might be in the funny farm when Liberty's effigy arrives? No, sweetheart, that's another twist altogether.'

She stared morosely into her coffee. 'So somebody else . . .? I'm lost, Simon. Utterly and totally lost.'

'My crystal ball's a little cloudy too,' I told her, managing a smile.

'Catherine always believed it was Rupert Gibson.'

'So did Delgado. When the melodic phone calls began to conflict with his own interests, I reckon he decided to blue-pencil Gibson and fit me up as the executor. I've still to clear my name on that score. Proving my innocence means proving Delgado's guilt.'

She moved her head from side to side, dumbly. 'I—I suppose it is all feasible.'

'A lot of theory and very little fact,' I admitted, 'but when Wade opened up about Intruder it all interlocked. It took on just one shape —a pound sign.'

She nodded absently, as though she was too dazed to comprehend. She smoothed the material of her skirt and drew her knees up to her breasts, her face partially hidden by her hair. Only the delicate green of her eyeshadow and the tip of her small freckled nose were visible.

I stroked a finger along her cheek and explained how I'd foolishly set myself up on the morning I'd viewed the rushes of Highwayman's fall. 'As I left the theatre I asked Delgado for Amanda Stewart's address. Like a mug I gave him another chance to stitch me up and he took it by tipping-off Storm. The jealous husband bit. Lover caught in bedroom. Boy, did I fit the role.'

'And did you?'

'Did I what?'

'Fit the role.'

'Of course not,' I lied. 'Storm only reacted violently because he'd been primed.'

'I'm glad.' Her mouth opened at the touch of my lips.

I felt a heel as I kissed her. 'Keep saying things like that,' I breathed, 'and I'll begin to believe you care.'

'I worry about you, Simon. I care very deeply because you care about Catherine.'

That wasn't quite the answer I'd hoped for. I smiled bleakly. 'Sure,' I said.

'When will you tell her about Rex?'

'Just as soon as the breaks start running with me and I can turn supposition into evidence. Delgado has a celluloid alibi and I've got to crack it.'

'Promise me you won't take any risks.' Her sensitive hands fondled mine. 'First Rupert, then Patch . . . . I couldn't bear——'

'You won't have to,' I said reassuringly. 'As you say in this business, I'll just wait in the wings for my cue.'

'Which has just arrived, dear.' The distinctive voice of Julian Knight startled me. He stood framed in the barn doorway, his face displaying a quizzical, slightly amused expression. 'Sorry to break up the party but Sidney's calling for you.'

I shifted my legs. 'Problems?'

'Something to do with Catherine's saddle. The old bitch can't get her feet in the stirrups.'

'Don't be so boorish,' Karan glared.

'Sorry, sweet.' He glanced over my shoulder, finger-combing a strand of hair which fell loosely across his brow. 'Freudian slip. I meant the "old girl", of course.'

I shrugged into my jacket and asked Karan to give me half an hour. I followed Julian's mincing gait and tried to ignore the amusement in his voice as he made me the butt of his sarcastic little quips. 'Love the phallic symbol,' he sniggered, as we passed the Jag. 'I used to have one but mine was in Matchbox series.'

I leered at him and crossed the courtyard. We headed for a strip of woodland near the gallops.

'I have a question,' I said, pausing deliberately to light a cigarette as we came within sight of the film crew. 'Cast your mind back to an incident which happened just over a fortnight ago. You were filming here at Berkeley, it was a Friday night and you had trouble with a slipping saddle.'

He gave a grim little nod. 'How can I forget it. Those girths were slacker than a Curzon Street whore.'

'What time did it happen?'

'Why?'

'Because it's important.'

'To whom?'

'To me.'

He pursed his lips, his stance attentive, the tilt of his head enquiring. He smiled suddenly, a wide, rather unnerving smile. 'You know you're really quite attractive. A bit of a mongrel mixture perhaps, but appealing just the same. In time I dare say I could get to like you.'

'Are you making a bloody pass?'

'You flatter yourself, Drake. Your heterosexual hackles are showing. Besides, I'm off white meat. I have a good thing going with a negro film editor.'

I breathed smoke, glared.

'You won't get anywhere with Karan Langford,' he went on. 'Better men than you have ended up limp through trying—if you follow my meaning. Rumour has it she's harbouring the holy grail between her thighs.'

My temper snapped and I grabbed him by the throat. He let out a terrified squeal, his eyes began to water and his face suffused with blood. I expected him to swing wildly or at the very least kick out, but he did neither. He just stood there frozen into immobility, wheezing like a staved in geyser.

'You're pathetic, Knight,' I growled. 'A pathetic little poof who makes me sick to my stomach. Now either you start talking about big hands and little hands or I'm going to rupture your windpipe!'

'Eight . . . eight-f . . . forty-five.' His breath rasped in his throat.

'You're sure?'

'Ye-es.'

I let him go. The time reinforced Delgado's alibi. I'd seen the saddle slip on film and I'd seen the producer rush into shot. If Delgado had been at Berkeley Stables at a quarter to nine, then he couldn't have been in a boat house supervising my knockout jab. It was unshakeable. I repressed an exasperated sigh.

'Y-you're a maniac, Drake,' Knight muttered through strained breath, dusting the lapels of his safari suit. 'You . . . you won't get away with this!'

'What are you going to do—write me a letter on stiff cardboard?'

'Report you to the production manager.' He stumbled away.

I walked towards the woodland, picked my way through the light stands and found Newton-Smith.

'Simon, dear boy.' His expression was pained. 'It's Catherine's saddle. There's been a cock-up with props and we're having to improvise.' He held up a pair of stirrup leathers and irons. 'These are far too long for Catherine's comfort.'

I told him it was only a case of making a few more holes. 'Send somebody to the yard,' I added, 'find the head lad and ask him for a leather punch.'

His bald head nodded like a clockwork toy. 'Runner!' he bellowed.

Amanda Stewart was getting restless. The camera was trained on her and her horse but no activity was taking place. She slipped her feet from the irons and let those long unsurpassable legs dangle freely against the animal's flanks. The top button of her cheesecloth blouse came under considerable pressure as she lolled back in the saddle, inflating her breasts. I wondered how many hands had been on them since I'd fondled them last. 'How much longer, Sidney?' she asked, through a polite little yawn.

The director looked at his watch, swore vociferously, and arrived at a decision. 'O.K., take ten minutes everyone. And I mean ten—not a bloody weekend.'

There was an audible murmur of approval and relaxation en masse. Amanda dismounted, took a freshly lit cigarette from an ogling sound technician's hand and offered everybody her swift, wide smile. Everybody except me. I received a cold glance and a thin wisp of her perfume as she prowled provocatively past.

'I need a holiday,' Newton-Smith was saying. 'A month away from all the tensions created by this lousy business. I'll take it a few days prior to *Devil*'s release. That way I won't have to grin and bear the malefic reviews.'

'Not even a spark of optimism?'

'Not the faintest glimmer. As George Cukor once said, give me a good script and I'll be a hundred times better as a director.'

'So you'll forget all about it and fly off in search of the sun.'

'Not fly, Simon, sail. I own a thirty-five foot ketch. It'll be Cannes or Nice or——'

'A boat?' I interjected.

'Named after my first wife. What a mistake that was—the marriage I mean, not the boat.'

I caught his expression and grinned. 'Constance?' I asked casually, grabbing the first name that came into my head.

153

'Arabella,' he said.

A tremor ran through me as I did a mental playback, watching the lifebelt roll across the boathouse floor, remembering how the lettering had been partially obscured by spray dust. *Arabella*. It had to be that. It was too damn close to be coincidence.

I let a few seconds slip by. I didn't want to appear anxious for information and a hasty question might bring suspicion. I smiled and said hello to the continuity girl. She had a flat chest, over-muscled legs, and a face like Whistler's grandmother. I watched her fiddle a cartridge of film into a Polaroid camera and then I turned back to Newton-Smith.

'I've always fancied a boat,' I said, keeping my voice even, 'but one hears so much about high mooring fees . . .'

'It can be expensive,' he agreed, his bald head again bobbing mechanically. 'Arabella's moored at Staines. Rex owns a riverside cottage with a fairly large boathouse. He only uses it during the summer, so for six months of the year I can dock there rent free.'

'Very convenient,' I said softly, pleased with his answer.

He stirred impatiently, slapping his palm against his thigh. 'Where the hell has that damn runner got to!'

Catherine Forrest and Rex Delgado were forging towards us. Catherine was leading a chestnut gelding, tacked, apart from leathers and irons, and she appeared in good humour. Delgado was talking to her. The new Delgado. A man I was seeing for the first time. This was the dedicated, ruthless, supremely confident model. The con-man, the killer. I could almost hear the thoughts buzzing behind that high forehead, plotting the moves ahead with chess-like precision. I watched the muscles flex in his jaw as he spoke; I heard Catherine laugh, that distinctive forced laugh of hers. She was wearing cream jodhpurs, a suede jacket and a silk scarf knotted loosely around her throat. A hoop of grey velvet secured her hair. She looked radiant but it was a delusory radiance created only by the meticulous make-up of her face. An expert covering of studio cosmetics to obliterate the pallor, the tensions, and the agitations which lay hidden beneath its delicate surface.

'Simon, darling,' she said in her breathy, emotion-charged voice. 'I have a horse and I have a saddle. I can't use either if I'm expected to ride with these ridiculous stirrups.'

'All under control,' Newton-Smith assured her. 'As soon as the necessary gadget arrives Simon will punch some extra holes in the leathers.'

'We can't afford these delays.' Delgado heaved a sigh. 'If it's not Patch Hunter knocking himself senseless in a shower cubicle, then it's minor irritations with props.'

'That sounds very callous, Rex,' Catherine said.

'Hunter drank too much, my dear. He only has himself to blame for his predicament.'

He has *you* to blame, I thought sourly, watching his lips compress as he lit a cigarette with casual deliberation. *You* organized Hunter's departure because you knew I was going to question him. *You* played on his weakness and sent him a case of booze. He almost died because of *you*.

'Something the matter, Drake?' He must have caught the look in my eyes.

I balled my shoulders, twisted my mouth into a smile. 'How's the ulcer?' I asked.

'Tender but tolerable.'

'You look damn well on it.'

'I won't drop dead on the set if that's what you're thinking.'

'I'm sure Simon isn't thinking anything of the sort, Rex,' Catherine put in impulsively. 'He's concerned about . . .' She faltered on finding her stepson at her elbow.

He wiped sweat from his eyes with the sleeve of his shirt, heaved a spade off his shoulder and stabbed it into the turf. 'Work completed,' he said to Newton-Smith.

'What work?' Catherine's eyes jerked from the boy to the director.

'Anthony's been helping to dig the pit.'

'Over by that clearing.' Delgado gestured with his arm. 'We're mounting a camera down a pit to get a ground level shot of the horses. Galloping hooves—mud flying in all directions—you know the technique.'

'Y-yes, yes I do,' her eyes flickered to the clearing, her tone abstract and distant.

'Is something wrong, Catherine?' Newton-Smith's forehead corrugated into a frown. 'I'm sorry if my making use of Anthony has offended you, but he did offer and I didn't think——'

'Of course not, Sidney,' she tried to hide it but her face showed a definite discomfort, almost repulsion. She composed herself and

155

managed a thin bubble of laughter. 'It's me . . . I'm just being silly.'

'Neurotic, more like,' Anthony murmured.

'No friction, please!' Delgado spoke briskly in an attempt to assert his authority. 'I will not have your mother upset by——'

'*Stepmother*,' he corrected quickly, yanking at the spade handle and once again slashing the blade into the turf.

'Ant . . . please . . . I beg . . .'

'Beg, Catherine?' There was a faintly aggressive assurance in the boy's stance. 'Why are you begging? What is it about me that disturbs you?'

'It's not you, it's . . .'

'Yes?'

'It's . . .' She switched her gaze to a point just above my left shoulder. She seemed to be shrinking.

I felt something move behind me. I turned.

It was the stunt arranger and a guy I hadn't seen before. His presence was having an unnerving effect on Catherine, and it wasn't difficult to see why. Pale, efficient-looking eyes, spectacles, greying hair. Although slightly younger and taller, he bore an uncanny resemblance to Rupert Gibson. The stunt arranger saluted with a nod, and spoke directly to Newton-Smith:

'Ed's padded and ready for the drag. What time is the take?'

Catherine stared, gulped, and demanded, 'Who—who is this man?'

Delgado frowned. 'Bill Cooper,' he said, 'I thought you knew—'

'Not Bill. Don't be inane! It's this . . . this . . .'

'Ed Sturgess,' Cooper put in. 'He's dragged by his horse when you shoot him.'

Sturgess bowed, grinned widely.

'You're the one who attacks me?' A muscular reflex caused her mouth to jerk.

'Yes, ma'am.'

She turned on Delgado. 'I'm always consulted on casting. This man is . . . I can't work with him, Rex . . .'

'But it's only a bit-part, Catherine. Ed's a stunt rider——'

'I don't care who he is!' She swayed slightly and clutched at my arm. 'Simon. Oh, God, Simon! You understand, don't you?'

I reckoned I needed a computer to keep ahead of the workings of her mind but as Anthony pulled on the spade and once again drove it into the turf, it all came together.

'Neurotic,' he said again, sneeringly.

Catherine's eyes vamped whitely as they followed the blade. She clung to me, trembling, stricken with facial paralysis, her make-up suddenly falling apart. 'You're going to kill me!' she yelled at Sturgess. 'In the woodland! Y-you're going to kill me with that spade!'

He looked at her, lips agape. 'Miss Forrest, I——'

'Don't deny it you filthy liar!'

'Catherine—for heaven's sake!' Delgado said firmly and forcibly. 'What on earth's got into you?'

She swallowed. 'I won't do this scene. I won't—I won't succumb to this machination.' She swallowed again. 'Oh, God. I feel dizzy. Take me back to the caravan—take—take me home.'

Delgado mopped his face with a handkerchief. For a second I thought I saw a look of genuine concern in his eyes. I also thought I saw Anthony's mouth twitch with a gesture of satisfaction. I discounted them both on reasoning it was all too easy to read false emotions into fleeting gestures. With all the rigours of the past weeks my cerebral forces were hardly at their judicial best.

Technicians and members of the cast were beginning to stare. Catherine, her countenance gone, turned to face them. 'Who are you all gaping at?' Her voice pitched into something close to hysteria. 'I'll tell you who—Catherine Forrest, the star of this picture. Make no mistake—I *am* this picture. I have a pedigree . . . a career spanning more than sixty films. In '39 I was earning six thousand dollars a week and had twenty-five fan clubs totalling thirty thousand members. I was worshipped. *Worshipped*, do you hear me!' She shook her hair into a state of dishevelment. 'I will be worshipped again! Not—not posthumously! There will be no ride in the woodland. This *STAR* doesn't feel in the mood for dying!'

There was silence. Nobody moved. All eyes were on the actress, the words of her flawless performance still ringing in their ears. She relinquished her hold on me, back-stepped, and was caught by Delgado.

'Kee-rist!' Bill Cooper let out his breath as the pair receded from view.

Newton-Smith shook his head, clenched his teeth. 'She's unhinged,' he said bluntly.

The runner appeared with the punch. 'Phone call at the stables for Mr Drake,' he announced.

I looked at Newton-Smith.

He raised his eyebrows to signify assent. 'Nothing doing here,' he muttered.

I was glad of the breather. I eased off my jacket and strolled back to the yard. Horses and lads came and went as if they'd never heard of an actress called Catherine Forrest. Lucky them. As I entered the tack-room I heard the tinny voice of Len Potter uttering little curses and mild obscenities from the pay-phone earpiece. I stooped and picked up the dangling receiver with a queezy foreboding.

'Yeah?' I grunted.

'Drakey, this is——'

'I know. What's the panic?'

'Captain Marvel.'

A weakness took me in the belly.

'The poor bleeder's bin drained of 'is powers—jus' like in the comics. 'E's bad, real bad. You'd better hoof it back before the flies get 'ere.'

Chapter Eleven

THE SPEEDO needle danced illegally between seventy and eighty as I despatched the Jag towards Alverton. Traffic was no more than a trickle and I made good time. My palms were clammy with the sweat of tension and under my ribs I could feel a pressure on my breathing. I tried to keep my thoughts on driving but the threshold of my mind kept delving into my limited veterinary knowledge, presenting an innumerable variety of ailments and diseases to fit Potter's obstruse summary of Marvel's symptoms.

Len Potter. A burr under my saddle.

Worse than useless.

When they'd dished out intelligence modicums he'd joined the wrong queue.

I heard the tyres howl out as I scorched through the studio gates. The gateman didn't present himself. No confidence in the car's braking system. Me, the Jag, and grievous bodily harm were synonymous as far as he was concerned.

I found Potter slumped untidily over the bottom half of Captain Marvel's box door. He was scratching at a sinewy forearm and gazing abstractedly inside. A furred tongue crept out to lick his lips and I heard him mumble, 'A little bit of lead'll put you right cocker. Cures everythin' that do. A little bit of lead—right between the eyes.'

'That's your remedy, is it?' I caught the collar of his grubby shirt and gave him a sharp jab below the left ear. 'Well thank you, Lennie, that saves me the trouble of calling in a second opinion.'

He let out a yelp and pitched forward. 'Drakey . . . You—you scared the livin' crap out of me. I aint done nuffin'. 'Onest I aint.'

'That's exactly what I'm afraid of.'

I dragged him to one side and peeled back the door.

At the sight of Marvel, perspiration prickled my skin. His condition was pitiable, far worse than I'd feared. He was staggering drunkenly about the box, coat saturated, head hanging limply below his shoulders. His stomach was distended, saliva was dribbling profusely from his mouth and from the smell and sight of his bedding he seemed to have no control over his bladder.

'Jesus,' I breathed.

'Gonner, aint 'e?' Potter muttered.

'How long has he been like this?'

'Didn't eat his morning feed. Bin gettin' worse sorta gradual.'

'Why the hell didn't you phone earlier?'

He pulled a face, drilled his ear with a forefinger. 'Didn't fink it was serious. Touch of the gripes I reckoned, so's I gives 'im some linseed oil and a bran mash.'

I reached for the animal's jaw, feeling gently for the submaxillary artery. The pulse was sluggish, weak.

' 'Bout lunch time 'e starts sweatin' real bad and piddlin' all over the place. I starts finking then that it might be colic.'

'And what do you think now?'

'Dunno. Anthrax, maybe.'

'Anthrax my arse. His pupils are dilated, his balance is haywire, and he's manufacturing an excessive flow of saliva. This horse has been poisoned.'

'P-poisoned?' he stammered. 'You lost yer bottle or somethin'?'

'How long before the vet gets here?'

'Phoned 'im same time as you—but look, Drakey, I aint pois——'

'I haven't time to argue. We need an alkaloid. Tannic acid—strong boiled tea or black coffee.'

'The canteen?'

'Of course the bloody canteen. Have you got a drenching horn?'

'A w-what?'

'A long-necked vessel for feeding the liquid down his throat.'

'Oh, one of them. Yeah, yeah, I 'spect so.'

'Well, don't 'spect—*look*!'

'Oh-kay.' He curled his lip and slouched off.

The horse was deteriorating fast. He backed away painfully, his neck bobbing now like a cork in water, his haunches trying desperately to maintain an upright stance. I looked on helplessly, recalling the time I'd seen those seventeen hands in action at Aintree. He wasn't a world-beater, but he was always a fighter; always willing to run himself into the ground so that a few idiot punters who'd wagered their lot on him could go away smiling.

I was acutely aware that beneath those moist eyes lay obedience, trust and intelligence; that beating within that robust rib-cage was a heart far larger than any National fence. But a fence he could see, he could judge, he could conquer. A weakening toxin wasn't countered by courage but by drugs. The tannic acid would help, I told myself. It had to help. Straws? They weren't really there to be clutched. Evading the truth only manifested itself in an inner sickness of self-deception. My stomach knew it was too late. Knew that the only thing the tea or coffee would help was my idle hands, my feeling of uselessness.

I paced the box, waiting. I picked up the water bucket and sniffed the remaining half gallon. Not a trace of odour. Did most poisons carry a smell? The only one I knew that did was prussic acid, commonly known as cyanide, and if Marvel had sucked that down his gullet then he'd have been dead long before now.

The hay net bulged with fresh hay. Dark green, with the right 'nose' and the right feel. Nothing amiss.

I turned to the manger. True to Potter standards it hadn't been cleaned. I scraped various dried debris into the palm of my hand for inspection. Oats, bran, and half a feeding cube were all easy to identify. That left me with a reddish-brown grain, or was it a seed? I rolled it between thumb and forefinger knowing it to be familiar yet unable to recall why. Thinking in terms of food supplements only created a mental block. I turned my thoughts towards poison and the words *meadow saffron* streaked across the forefront of my mind. I'd once seen a whole army of farm hands hoeing the bulbs out of a pasture. I'd been shown the seeds and corms and a dairy cow and calf who were dying on their feet less than a day after eating them. The meadow saffron or autumn crocus was a common woodland inhabitant. It was also pretty when in flower, highly palatable, and very very lethal.

'Canteen's 'bout as good as tits on a bull.' Potter's whining interrupted my thoughts. He stumbled into the box clutching a drenching horn and funnel and slopping a bucketful of brown fluid over his filthy shoes. 'The old mare behind the counter got quite narked when I asked fer stewed tea—kinda took it personal.'

I told him to keep his face shut and his hands still as I transposed half a pint of liquid from the bucket to the bottle. Marvel's movements were slack and dragging as I gently lifted his head, whispering entreaties into his ear. I coaxed the drench on to the back of his tongue, sighing with relief as I felt the rhythmic swallowing movements at the lower side of his neck.

'Atta boy, Captain,' Potter breathed. 'Vet'll be 'ere soon.'

'Meadow saffron poisoning,' I said.

'Eh?'

'You've been feeding him the killer crocus.'

'I've bin . . .? I aint never. I wouldn't . . .' His eyes leapt from me to the horse in a frantic search for corroboration. Marvel kept swallowing. Potter set his jaw. 'Are you accusin'——'

'No, I'm merely stating a fact. I found a saffron seed in the manger. It didn't walk, Lennie, so how?'

'I dunno,' he murmured through barely moving lips. 'I jus' dunno.'

'You gave him a bran mash——'

'Out've a bucket. Never went in the manger.'

'So his last proper feed was last night?'

'Yeah, 'bout five-thirty.'

'Then that feed must have contained the meadow saffron.'

'It can't 'ave,' he protested. 'The Captain aint the only 'orse 'ere y'know. They all get the same chow.'

'No variety in diets?'

'None.'

I had to be missing something. It wasn't just a blind guess. The time factor and symptoms tallied. The more I thought about saffron poisoning, the more it made increasing sense. 'How do you prepare the feed?' I asked.

'I mixes it all up in a plastic dustbin and goes from box to box.'

'Consecutively?'

He squinted at me.

'You start at box one and finish at box six?'

'S'right.'

'And Marvel's in box six so you'd do him last.'

'S'right,' he said again.

I played a hunch. 'Could somebody have got at the remaining feed while you were doing box five?'

'Not a chance. Ask the four by two, he'll tell yer.'

I looked at him blankly. 'The . . .?'

'Four by two—Jew. Rex Fandango or whatever 'is name is.'

'Delgado—he was with you?'

162

Dull colour flooded the sallow cheeks. 'W–well sort of.'

'For how long?'

'Oo–er . . . just a few secs,' he added, the lying little bastard. 'He came to see Hot Mustard—the replacement 'orse fer Highwayman.'

'But Grant specifically told you——'

'This geezer's the producer, Drakey . . . I never let 'im near Marvel . . . 'sides 'e said 'e 'ad your permishun.'

I let out a strangled breath. I guess I looked sick.

'You're not thinkin' . . .?'

I'd have gone nap on it, but I shammed a smile and said, 'No, no, of course not.'

Suddenly Marvel's tongue writhed protestingly against the remainder of the drench. Rivers of sweat ran down his ribs and his whole body began twitching in violent involuntary jerks. His legs splayed, his shallow breathing became virtually non-existent, and I found my fingers covered in a slime of saliva as the big horse slipped torpidly from my grip. The floor shook, sending up an eruption of straw dust. A final surge from his lungs fluttered his nostrils. The ensuing stillness said his misery was over.

I dropped the drenching horn and turned away, sadness and impotence burning in the pit of my stomach. The sound of a car engine heralded the arrival of the vet.

Too late for drugs.

Too late for hope.

Just too damned bloody late.

'Poor bleeder never 'ad a fart's chance,' Potter murmured.

For once in my life I found myself agreeing with him.

Catherine Forrest peeled the impregnated cotton-wool pads from her eyes and fished a cigarette from a monogrammed silver box. She'd been smoking heavily. The crystal ashtray at her elbow was glutted with lipstick-stained butts.

'So it's finally happened,' she pronounced, traversing the lounge with her cigarette, taking quick nervous little puffs. 'Fiona, Highwayman, and now Captain Marvel. When will it end, Simon? How much more of this heinous persecution have I got to endure?'

She seemed to float rather than tread, her white cut-away silk gown billowing coquettishly across the carpet. Beneath the smooth sweep of dusky hair the strained, mercurial features were thrown into soft focus by strategically placed table lamps with coloured shades and flattering low-wattage bulbs. She still had a whole lot of what it took. A flick of ash, a tilt of head, a practised hand movement as she waved me eloquently into a vacant chair. The era might be bygone but the femme fatale who dominated it gathered deftness, not dust.

'I'm being constantly pestered by the Press,' she added bitterly, sinking exhaustedly upon the sofa and heaving a prolonged sigh. 'They're dropping subtle innuendoes about my stability. It's film crew gossip that's tickling their palates. Everything they say sounds as though I'm certifiable. God, I feel so trapped!'

'About this guy Sturgess——' I began.

'Rex is getting rid of him. If he's seen anywhere near the set then the police will be called.'

'I think he's harmless. I've checked——'

'Harmless?' Smoke dribbled from her lips as she laughed thinly. 'I'm only alive because I refused to do the scene. Without the wood-land premonition——'

'What premonition?'

'The woman on horseback. The man—Sturgess, hitting her with a spade.'

'There wasn't anything premonitory about that. You saw it happening and I saw the hoof marks.'

'It—it seems like a dream,' she said, falteringly.

'At the time you were convinced it was Rupert Gibson.'

'I made a mistake. Sturgess looks remarkably——'

'That mistake probably cost Gibson his life.'

'Don't be ridiculous.'

'I'm trying to be logical.'

'Well if we're going to be so devastatingly logical, try telling me why a man who resembled Gibson should be booked for a death scene and then make an on cue entrance just as Anthony decides to tear my nerves to shreds by wielding a spade.'

I was out of cigarettes so I helped myself to one of hers. 'Anthony worries me. How are things between you?' I could play the questions game too.

'Things? Between us?' She uttered the words as though she hardly knew their meaning. 'Ant can be tiresome at times. He—he's at a difficult age.'

'Any resentment?'

'You mean on my side?'

'I mean on either side.'

'No, of course not.' She waved the suggestion away blithely.

Karan came into the room. She'd changed into a towelling jump-suit and washed her hair. The chestnut locks were combed straight back from her forehead and hung in thick ringlets about her neck. She stood before me looking voluptuous, evocative. My eyes instinctively traced the zipper, buttons and snap fasteners of her suit. It clung to every curve and looked nigh on impregnable. Designed by a woman for a woman, I thought, returning her smile. I contemplated the outline of her briefs as she leaned forward to whisper something into Catherine's ear. Undoubtedly diminutive, and black at a guess. Bide your time, a small balanced voice inside me said. Women's pants were like unfranked stamps on envelopes. More had been slipped off with a little patience and dexterity than had ever been removed with over-anxious hands.

'Please excuse me, Simon,' Catherine twisted out her cigarette and rose. 'I won't be more than a moment. Put on some music. Help yourself to a drink.' She swayed away from me, tracking Karan to the staircase.

I stretched my legs on a walk to the corner cabinet. I made a few dummy passes through the bourbon bottles and got to grips with the Smirnoff. Vodka scorched over my tongue as I looked consideringly at the man reflected in the mosaic of mirrored tiles. I toasted myself and smiled. The face smiled sardonically back. The lip had healed nicely but a bluish blotch rather like a faded ink stain stubbornly remained. I encompassed the room and dwelt idly on the fact that I looked and felt a bloody good thirty.

The hi-fi was one of those smoky perspex jobs with automatic this and that and a hundred and one slide controls. I fiddled around until a red light glowed and a definite hum emerged from the giant free-standing speakers. Lowering the volume slide, I thumbed through a selection of L.P.s and placed side one of a Sinatra album on the turntable. I wasn't a fan, but then Catherine's musical taste didn't stretch to John Denver.

A rich swell of strings, the inevitable piano—I settled back, waiting for the voice.

No voice.

No voice?

165

My senses swam. This was purely orchestral. This was Rhapsody in Blue. I flicked the reject switch. The stylus disengaged. The record label tallied with the sleeve: *Sinatra's Greatest Hits*. A dryness plucked at my throat as I repeated the process with the 1812 Overture, Handel's Messiah, and the incomparable Fitzgerald. They were identical. Side one, first track, all Rhapsody in Blue.

I stood confused, surrounded by a disarray of albums, my brain trying slowly and painfully to pull sense into the situation. When had Catherine last used the hi-fi? How in hell's name could Rhap . . .? I stopped. My brain didn't need the questions, my mouth needed to ask some. I drained the vodka and headed for the staircase.

Catherine's bedroom door was ajar. I went to knock but my knuckles froze as I glimpsed Catherine sitting rigidly on the edge of the bed. She was tearing open a cellophane sachet, removing a disposable hypodermic syringe. Karan steadied a little bottle as the actress carefully pierced the needle through the rubberized seal and withdrew a measured quantity of fluid.

A thick carpet deadened my footsteps as I entered. I don't know what I was thinking. I just stood there dumbly, my eyes fixed unblinkingly on Catherine as she teased the needle under the skin of her forearm, her tongue wedged between her teeth as she applied pressure to the plunger. Karan watched as the seconds passed. The needle was extracted and the hypo dropped into the waste bin. Catherine began pinching the punctured flesh to speed up dispersal.

I folded my arms, coughed.

Catherine's head jerked up. She gave me the kind of look people reserve for gate-crashers.

'Simon,' Karan began, 'before you jump to conclusions——'

'I've already jumped,' I said. 'How long has the lady been hooked?'

'She isn't hooked, she's——'

'Oh, but I am,' Catherine's mouth lifted in an abortive attempt at a smile. 'I've been *hooked* as you put it for most of my life.' She handed me the bottle, adding, 'The label's marked insulin—do I have to explain?'

I was thrown by the directness of the statement. A diabetic. It could be important. It probably was important. I should have been damn well told.

Karan thought the look on my face justified an explanation. 'It's not something we talk about, Simon.' Her voice was subdued and apologetic. 'It's very personal—only a few people know.'

'*I* didn't know.'

'There was no need——'

'There was every need,' I looked at Catherine. 'How many shots?' I demanded roughly.

She levelled her eyes square into mine, parted her lips. 'You're behaving very badly. I'm not sure I care for your manner.'

'My manner isn't on offer, you're hiring my expertise.'

'Don't be glib.'

'I'm not being glib, I'm annoyed. It's bad enough trying to un-tangle this mess without having important factors like diabetes kept from me.' I let my breath hiss through my teeth and repeated my earlier question.

'Twice daily,' she said.

'Always a fresh syringe?'

'Of course.'

'Are you sure this is insulin?' I asked, rocking the remaining contents of the phial, studying the holes in the rubberized seal.

'If it isn't I'd be in a coma by now. Each bottle contains three days' supply.'

'Fairly easy to lace it. Simply take a syringe, extract a small quan-tity of insulin and replace it with an equal amount of something more potent.'

'You're being obscure.' Her face betrayed a certain impatience as she sat before the rose-tinted mirror of her dressing table, leaning her elbows on the glass surface, patting at her hair.

'I'm offering you a plausible way of inducing nightly neurotic fantasies, delusions of persecution, D.T.s to order.'

'That's absurd, Simon. Nobody could tamper with those phials. You'd have to live here to . . . It's absurd.' She finished weakly.

I felt like a tired whale battling against the current. I looked at Karan wishing we could both just drop out of the sky and land on an uninhabited tropical island.

Catherine remained impervious to my fantasy. She dabbed at her face with a Kleenex, twisted the gold case of a lipstick. Shit or bust, I thought, and plunged on.

'You'd have to live here to pull the script switch.'

Her eyes flickered but she said nothing.

'And as for your collection of L.P.s—well they've got to be heard to be believed.'

'L.P.s?' She paused, the lipstick hovering an inch from her mouth. Karan frowned at me. I explained.

'Y-you've heard them too?' Catherine forced the words through tightly clenched teeth. 'I thought it was me—my mind. Whenever Ant played them they were perfectly normal, whenever I played them they were . . . Oh God, Simon, don't tell me it's Luke. I've heard he's having an affair with Amanda Stewart—but he wouldn't—not cruelly——'

'Drive you out of your head?' I provided.

'I don't believe——'

'You don't want to believe.'

'Please . . .'

'Scripts don't switch themselves, record labels don't——'

'No!' she shrilled harshly, and then she stopped. Her eyes widened to the point of bulging as she gaped at her reflection in the mirror. The lipstick stroked a red stain across her chin as it fluttered from her fingers. Bright blood splattered lavishly from her lips, pitting the dressing-table, scoring a vitreous trail from her mouth to the cleavage of her gown.

Predictably she screamed.

Suddenly the swimming redness was everywhere.

Karan gasped, transfixed. My senses were dislocated too, but I managed to unscramble them as the lipstick rolled across the carpet and made contact with my shoe. There, embedded in the tip of the cosmetic, was a sliver of finely honed razor blade.

'Help her to the bathroom,' I ordered, thrusting a handful of tissues towards Karan. 'Her bottom lip's split like a banana skin. It'll bleed like crazy and you're going to have to work like hell to stop it.'

Catherine sagged over the dressing-table, put her elbows down hard on it, held her mouth in a crimson-soaked wad of Kleenex and shuddered.

'*Who?*' she demanded painfully.

'The bathroom, Karan,' I repeated.

'Luke wouldn't—he wouldn't——' Catherine's eyes strayed fearfully back to the mirror. 'Not—not to my face.'

I wasn't thinking about Luke. I reckoned he was capable of most things, but this was crude, malicious, almost juvenile in design. The work of an immature mind filled with a sickness of hate. Anthony Taylor had that sickness. I'd seen it in his eyes as he'd slashed the spade into the turf; caught the bitter intonation in his voice as he'd amplified the word *stepmother*. It wasn't something I'd wanted to believe. I guess I'd even ignored the possibility. The revelation, 'Whenever Ant played the L.P.s they were perfectly normal', plus a mirror tarnished with the drying blackness of Catherine's blood, had finally won me over. I got motion into my legs and headed for the boy's bedroom.

It was more like a self-contained flat. Colour TV, shower, telephone, blow-up furniture. I drew the blinds, switched on a table lamp, not really knowing where to begin. The obvious seemed as good a place as any, so I started with it and struck gold. The kid might be adept at musical contrivances but when it came to clandestine behaviour, he hadn't graduated beyond the 'under the mattress' routine. Within minutes I'd uncovered an assortment of soft porn magazines, a cassette recorder still with brackets attached, and a syringe, needles, and ampoules wrapped in a polythene dry cleaning bag. If I hadn't flicked the cassette to PLAY I might have been aware a little earlier of the figure in the doorway.

'If music be the food of love . . .' the boy said, lounging against the jamb, apparently unperturbed by my presence.

I stitched together a smile. 'Is there any?'

'Any?'

'Love.'

He grinned in sick contempt, his wide eyes mocking me with their bogus innocence.

'You could have killed her,' I said.

'It wasn't for want of trying.'

'What were you hoping for—suicide?'

'In time maybe. She's very resilient. She should have really freaked when she saw Sturgess. Anyone else would have gone right off their box.'

I switched off the tape, spread my hands questioningly. 'Sturgess was a nice touch. I figured you set him up, but just how . . .?'

'Careful planning, that's how. I combed the script until I found a suitable sequence—Catherine being chased by a stunt rider—pit-mounted camera. It was too beautiful to be missed. I checked the cast list in the production office and came up with Sturgess' name. All I had to do then was find out what the guy looked like.' He paused, chuckled. He was enjoying himself. 'Have you heard of a trade directory called *Spotlight?* It's a casting director's bible. Ed Sturgess' photograph was in there. The fact that he happened to look like Gibson was a bonus. A swell one, eh?'

I didn't offer any congratulations, my imagination was already beginning to fill in the blanks. 'So it was you Catherine saw in the woodland?'

He nodded. 'Me disguised as Sturgess—horse hired from a local riding school—wig, spectacles, and make-up courtesy of Alverton Studios.'

'And the blonde?'

'A dummy from props. I dressed it in one of Catherine's gowns, strapped it into the saddle, and filled the head with synthetic blood. It split like an eggshell when I hit it with the spade. The stuff ran everywhere. Over me, over the horse, everywhere. What a godawful sight. I almost frightened myself. Jeez, you should have heard Catherine scream.'

'I did hear her scream. I was the mug who brought her home.'

'Yeah,' he chuckled again, 'so you were.'

I looked at him silently. I wanted to say something but words failed me. The generation gap hung between us. A void. He'd never paid to see an Alan Ladd movie, never followed a Jane and Garth strip cartoon. He'd never queued for Saturday morning pictures or played with a Meccano set. At his age my definition of pot was the one stated in the New Oxford Dictionary, and an underground magazine was a copy of *Titbits* left behind by a Circle Line commuter. Todays' kids were weaned on Robbins not Dickens; they campaigned for abortion on demand and suffered from sex fatigue at fourteen. Communication wasn't easy. The seconds stretched into minutes, then he said:

'I thought you had me in the car. Me sitting there with the cassette in my duffle bag, soaking bloody wet, watching you fiddle with the main beam lever. You fair gave me the squits.'

There was going to be an encore unless he took that grin off his lips, that matter-of-fact tone out of his voice. 'Aren't you concerned,' I asked, 'knowing that I know?'

'Is this a bust?' The grin remained under superb control as he dug a pack of cigarettes from his pocket. 'I'm a juvenile, Simon. What are you going to do—slap my legs, make me stand in the corner?'

'Illegal possession of drugs, stealing studio property, malicious wounding,' I mulled over the various charges.

'Malicious . . .?'

'A razor blade in a lipstick. I take it that was another of your sick novelties.'

'Yep.' He snapped his lighter under the dangling cigarette. 'It's just made contact, huh? That's cool. It must have been in there for three weeks. They sure are making cosmetics to last these days.'

I shifted angrily. 'Catherine's not paranoid, sonny boy—you are.'

His eyes went lazy and slack. He managed a shrug. 'Cut her, did it?'

'Yes, it cut her.'

'Bled plenty, I suppose.'

'Plenty,' I echoed.

He nodded slowly, inspecting me in a long silence. 'It must have hurt,' he said finally. 'How much do you reckon it hurt?'

I reserved an opinion until he came into range. A hand went lazily to the zip of his jacket and he glanced at his watch. As he loped towards the TV I lifted myself off the bed, grabbed his hair at the neck, and punched him hard in the kidneys.

'About that much,' I gritted. I released as he doubled up and drove my knee into the soft flesh of his buttocks. He belly-sprawled in a tousled heap on the bed.

'Nobody h-hits me like that,' he whimpered.

His cigarette was smouldering on the carpet. I stamped it out.

He turned to look at me, clutching his side, his high intelligent forehead covered now with a fine beading of sweat. He said fast, jerkily, 'What would you know about anything—you lousy god-damned motherfuc——'

'Save the compliments,' I growled, making a tourniquet with his shirt collar, halting the invective.

'You're chok . . . I want to say . . .'

'You've got nothing to say that could possibly justify——'

He flopped around helplessly, holding up his hands in supplication, eyes protruding, mouth twisting in a spasm of pain. 'Catherine Forrest killed my mother . . . She—she *killed* my mother . . .' The words tumbled out in a sudden lamenting rush, pitched high.

My fingers released involuntarily. He scrambled away from me, turning his back, burying his head in his hands. His shoulders shook. He was weeping.

This was one helluva mixed up kid.

I said, cautiously, 'Your mother killed herself, Anthony.'

'She slashed her wrists,' he sobbed, his speech decelerating. 'I found her hanging over—hanging over the bath. She was crying and the blood was pumping out with every breath. Swirling and pumping. Eddying around the drain hole. I asked her *why* but she just kept crying. I cried too. I cried long after she'd stopped, long after she'd died. I wanted my dad—Oh, Christ, how I wanted my dad . . .'

'But he was in Florida,' I murmured softly, recalling the facts in Grant's file.

'Catherine Forrest stole him and destroyed my mother. Have you ever seen a human being coming apart before your eyes? I saw it. Seven years ago I saw it and I've been hating ever since.'

'It takes two to cause a marital break-up—or are you saying your father was blameless?'

He dropped his hands, squeezed his knees together to stop their trembling. 'I—I guess he was overwhelmed by Catherine. I guess he didn't know what was happening until it was too late.'

'That's a rather naïve assumption.'

'That's how it must have been.'

'Or how you hoped it was? Catherine black, Luke white. That was the most acceptable casting so that was the version you chose to believe.'

He ignored me, deciding to take sanctuary in an animated dialogue with himself:

'*You won't be able to punish her anymore, Anthony. Not now Simon knows.*'

'*I guess I goofed, huh?*'

'*You should have kept it simple—like the studio accidents. Loosen a spotlight clamp here, a staircase reinforcing bar there. They didn't all work but those that did had a spectacular effect.*'

'*The adjustment to the script was simple—she flubbed her lines.*'

'*But it drew suspicion away from Storm and Knight. Only someone inside this house could pull a stroke like that.*'

'*The record labels too, I suppose.*'

'*Steaming off and switching? An expensive and risky business.*'

He nodded to himself, his expression faintly contemptuous as he added,

'*The lipstick was the biggest giveaway of all. You should have resisted the temptation.*

'*I couldn't—I just couldn't. The razor blade cutting through skin was symbolic. I wanted her to bleed—I wanted her to bleed just like ma.*'

I pushed a cigarette between his lips. In the flare of the match I could see his eyes were streaming. He cuffed the tears away, inhaling gratefully.

'What's in the ampoules?' I asked, attempting to get through to that maladjusted mind.

'The juice of the cactus. A drug called Mescaline.'

It registered as an L.S.D. equivalent; an unrivalled front-runner in the heebiejeebies syndrome.

'A guy at school had some real bad trips after he'd gotten on the stuff.'

'So you hit on the idea of a Mescaline cocktail?'

'I experimented. I was careful not to overdo it.'

'Catherine's just had a shot. Was that contaminated?'

He shook his head. 'Pure insulin.'

I breathed out, relieved, pondering my next move. I felt like a bookie's runner with bets to hedge but not knowing where or how to place them. Everything had suddenly dovetailed, but it was an unbelievable mess. The telephone chattered, disturbing my thoughts. It gave three rings, then stopped. Karan must have picked up an extension and that prompted another question.

'There has to be more than one line,' I said. 'I remember getting a melodic phone call while you were in residence.'

'Dad's study,' the eyes drifted to an opposing wall, 'he has a business connection.'

I smiled vaguely.

'Aren't you going to ask me the obvious?' he prompted.

'Let's pretend I have.'

He hesitated for a moment, ran his tongue across his teeth. 'Do you know why I used Rhapsody in Blue?'

'At a guess I'd say you cashed in on coincidence.'

'Pretty good guess.'

'Damned good memory. The rhapsody was playing when the poodle died. That was straightforward—nothing sinister—the hi-fi was on so something musical had to coincide with Fiona's death. On the second occasion—pure chance, not Anthony Taylor, sent it through the studio restaurant's loudspeakers. A random selection of melodies and Catherine happened to be there at the wrong time. You saw her abhorrence, you grasped the reason why, and from there on in you capitalized on it.'

'That was most explicit, Simon,' the voice came from the doorway. Catherine stood as though mummified. Her bottom lip had ballooned and was covered in a veneer of Elastoplast and congealed blood. She winced as she spoke, trying to control pain twitches. 'Y-you're wanted on the telephone. You can take it in my bedroom.'

Anthony looked as though he was going to slide right down between the floorboards. He backed away, his waterlogged eyes huge and frightened. Suddenly he blurted out, 'Don't go, Simon. Take the call on my phone. Please—please don't go.'

I turned to Catherine. 'There's a lot to be explained——'

'This boy tried to put me in an asylum—a padded cell—can you explain that?'

'There are certain facts——'

'Which I will listen to *later!* Your caller must be getting impatient. I repeat, Simon, take the call in my bedroom.'

I puffed my cheeks at Anthony, nodded, and went.

Karan was gathering up soiled tissues and wiping bloodstains from the dressing-table mirror. She managed a brief flicker of a smile, then dropped her gaze anxiously to the telephone. 'It's Frankie Wade,' she said softly. 'He's ringing from the hospital.'

I took a long, deep breath. 'What's happened, Frank?'

'Patch is dead, Simon. He never regained consciousness.'

'When?'

'About ten minutes ago. I was——' He paused, gathering his strength. 'I was with the poor bastard. I'm gonna get Delgado for this, Simon. I'm gonna——'

'You're going to come back here—now!'

'What the hell for?'

'Me,' I said bluntly.

Chapter Twelve

'ANT'S GONE,' Catherine announced, blundering into the lounge.
'Run away with his tail between his legs. Too frightened to face me.
Too stubborn to apologize. My God, he ought to go down on his
knees, begging forgiveness for what he has to answer for. The weeks
of torment—this final act of savagery—the viciousness, the vileness.
What have I done to deserve a stepson like that? Answer me, Simon.
I've always—I've always——' She passed a wall mirror, catching the
reflection of her soiled dress, her ghastly face. Her pride revolted. A
shudder ran visibly through her. 'Is this Catherine Forrest? Is this the
Hollywood legend? Is—this—what—Anthony's—done—to *me*!'

I said, 'Stop feeling sorry for yourself—the boy's hurt goes deeper
than any cut lip. I'm not condoning what he's done, but perhaps if
you'd had a little more time, shown a little more interest, not been so
bloody self-centred——'

'He's turned you against me too!' She ran her hands through the
silky dishevelment of her hair, lit a cigarette, and stared out at me
from behind a veil of smoke.

'Try loving him a little instead of loving yourself a lot.'

'That's unfair, Simon,' Karan cut in. 'You're making Anthony out
to be the injured party.'

'He blames Catherine for his mother's suicide—perhaps with good
cause, I don't know. He's sick. He needs help, not hounding.'

'You don't believe that I . . .?' Catherine's voice was low, throaty.

'If you care one iota for the boy, start worrying about where he is,
what he might do. He doesn't want to worship a screen goddess, he
needs the affection of a mother.'

'He'll have gone to the Olympus. He-he'll be with Luke.'

I had my doubts. In defending Catherine I reckoned I'd shaken the
boy's confidence in his father. I hoped I was wrong but I couldn't
afford time for abstract thought. There were more pressing matters.
Wade was on his way over and my mind had shifted into high,
construing a plan of action.

In a now lifeless voice, Catherine asked, 'Did Ant send the effigies?'

The next bit wasn't going to be easy. It was going to be as difficult for me to explain Delgado's culpability as it was for Catherine to accept it. Time didn't allow for a lengthy break-it-gently oration. I had to be brief, concise, and above all, convincing. I began by unfolding the mechanics of the scheme—the motive behind the effigies—the methods used to make them work—how Anthony's musical meddling had been counter-productive and inadvertently cost Gibson his life.

I expected her to challenge every word, sift every sentence, question every nuance. To pace the room making theatrical gestures. To gurgle, hiss, deny, protect, and eventually take shelter in an attack of hysteria. To do anything in fact rather than listen.

I was wrong. She seemed physically and mentally immobilized. As I told her about Patch Hunter, her bosom heaved and she stared at the glowing tip of her cigarette. 'God,' she said softly, and swallowed.

'Had Hunter lived he could have given evidence,' I pointed out.

She nodded. She'd accepted the verdict and wasn't going to appeal.

'Are you all right?' Karan asked her.

'I need a drink.'

'Coffee?'

'A double jigger of cognac. To hell with the blood sugar—I suddenly feel very cold.'

I evened my voice. 'How long have you suspected Delgado?'

'Rex?' Her head jerked up. 'I haven't—I——'

'You were shocked just now, but not surprised. Delgado's been a lifelong friend. Nobody, least of all Catherine Forrest, sits in total silence while I tear away those years and brand him with the Judas kiss.'

'I—I didn't want to believe.' Her voice was flat and tired. 'I couldn't see any motive, so I put it out of my mind. My whole world's been turned upside down, Simon. I'm just not able to think——'

'But you did suspect him?'

'At one time—fleetingly. Shortly after you accused me of handling the effigies.'

'Why?'

'Have you ever been in Rex's office?'

'Once.'

'There's a cabinet full of souvenirs, relics from past productions.'

'I've seen it.'

'One's missing.'

An alabaster base with a spiked centre flashed through my mind. The wording on a little white card pressured my subconscious, demanding recognition. And then it clicked. 'Your first film. It was to do with the Colchester martyrs. You played Rose somebody or other.'

'Rose Allin. Rose was accused of heresy in 1557. The scene in the movie showed a tyrant called Edmund Tyrell burning her hand with a lighted candle. It was her right hand, Simon.'

The lesson distilled favourably. 'A dummy hand—the missing trophy?'

'Made in latex by special effects and cast from my own hand. It was perfect in every detail, right down to the——'

'Fingerprints,' I said decisively.

'And that was over forty years ago. Can you blame me for not giving it more than a second's thought? It's hideous. Rex Delgado, the man who took me and moulded me into a star. When I think how close, how very close, he came to mentally destroying me.' She took a healthy swallow of the brandy, carefully tilting the glass so that none of the fiery liquid came in contact with her injured lip. She coughed, shuddered, bitterness and revulsion jockeying for first place. 'Two men are dead, Simon. Why for God's sake? Because of a horse race?'

'That's about the size of it. I phoned Grant before I left Alverton, got him to make a few discreet enquiries. Four months ago Delgado's bank statement showed a credit of twenty thousand pounds—today it shows a deficit of a few hundred. Where's it gone? It's riding on Intruder. Spread at an average ante-post price of what . . . 25–1.' I did some mental arithmetic, whistled through my teeth. 'He stands to collect a cool half million.'

'Minus betting tax,' Karan put in simply.

'Cute kid,' I said.

'The amount is hypothetical,' Catherine announced impulsively. 'There's no question of My Liberty being scratched, not now. Let him send a legion of effigies. I'll melt them down and make candles for Halloween.'

'Wrong tactics,' I told her. 'In desperation he could resort to more orthodox stopping methods. I have a plan which could prove his guilt, perhaps even extract a confession, but it carries an element of danger. You'd be the key participant in the scheme. I think we could eliminate most of the risks, but there's always the chance——'

'I'll take that chance.' Her voice was small but determined. 'Besides, whoever heard of Catherine Forrest being offered anything less than the lead.'

I felt a smile form on my lips. 'Who indeed,' I agreed.

Sleety rain had started to hammer the windows. Karan crossed to pull the drapes. She leaned over furniture, stretching and parting her legs, thrusting her breasts at the heavy brocade curtaining. I watched the supple movements, tantalized, feeling an urgency plucking at my groin, knowing it could never be shared until I'd dulled the edge of her inhibitions.

Catherine stirred impatiently. I lit a cigarette, swallowing thoughts of sex along with a lungful of smoke. Karan returned to the sofa, crossing those long legs gracefully at the ankles, flicking away a strand of hair that had dared to caress her delicate nose. I blew a smoke ring and outlined the plan.

It was simple and only possible now that Hunter had died. Catherine would phone Delgado, break the news, and tell him she had been called to the hospital because Hunter had been constantly repeating her name. At his bedside she'd heard a disjointed confession which implicated the producer in a conspiracy aimed at the withdrawal of My Liberty from the Champion Hurdle. Were these just nonsensical ravings uttered by a man who'd emerged briefly from a coma? Or did they have some basis in fact? I've got to see you, Rex, she'd say. I've got to talk to you before I talk to the police. And of course he'd agree. He'd come with a counter-plan and he'd bring Bernard and Stiletto along for company. I'd have Wade, Grant, and half a dozen T.S.D. men to cover the meet. The rest wasn't scripted. Strictly ad-libbing. Delgado's ulcer against my butterflies.

'Let him name the time and the place,' I emphasized, as Catherine's forefinger tapped the digital sequence of the producer's London number. 'Don't cajole or he'll smell a fix. You're torn, shaken, bewildered. You don't want to believe he's guilty. Fill your voice with——'

The briefing was unnecessary. As Delgado answered she launched into the deathbed confession with such credence, that I could almost hear Hunter's small voice clearing his conscience. Her lip was obviously giving her pain, but she didn't let it show. She paced the lounge, trailing the telephone cord, her rippling diction and seismic hand movements faintly mimicking the style on which Bette Davis holds the patent. But the quality was inimitably Forrest. This wasn't just another scene. This was get-it-right-first-take time and it demanded cool professionalism. She stopped her pacing and let me share the earpiece.

'Of course we must meet,' Delgado was saying. 'These accusations are really quite groundless, my pet. Do all the years we've known each other count for nothing? I'm incredulous, Catherine. To think our friendship could be put in jeopardy by the mutterings of a mortally ill man. And this silly notion about going to the police . . .'

'I don't want to, Rex. I—I don't know what to do for the best. If Simon was here he'd be able to advise me——'

'So you haven't mentioned this to Drake?'

'I can't find him.'

'Or Luke?'

'No.'

There was a levelling of breath. The anxiety lifted. 'Promise me you won't talk of it to anyone. It's lunacy, Catherine—the poor man's mind was disordered.'

'Maybe you're right. It's just that——'

'Promise me.'

'Yes—yes, I promise.'

'Are you feeling well enough to drive?'

'I'll cope.'

'I've guests staying here, so my apartment's out of the question. How about my riverside cottage—say ten p.m.?'

That gave us an hour and a half to get things organized. Catherine's eyes were asking for confirmation. I nodded.

'Karan and I will be there,' she said.

Karan? I shook my head violently.

'I thought there would be just the two of us,' Delgado didn't sound overjoyed by the idea either. 'Surely we can talk this over without——'

'Karan will be accompanying me, Rex.' She was adamant.

Silence for a moment, then, 'Very well, my dear. If that's what you want, then that's the way it will have to be.'

I was frantically signalling my disapproval, but to no avail. She broke the connection.

'That was bloody stupid,' I said.

'Karan goes everywhere with me.'

'You've doubled the risk.'

'I've made the whole thing more credible. Agreeing to go alone would have been totally out of character.'

'That's as maybe.'

'That's fact. Rex is very shrewd, don't belittle his intelligence.'

'O.K. . . . O.K. . . .' I flapped my hands at her. 'I haven't time to argue. Get yourself changed while I make the arrangements with Grant. Slacks—a trouser suit—something practical.'

'I'd prefer to look elegant.'

'You're not attending a première. Delgado might just decide to kill you. I don't want you hampered by a hem-line.'

She turned a key in a bureau, slid open an inner drawer and pulled out a small ·25 automatic with pearl grips. 'I'll be carrying this for protection,' she said coolly. She pressed the magazine release button, checked the clip was full and snapped it back into the butt. She disengaged the safety catch before dropping the weapon into her purse. I figured she knew how to use it.

Howard Grant took down the riverside address with methodical slowness. He informed me that plans made in haste had a notoriously high failure rate and that exposing Catherine in this way was madness. I told him I agreed and blamed Hunter for dying without prior warning for the catch-as-catch-can showdown.

'Your case against Delgado is mostly circumstantial. He'll have to verbally unveil the Intruder plot for us to make anything stick,' he added.

'Just be there to hear it. Catherine will do the rest. I only hope to Christ she doesn't intend to shoot him.'

'Are you saying she'll be armed?'

'She's packing a decorative little pistol and it isn't the kind that lights cigarettes. Thirty years ago she probably wore it tucked in her garter'.

'Oh, my God.'

'Play with your rosary later. Right now we need at least three men covering that boathouse.'

'You'll get them.'

'Wade and I will shadow Catherine to the rendezvous. We should outnumber the opposition two to one. If I was a handicapper, I'd say we had a stone in hand.'

'No heroics, Simon. Catherine's safety is paramount, so let me be blunt. If anything goes wrong, you'll find yourself permanently suspended from the Division. I think you're hitting the front too early and all your zeal will get you is a zero to the left of your name on the racecard. I only hope I'm wrong.' The dial tone buzzed in my ear as he hung up.

Frankie Wade sat stiff, motionless, his lips compressed. I'd spent ten minutes outlining the plan and was now waiting for his reaction. He blew gently on the ember of his cigarette and muttered something about Hunter always being a bundle of laughs and the Berkeley yard not being the same without him. A further minute elapsed while he held a silent requiem for the jockey. Finally he dragged back the cuff of his bomber-jacket and announced, 'It's nine-thirty, we'd better think about leaving.'

The telephone shrilled and Catherine's hand reached delicately to silence it. She was dressed in a lime-green trouser suit, not particularly becoming, but sensible. She brought the telephone mouthpiece to her lips and uttered the number. The lips quivered slightly.

'Yes—I understand,' she said shortly. 'Now? Yes—yes all right.'

Wade's eyes strayed to me. I shrugged and looked at Karan. She looked blankly back.

Catherine turned towards the wall. She spoke softly, articulating each syllable. 'I—said—all—right. Yes. Goodbye.'

'Is anything wrong?' Karan asked.

'Luke.' Catherine's smile hung a little crookedly on her mouth. 'He—he's on his way home. Anthony's with him. Everything's fine.'

'Then let's go.' Wade doused his cigarette and stood up.

I said to Catherine, 'Take a slow drive through Old Windsor and pick up the river road to Staines. Frankie and I will peel away just before you and Karan reach the cottage.'

'I've decided to follow your advice,' she said obscurely, gathering up her coat and purse. 'I can be very impulsive. You were right and I was wrong. I admit it.'

'You admit . . .?'

'The danger, Simon. It would be very foolish to involve Karan.'

'I'm glad you've seen sense.'

'Might I be asked?' Karan placed obstinate hands on her hips. 'If I'm forced to stay here, I'll be sick with worry. I want to come.'

'As your employer, I forbid it,' Catherine retaliated.

'But surely——'

'I said I forbid it!' She drew herself up to her full height, pushed back a falling lock of hair. 'Please don't make things more difficult than they already are.'

'How about a compromise?' Wade suggested. 'Karan can come with us in the Jag. She'll be safe enough just so long as she stays in the car.'

'I—I don't know. I really——'

'She can lock herself in. Make herself useful as a sort of lookout. A coupla blasts on the horn for impending danger—like they do in the movies.'

'Please say yes, Catherine,' Karan coaxed.

'Oh, for God's sake—Yes! Yes!' She slid the heels of her palms up her forehead in frustration.

We trouped out to the driveway. Wade released the up and over door of the car-port and Catherine slid behind the wheel of the Aston. A quick, stark fork of lightning crackled and emblazoned the sky. Distant thunder rumbled in its wake. After the stuffiness of the house the rain felt cool, sobering, bracing. I requisitioned Karan's wrist-watch. Nine forty-five. Time to move. No room now for second thoughts, no improvising. The little headlight wipers whirred, dusting away the droplets that dared to undermine the lamps' efficiency. Catherine let in the clutch and the car moved slowly forward. It drew level with us and stopped, the motor idling.

Catherine's face was set. She evaded my eyes, staring out at the ribbon of road ahead. Something was very wrong, I could sense it.

Suddenly she turned, arching her long delicate neck. 'Forgive me,' she said simply.

I went to reply but the electric window hummed, the elevating glass barring further communication. With a downward drive of her foot, she gunned the vehicle forward, cramping the wheels viciously as she swung the power-steering into a fierce lock. The $5\frac{1}{2}$-litre thrust from the exhaust smacked at my knees and left me enveloped in fumes. Karan and Wade scattered as the Aston ploughed an exit.

It's rear end reeled slightly on the slippery surface, tyres chewing up a cumulus of soggy gravel as the thirsting carburettors pitched it into infinity.

'Has she gone bloody crazy?' Wade yelled, shaking a puddle-doused ankle.

I hunched my shoulders against the rain and pointed him towards the Jag. Confusion battered my mind. It was as if my brain had slowed down, hanging one step behind the music. What the hell was she playing at?

Karan looked dazed, unable to take her eyes from the fast diminishing tail-lights. 'The phone call,' she murmured as I ushered her inside. 'It changed her, Simon. It changed her mind about me and did something . . .'

'To balls-up the scheme,' Wade provided bitterly.

I hit the switches and kicked the stick into low. No rear wheel spin, just smooth acceleration as I went through the box. The tempo of rain was increasing, little icy pellets flinging themselves against the windshield, hammering the glass like ack-ack fire. Dark, dripping figures scurrying along pavements. Sallow faces eclipsed by yellow lamp-light, huddled under umbrellas. Colour TVs beaming from rental shop windows, playing to empty houses. A smattering of undaunted tourists risking pneumonia in order to get a glimpse of the castle.

'She's caught at the lights,' Karan's voice confirmed what I could see.

'Motorcycle cop,' Wade said.

I nodded, eased back the throttle. Lady Luck had intervened. The shiny white bike was alongside the Aston, rescinding any thoughts Catherine might have been having about crashing the signals. We cruised up behind her just as the lights turned green. The cop gave us a glance then peeled off right. Catherine saw the danger vanish and hustled the Aston forward. I did likewise, pinning the Jag to the silver-wet tail. The street lights of Windsor receded in my mirror. A roundabout loomed ahead.

'She—she's taking the Ascot exit,' Wade's voice was barely audible as the car lurched, throwing him heavily against the side window. I wrestled with the steering, the tyres rippling over the shiny tarmac, slewing for adhesion. The suspension groaned protestingly. 'I just love roller coasters,' he added.

I felt Karan's fingers stiffen on the back of my seat. I expected a sob, a shout, a scream, a prayer, some typical female reaction. Instead I heard a small calm voice indicating that Catherine was entering Windsor Great Park.

'She's forking left at the Rangers' Gate.' Wade regained his equilibrium. 'If she's not heading for Staines, then where the hell . . .?'

'Right into the obituary column if she goes any faster.'

The Aston bored past a 'no vehicles allowed' sign, swamping my vision with a kick-back of muddy spray. It didn't just surge ahead, it evaporated. I laid on the right boot until there was no place left for it to go.

'Just look at that baby fly!' Wade enthused.

'Yummy, yummy,' I grunted, flicking the main-beam toggle, the oversplash of lights wisping against saturated tree bark and greenery flanking the route.

'Slow down, Simon,' Karan said suddenly.

'Are you kidding?' Wade interjected. 'We'll lose her.'

'We're pushing her to the limits.'

'She can always stop.'

'She won't stop! She—she'll kill hersel-*l-l-l* . . .' The word stretched into a gasp. I glanced in the rear-view, saw Karan with her hands to her mouth, staring mesmerized over the bright fringe of her nails.

'Simon—the Aston!' Wade's voice was urgent.

The brake lights blinked on. The tyres screamed for traction, but the rear end was already into a slide. The car canted to one side, its silver nose lifting then plunging violently. There was a dull thud as something hit the Aston's front fender. A big brown bundle richochetted up and over the roof. It caught briefly in my headlight beams as it spiralled towards us.

'What the . . .?' Wade's mouth went loose.

I stabbed the brakes, felt the tyres snatch then skid. The bundle plummeted on to the bonnet with a noise like a muffled explosion. The wipers swept away a brief stippling of blood—then suddenly there weren't any wipers—just shards of glass as the object ran over the carburation vents and burst through the screen.

Karan let out a guttural cry of terror. A pair of antlers skewered through the dash padding and hooked themselves around the wheel. The broken neck of a stag dangled over the column, hanging by what little sinew still existed. The body still twitched. A warm, pulsing flow of blood leaked in twin rivulets from the moist nose, sousing my knees. My hands were covered in shreds of flesh and hair. As I managed to get a turn on the steering, the head twisted like a ball-socket showing the reflection of my tightly clenched teeth in the depths of its unseeing eyes. I spat away blood and rain as it swept through the yawning hole in the windshield. I bottled up my fear and somehow wasn't sick. The Jag was bouncing all over the place. Earth was scrunching against the metal floor, hammering the silencer boxes, branches snapping and scratching over the roof and doors.

Wade grappled with the antlers, trying to disengage them from the wheel. A muscle rippled along his jaw. 'Fuckin' hell,' he said quietly.

Karan wasn't saying anything. I felt the tear streaks at the corners of her eyes as she pressed her face hard against my neck.

The Aston's silver bodywork sprang out of the darkness. It was broadside on, trapped in our beams, illuminated like some piece of theatre. My stomach and spine tensed. We were going to collide. Catherine was too horrified to move and our steering was now fully jammed. My fingers wrenched ineffectually at the wheel.

'Give, you bastard. *Give!*' Wade pulled at the antlers with all the force he could muster. An aluminium spoke sheared under the pressure, jarring his hand against the glass. Blood ran down his wrist. '*Now!*' he yelled.

The wheel was sufficiently free to complete half a turn. I yanked it over. The broken spoke severed the stag's neck from its body. I saw the limp appendage on the bonnet slide off into the blackness. We missed the Aston by a watch-tick, zigzagging crazily past, uprooting a sapling, the nearside wing taking the major brunt of the impact as we sliced into a grass banking. Karan lurched against me as we stopped. I turned away from the gory decapitation and looked at her. I had expected to find revulsion in her face, but there was none, only relief and concern now for Wade. She released his seat belt and offered attention to his wound.

'But there aren't any stags in Windsor Great Park,' he was saying. 'No stags, no does, no deer of any kind.'

'Try telling that to the park superintendent,' I said. 'The hunk of venison looking at us from the windshield happens to be Crown property. He probably wandered from the private estate. It's not unknown.'

'He lost by a short head.' Wade grinned.

The Jag was becoming claustrophobic. I climbed out. I told Karan to tie a makeshift dressing around Wade's wrist and then get herself and him over to the Aston. Catherine's car, I added obviously, was now our only means of transport.

Rain settled on my lashes, blurring my vision as I tramped towards the silver machine. Catherine's hands gripped the wheel tightly, bleached knuckles pressed hard against her forehead, her face barely visible beneath the tangle of hair. I looked briefly at the deplorable state of my trousers and the white luxury of the Aston's lambswool upholstery. Even contemplating entry seemed like irreverence.

'If I'd known there was going to be a stag party I'd have come properly dressed—rubber apron, galoshes . . .'

Her face came up. 'That's not funny,' she said.

'That's what I thought when the Jag's speedo needle keeled over in a swoon.'

'I didn't ask you to follow me.'

'No, you asked me to forgive you. Why?'

'I-I'm not going to Staines.'

'I'd already worked that out.'

'The scheme—it's too dangerous—an absurdity at my time of life.'

'So is punching a high performance car on wet roads. You could have been killed. We all could have been killed. The Jag's taken a pretty bad beating.'

'I repeat, I didn't ask you to follow me. I'll buy you another car— I'll buy you a dozen cars . . .' A rapid pulse began fluttering in her throat. 'Simon, please . . . for God's sake just leave me *alone*!'

'To do what?' I asked wearily.

'Whatever I choose.'

'Whatever Delgado chooses would be more accurate. He's rolling the credits and we haven't got a billing.'

'That's ridiculous. I—I've simply changed my mind.'

'The phone call changed it for you. It was from Rex not Luke. He altered locations and you agreed. That's why you tried to shake us off. He's managed to frighten you and now——'

'Get out of the car!' The snout of that little pearl-handled automatic came up like an adolescent's erection. There was a feverish determination in her eyes. I doubted if she'd shoot to kill, but a plastic knee-cap certainly seemed within the realms of possibility.

'At least tell me where you're going,' I stalled.

'No,' she said flatly.

I let out my breath, watching it plume and condense on the windshield. A jagged streak of lightning flickered and stabbed through the darkness, momentarily illuminating the Aston in its blinding glare. Catherine's face tightened, anticipating the roll of thunder. It came, she winced and suddenly I was holding the gun.

'I want to be around to collect my fee,' I said dryly, clicking on the safety and slipping the weapon into my leather jerkin.

'Damn you, Simon!'

'Some other time. Let's run over the dialogue again—from where you offer to buy me a dozen cars to where you tell me to get out of this one.'

She compressed her lips, remained silent.

I tilted my seat back, cushioning my neck against the head rest. 'O.K., have it your way. We'll just sit here and wait for the park rangers. They patrol this area at regular intervals and——'

'No—I must——' She glanced at the dash clock.

'Keep an appointment?'

'Yes.'

'With Rex Delgado?'

She gave a small nod of confirmation.

'But not at Staines.'

'No, not at Staines. Oh, Simon, please . . .' She put her hands to her eyes, tears seeped through her fingers. 'He wants me to meet him at the studios—at E stage. I have—I *must* go alone. Please, please, don't try to stop me . . .'

I felt her body convulse as she buried her face on my shoulder.

'What's he been saying? What the hell's he duped you into?'

'He—he knows.'

'Knows?'

'That you were at the house when I phoned him . . . that I lied.'

'How can he know?'

She looked up, met my gaze levelly. 'When Anthony fled he chose to go to Rex rather than to his father. He must have talked about you and——'

'He guessed we're trying to stitch him up,' I cut in.

She clutched her cheeks hard between her palms. The skin strained thinner and paler with mounting tension. 'Rex is using Anthony as a sort of hostage . . . to make sure I come alone.'

'And if you do?'

'He says he'll release him.'

'That sounds like a bookie telling you he's got a social conscience.'

'I'll have to go. I haven't any other choice.'

'Is this Catherine Forrest—the caring stepmother?'

She answered with slow deliberateness. 'I know what you're thinking, Simon, and a few hours ago you would have been right. For the first time in my life I'm not being selfish—my career suddenly seems ridiculously irrelevant. Luke would never forgive me if anything happened to Anthony. I love my husband and I'm responsible for his son. It's taken me a long time to realize it but now that I have I desperately want a second chance. Have I left it too late?'

'Welfare isn't in my line,' I said. 'Snap on the ignition and let's pick up Karan and Wade.'

The motor whirred, her hand hesitated on the gearshift.

'Give way to stags,' I added.

Chapter Thirteen

MY HAIR brushed the zipper at Karan's cleavage. My head shifted on her breast with the motion of the car. A little metal tongue marked *Lightning* played havoc with my left nostril. Under different circumstances it could have been fun.

We were pressed tightly together, hugging the Aston's carpeting as the car puttered up to the studio entrance. Wade being the shortest had taken the front passenger side, while Karan and I lay snugly in the rear. An electric window purred as Catherine exchanged words with the gateman.

'You're late, Miss Forrest.'

'I beg your pardon?'

'I said you're late. Mr Delgado's been worrying.'

'Then he'll have to worry a little longer. I'd like to use your telephone.'

'I'm afraid I can't oblige.'

'I want to call my husband.'

'Out of the question.' Timber groaned as the barrier pole was raised.

Karan blinked, whispered, 'I don't know that voice.'

The face wasn't familiar either. I caught the guy's reflection in a side window as the Aston eased forward. Mid-thirties, thick lips, plenty of lard around the jowls.

Catherine said, 'Where's Bob Draper?'

'Sick,' came the curt reply.

'I insist on using the telephone.'

'You're in no position to insist on anything. Now move over. My instructions are to drive you to E stage.'

Karan's body tensed against me as I eased the tiny automatic out of my pocket, gathering the slack in the trigger. I could almost hear Wade's heart thumping in his rib-cage.

'I'm perfectly capable——' Catherine gestured vainly with her hands.

'I said move over!'

His fingers were on the door handle. Any moment the courtesy light would click on and then he couldn't help but see us. I lifted the pistol. The angle wasn't good but I reckoned the bullet would take him in the head if he did anything less than freeze.

The telephone shrilled a reprieve.

'Stay put!' He reluctantly released the handle. 'That'll be Rex now.'

The footsteps receded. I heard the gatehouse door open, the phone was silenced.

'Make a fuss,' I whispered against Catherine's seat. 'Get out, leave your door open, and do anything to draw his attention away from the car.'

'He'll see me if Catherine leaves the bloody door open,' Wade croaked.

'He'll see the courtesy light come on if she doesn't,' Karan pointed out.

'He'll see neither.' Catherine prodded a dash switch as she snapped open the door. She swung her legs over the sill and began hurling unladylike vocabulary towards the gatehouse. The door slammed shut. The courtesy light stayed on.

We slithered out on all fours, scudding across the rain drenched asphalt, keeping low until we reached the administration block. Hiding in the deepest shadow we could find, we stood in silence as the black louring clouds hurled their contents pitilessly in our faces. We watched Catherine struggle as, gripped by the wrists, she was dragged brutally to the car. Her hair whipped free as a strong gust of wind wrenched loose her green bandeau. She almost fell on to the passenger seat. The door was locked, the barrier lowered. The guy turned over the motor, blipped the throttle, and selected a gear. The Aston snaked off towards the stages.

'Karan,' I said softly, 'Catherine's attempt failed so it's up to you to get to a phone. Get hold of Grant, tell him what's happened, and then hide yourself in a safe place.'

'I understand.'

'This isn't toytown. Stay put or you'll scare the pants off me.'

'And you . . .?'

'E stage, hopefully protecting Catherine's interests.'

'We'd better move, Simon,' Wade said.

I tore my eyes away from Karan and nodded. With senses

heightened by tension, we forged a course towards the stages. The Aston cruised slowly back as we reached the scenic department. The bogus gateman was the only occupant. Catherine had been deposited.

We circled wide, keeping away from roads and the numerous arcades which were a far more direct routing, but which were to be avoided for that very reason. Past the cutting block, J and K stages, the carpenters' shop, and the R.C.A. theatre. Across an expanse of grassland, dodging between discarded flats, rusty scaffolding, and a host of soiled props from long forgotten productions. A few minutes more brought us to the rear of the cafeteria and within sight of E stage. Two studio trailers and a tow-tractor made an effective screen as we softshoed cautiously towards the tall grey structure.

Wade's hand plucked at my sleeve. 'Our troubles are not going to be little ones,' he murmured.

I hitched an eye over the wheel of the tow-tractor. A torch beam was lancing from the stage door making a sweeping reconnaissance of the surroundings. I ducked down as the yellow glow rippled through the gaps in the machinery, sending a macabre play of shadows over my face and hands. The sweep was completed and the light extinguished. Wade hunched his shoulders to bring the collar of his jacket higher around his ears. 'We'll never make it to that door,' he said grimly.

A twenty yard span of open ground lay between us and the two hundred pounds of muscle guarding the stage. I probed the blackness, mulling over ideas, feeling increasingly uncomfortable as the sleety rain gathered on my hair, resting momentarily before finding its way to my scalp. Minutes elapsed. I began to shiver.

'How about a diversion?' Wade suggested.

'Such as?'

'Horses.'

'Horses?'

'From the stable block. They'd come right past here if I stampeded 'em.'

I followed his eyes. The avenue led directly to the horses. There were no intersections so they couldn't diverge. The thought touched my mind that Delgado might hear the rumpus and react accordingly, but then I remembered the stages were totally soundproof. He was insulated from all outside noise. It was perfect.

'Give me ten, Simon, then watch that goon——'

I overrode him. 'Take it easy or you'll end up as corpse-meat.'

'Karan can always revive me. A quick rub down with *The Sporting Life* works wonders.'

'Yeah, the *Sits Vac* page—now move.'

He grinned and scrambled off into the pitchy darkness.

I guess the rainfall went up by a couple of millimetres as I waited. Every few minutes a squall would sweep across my face. It almost blinded me and it was all I could do to stop my teeth from chattering. A sudden tightness in my chest and throat offered an adequate cure. I heard a movement then felt the tip of a stiletto piercing the flesh between my hip and lowest rib. A soft chuckle promised that a new undreamed-of nightmare was about to begin.

'Careless, Drake. Very, very careless.'

I stiffened, feeling a little like the guy who'd just received an unwanted parcel which had just started ticking. A hand crept to the pocket flap of my jerkin. Catherine's tiny automatic was extracted.

'Pearl grips—mm, very nice. A bit effeminate, but nice. Standard T.S.D. issue?'

'Go jump,' I growled.

He grabbed me by the hair, made an incision at the collar of my jerkin and skimmed the blade down my backbone. Steel whiskered over flesh as the point cut effortlessly through the leather. It took my shirt with it rending the cotton to the waistband of my slacks. Fleshy fingers folded themselves around my neck and in a single fluid pull my shirt and jacket were suddenly lying at my feet.

'Skill, Drake,' Stiletto congratulated himself.

I heard a muffled little whimper. I turned.

It was Karan. The gateman had her two wrists clamped in one hand and her mouth covered with the other. There was blood on her breast. The sight of it caused anger to break over me in feverish waves. She saw the look in my eyes and shook her head violently. The gateman tightened his grip, showed me his profile. The skin from his temple to his neck was torn in bloody lacerations.

'Caught this little cow in the admin block.' His voice was cracked and distorted as it left his damaged mouth. 'She was on the phone—trying to reach some guy called Grant. I stopped her, Kirk—just. Look at my cheek. Can you see? Can you see what the bitch has done to my bastard cheek?'

'Yeah, I can see.'

'I want something in return. I'm gonna . . . He snatched a tight fistful of her hair, forcing her body over the wheel of the tow-tractor, kneading her breasts, trying to get astride her. Karan's pelvis twitched and jerked. A silent scream formed on her lips.

Kirk said, 'Let the broad go or you're going to need a doctor to get my boot out of your mouth!'

'I'm gonna . . .' He began trembling in anticipation, unable to complete the sentence. He was going to take her then and there. Against the tractor. In the pissing rain. Her teeth flashed carnivorously as she fought against the anxious fingers which wormed their way towards her pubic region. She hammered her tiny fists into the lust-crazed eyes, only to receive a blitz of forehand and backhand slaps which shook her head like that of a broken doll.

'Get that bastard off her!' I yelled, balling my fists.

The stiletto pricked against my side, gently reminding me that Kirk was still very much in command. I sought out the small eyes which lay beneath an overhang of thick eyebrows, followed the deep creases which ran from his wide-nostrilled nose to his sneering mouth. He skilfully switched the stiletto from his right hand to his left and pulled Catherine's automatic from his waistband. The ironmongery was levelled at the gateman.

'Get your sex some place else, Harv—in your own time, not Delgado's. He's paying you to cover the gate, not get your leg over a broad.'

'Screw the gate,' he panted, perspiration sitting heavily across his face.

'Screw whatever you like, Harv, but not this girl and not now. Button your flies or you're gonna have two holes in your goddamn arse!'

'Sweet Jesus—take it easy, huh.' His voice rose a pitch.

'Back off!'

'O.K.—I'm backing, I'm backing.'

He released Karan's arms, allowing her to cover her now naked breasts. Her face was puffed and there were teeth marks on her neck. She looked at me silently. A tear welled in the corner of one eye, balancing fraily before streaking down her cheek.

Kirk lowered the pistol. 'Now keep that gate manned,' he rasped.

'Like making love to a bloody stiff,' came the reply.

In the recesses of my mind there was a brief conflict between rashness and caution. Rashness drew clear and the bowstring that checked my temper gave way. I felt a brutal satisfaction as my knuckles slashed into the gateman's face. A shock wave rippled through his jaw, rattling his teeth and tugging at his jowls. The ensuing scream and the trickle of blood from his nose offered compensation of sorts. He bounced against the tractor, his face contorting as his upper lip dragged against the mudguard. I watched him drop dazedly on to his backside and then I braced myself for Kirk's retaliative move.

The flash of pearl grips, and then the weight that went behind them.

Measured weight. Enough to take away my legs, but not enough to render me unconscious. It slowed down my brain, numbed my reflexes, and blurred my vision. I lay leaden. My tongue probed to drag moisture into my dry mouth and found only the gritty filth of the tarmac. One operable eye was receiving pictures of Karan. She was kneeling, pressing a moist cheek against my navel. With a forefinger I touched the warmth of her lips, grimacing at the sight of the ugly red welts that discoloured her face.

'Up!' The voice came from a flashlight that was arcing down on to my eyes. A toe-cap jabbed at my cheek.

I started shakily to my feet, only to be helped by a waist-hold that threatened to tear my ribs from their moorings. The strength belonged to Bernard. The flab from his oversize gut pressed into my back until my bones creaked.

Kirk seized Karan's right arm and bent it behind her back. A small white scar on his chin twisted palely as he smiled. He flipped the stiletto into the air and caught it so that the handle rested against his sleeve and a couple of inches of steel protruded between his thumb and index finger. He teased the blade under the nipple of Karan's right breast, studying the quivering delicate orb.

'I am motivated by money, Drake,' he said smoothly. 'My every action is lubricated by it. I terrorize and kill for it. I maim for it. In my business there is no room for compassion, no margin for sentimentality. I curbed Harv's impulses because apart from one man's satisfaction it would have achieved nothing. Thrills are cheap. I don't go in for cheapness.'

Karan's mouth opened as the tip of the stiletto tweaked, toyed, played. Her tongue circled her lips.

'For Jesus' sake,' I muttered.

'Co-operate, Drake, and the lady stays unmarked. Play hero, and not only will she lose her sex appeal but she'll suffer unimaginable pain.'

My skin crawled. I nodded.

Bernard released the hug-like grip. Kirk handed him Catherine's pistol and he laughed contemptuously as he pocketed it. He flicked open his macintosh and pulled a ·32 Browning automatic from a speed rig. He gestured towards E stage. 'Let's go find Rex,' he said.

I could feel the horses long before I could hear or see them. The tarmac seemed to shiver under my feet. A gentle pulsing at first, then a great tremor of motion. Kirk halted dead in his tracks and listened. He looked strangely unnerved as the vibration grew into the sound of thundering hooves. He stood rooted, eyes screwed against the rain, lips drawn back against his teeth with intensity as the barrage of galloping horseflesh suddenly materialized.

Fluttering nostrils, streaming manes, and the unpredictable glaze of a dozen eyes caught in the beam of Bernard's flashlight. He lifted the Browning to the heavens and loosed off two rounds in rapid succession. It was obvious strategy, of course, and it broke up the group, even slowed one or two down. Sparks jumped from plates as horses swerved, buffeting against each other in an attempt to change direction. A shoulder clipped a pyramid of garbage cans, upending them and sending them clattering towards us amidst a lava of reeking swill. Bernard took one in the chest. He let out a thin wail of a scream as he was deflected backwards. A horse, its forelegs splayed and sliding on its haunches bore into him like a locomotive. I caught a flash of white feet and a tongue writhing briefly against stained teeth as the impact jarred breath from his body, carrying him towards the cafeteria. His hands clutched wildly at the animal's neck, momentarily preventing him from being dragged under the vast belly and towards the crippling power in those hind legs. The Browning rattled across the tarmac as he was swept off into the darkness. Just a blur. His straining fingers released and his own momentum took over. There was a split second lull as hooves found their grip on human flesh. The resonance of steel plates muffled in an insular moment that spelled pain.

In the mêlée Karan had wriggled herself free. Kirk was too occupied dodging horses to think about recapture, or even retrieving the

Browning. It was as though he was irresolute, paralysed in thought and action. The stiletto swung vaguely in the direction of my windpipe but it was the move of a desperate man with disorientated timing. I parried it with a savage kick and sent the blade spinning from his nerveless hand. A mowing blow from my right fist snapped his head sideways. The skin burst by his mouth and blood leaked down his chin. His eyelids flickered as he sagged. Water whoofed over my shoes as he reeled through a puddle and lay still.

'Simon!' Karan's voice was shrill. I turned away from Kirk and saw her standing very straight, breasts heaving, hair trembling, the Browning clenched tightly in both hands. The muzzle wavered menacingly in my direction.

'F'Chrissake . . .?' I gasped.

She closed her eyes, bracing herself for the recoil. The barrel jerked upwards as her forefinger pulled twice within the space of a second. The first bullet punctured a section of guttering some five feet over my head, while the second splintered the corrugated sheeting by my hip. Her aim was so haphazard that I didn't know whether to freeze or run. The dilemma was decided for me as streaks of pain knifed through my neck, ragged nails clawing for my jugular. The gateman's torn blooded face bore down on me. I grabbed a rasping lungful of air, twisted convulsively and managed a fair jab at his stomach. It didn't touch him. The pressure increased and a red mist began building before my eyes.

Another shot rang out. Breath hissed against my neck. The pain eased to the point where it was bearable and then flaccid bodyweight fell against me, knocking, then pinning me to the wet ground. I could see a splash of redness on my arm and for a moment I wondered whose blood it was. Then I felt the warmness flushing across my naked back as it pumped from the gateman's abdomen. I prised loose the still gripping dead fingers and risked a few grazes as I elbowed myself clear of the corpse.

Karan was sobbing uncontrollably, unable to take her eyes from the large messy exit wound in his back. I lifted the Browning from her limp hand and snugged it into my belt. A full clip housed eight rounds. Bernard would have had a full clip. That left us with three.

'Simon, I'm going to faint.'

'The hell you are,' I said roughly.

'But I've killed . . .'

'An animal. An animal who was trying to kill me.'

'I—I just picked up the gun, pointed it, and pulled the trigger.'

'You jerked the trigger. You should never jerk. You take aim and squeeze gently.'

'I didn't aim,' she said desolately. 'I don't know how to aim.'

'I'd noticed.' I nuzzled my chin into her hair, held her shivering body hard against mine. Stinging needles of rain hammered my bare chest, dissipating the pungent taint of cordite and the clinging stench of death.

'Catherine?' The word was a question.

'Just as soon as Frankie arrives,' I assured her.

I felt a tremor race along her spine as thunder rumbled overhead. The noise was an effective mask for a gunshot. Only the shrill whinny of a ricochet and rusty scaffolding flakes settling on my shoulders told me we were in somebody's sights.

I pulled Karan to the gound, scanning the murky darkness, feeling the adrenalin alert my senses as it surged to my nerve centres.

Another bullet winged into the door of E stage. Small calibre, thin report. Bernard with Catherine's little pea-shooter, I guessed. Lying out there in the darkness. Undoubtedly injured, but still left with sufficient stamina and application to drop us if we so much as motioned for that door. I eased out the Browning, seeking for a movement. The barrel made a radial reconnoitre and found nothing. With only three precious rounds in the clip I had no intention of blasting at shadows.

I forced clearheaded thought. 'We've no option but to head for the lake. My guess is he'll follow and that will leave the coast clear for Frankie.'

'But the lake is very exposed——'

'Which gives him a good reason to stalk us. We've got to draw him away from the stage door.'

'To allow Frankie to get in, yes I understand . . . but shouldn't he be here by now?'

I nodded gravely.

She looked in the direction of the stable block. 'No sign of life.'

I ignored the palpitation in my chest and the small voice in my mind that told me with numbing certainty that something had gone wrong. 'He'll show,' I said.

We rose cautiously, remained static for a couple of heart-beats, and then raced towards the tow-tractor. A flurry of clearly speculative shots seared wide as our feet slapped hollowly over the tarmac. Karan wanted to pause for breath but I dragged her on. Bernard was tracking us in a deadly game of hide-and-seek. His footsteps seemed unnaturally loud; slow but inexorable. The kind of calculated slowness that made you hold fear in your teeth like a bit.

Three more minutes of running, taking cover, and running again brought us to the lake. Another twenty yards were covered as we scuttled along the jetty. Karan lost her footing on the damp fungoid boards and landed heavily on her knees. 'I can't go on, Simon,' she said, her voice gasping and distressed.

Lightning crackled and flared. I pivoted with the Browning and found Bernard locked briefly in my sights. His face was streaked with dirt and blood and drawn in exhaustion. He was fiddling with a piece of machinery—a mobile generator—range fifty yards. My trigger finger squeezed twice. Both rounds spiralled off the generator in an elongated whine. The sky stayed alight long enough for me to know I hadn't touched him.

I got a hand under Karan's armpit and helped her to her feet. I indicated two speedboats straining at their mooring ropes.

'He—he'll only follow us,' she said hoarsely.

'Not if number two's set adrift.'

'He's trying to start the generator.'

'Which supplies what?'

'Power to the floodlights. It illuminates the whole lake.'

I didn't reply. I lowered her into the first boat, soberly aware that if the lighting came on we would find ourselves playing a very different game.

'Do you know how to start one of these things?' I asked.

'Is it like a car?'

My eyes flitted over the dash. 'It is when you've got an ignition key. We haven't.'

'So how . . .?'

'Manually.' I crawled aft and located the carburettor priming bulb. I pumped with one hand while I groped for the choke with the other. 'Open the throttle a fraction by pulling back the red-handled lever,' I shouted, as the priming bulb hardened in my palm.

'Like this?'

I heard the remote-control cable shift in its sleeve. I nodded, then beckoned her towards the outboard. 'This is the start cord,' I explained, showing her the T-shaped grip. 'You pull it gently until you feel the starter engage and then you yank with all the force you can muster.'

'Simon, I'm not so sure——'

'It's only a precaution. All being well I'll do the pulling.'

Her fingers closed tentatively on the rubber grip. She was shivering badly and she looked scared to death. I clambered on to the jetty and released the for'ard mooring. The bow swung out, the stern snatching on its rope as it took up the slack. No sign of Bernard. No floodlights. I flexed life into my benumbed fingers and began untethering boat two.

A saturated sheet of paper flapped at me from the windshield. A thick felt pen had printed the words: *STAR PRODUCTIONS, THE WHALE. BOTH TANKS FULL*, and the message had been hastily attached by two clips from a set of battery jump-leads. I began getting ideas. Explosive ones. I left the mooring ropes secure, removed the jumpers and climbed aboard.

'What are you doing, Simon?' Karan sounded panicky.

'Don't worry,' I yelled. 'Just stand by with that starter handle.'

Coldness corroded my bones as I sloshed around in about four inches of water, fumbling blindly for the fuel tank and battery box. I drew back two small bolts, released the rear seat, and explored the interior . The port side housed the tank, the starboard side the battery. The jump-leads would stretch with cable to spare.

I worked quickly, thumbing the last round of ammunition from the Browning's magazine, jamming it under the lip of the filler-cap and anchoring it firmly with a red-sleeved jumper clip. I coupled its mate, the black, to the other side of the cap and carefully played out the cables until I reached the battery. The terminals felt greasy and cold to the touch. I couldn't differentiate between negative and positive, but then I didn't have to. All it needed to cause a dead short was for the two remaining clips to each hug a terminal. The tank would get progressively hotter, the fuel would begin to vaporize, and the bullet's percussion-cap would detonate—I hoped. All this depended on the condition of the battery and a host of unpredictable factors.

I felt the sinews in my neck tighten as I cramped the red jumper on the furthest terminal. The final one, the all important black one, opened wide under the strength of my grip. I hesitated because I was shaking. I steadied my right wrist with my left hand, then snapped the crocodile clip hard on to the remaining terminal. A healthy spark smacked at my fingers as the teeth bit into the lead. I slammed the seat back into position and got the hell out of there.

I suppose I was mid-flight when the lights came on and a bullet took me in the shoulder. A moving target caught in a frantic leap from the foredeck of one boat to the gunwale of the other. I remember yelling for Karan to pull the start cord and I remember hearing the engine bubble and throb as it fired. After that events became orderless, caught up in a maze of pain. The boat pitched and rolled alarmingly. Its stern reeled in drunken arcs, its bows dipped into a trough of towering waves which smashed over the deck with stunning impact. I was tossed involuntarily aft. My lungs hurt, my ears ached, and a gale force wind was tugging fiercely at my hair. My eyeballs had the sensation of having been deep frozen then rush thawed. Water was everywhere. The deluge swamped my neck, shivering my shoulders as it cratered under my armpits. Karan was forcing the wheel to starboard, yet unbelievably the boat heeled to port. The wind was driving it that way—the wind and the noise. An incessant whirring, whistling sound that rose above the rumbling thrust of the outboard.

I scrambled along the crazily shifting deck in an attempt to reach Karan. The fingers of my right hand tried to staunch the blood which pioneered its sticky route down my left arm. My shoulder was beginning to stiffen.

Karan brushed water away from her eyes and shouted, 'Wind machine, Simon—I can't hold——'

The throttle lever was only two thirds open. I fisted it wide. The hull began creaming the water, the nose lifting under the rushing buoyancy. I got a hand to the windshield and managed to stay vertical as the boat broke free from the mechanically produced squall. I could see the wind machine now—a huge piece of apparatus some ten feet in diameter a silver propeller spinning in loud constant effort behind a half-moon of safety grille.

'You're bleeding,' Karan announced gravely.

'A few more inches to the right and I'd be wearing a halo.'

'It needs attention.'

'Later.'

'Immediately.' She began tearing towelling strips from her trouser suit.

I took the wheel and glanced astern. Bernard had wasted no time in getting boat two under way. The hull caught only the remnants of the spume as it by-passed the wind machine. Both vessel's were equipped with 40 h.p. outboards but we appeared to be labouring while he appeared to be gaining. My eyes latched on to the rear mooring rope and the reason became instantly apparent. We were towing half the jetty in our wake.

Karan followed my gaze. 'I hadn't time to cast off,' she admitted, pressing a towelling pad against my shoulder. 'I felt sure the rope would snap.'

'Mooring rope doesn't snap that easily—which is more than can be said for movie makers' jett——' Pain cut off my breath as a strip of cloth was knotted firmly under my armpit.

'Keep still.'

'That hurts.'

'You're bleeding from two holes.'

'Good.'

'Good?'

'One entry, one exit. That means the bullet isn't lodged in my shoulder.'

'Is it very painful?'

'Right now I feel a lot better than the gateman. Start worrying when I begin screaming for morphine.'

Bernard was closing rapidly. He was getting ideas about ramming us—highly feasible ideas now that the prow of his boat was only feet away from our transom. I could see his gleaming knuckles on the wheel, the intensity in his eyes. I thought briefly about the jump-leads clinging to the battery and tank, short circuiting, generating heat. The thought was brief because the likelihood of an explosion seemed to be diminishing with each passing second.

Karan was tossed against the bulkhead as stem collided with stern. Once, twice, hacking wood away in large gouts. The wheel was snatched from my grasp as the outboard twisted and lifted, the throb changing to a scream as the prop surfaced, chewing doggedly at the air before plunging back into the icy water. Bernard swung out around us going a little wide, taking his time, increasing his speed until he was a good ten lengths clear. He took a few seconds to centre our boat in his mirror before heeling hard to port, engine at full lock, hull chinning the water in a calculated death run to slice us in two.

Starboard was the only place to go. We angled in sharply, albeit only briefly. The motor suddenly stuttered and died. We were back in the clutches of that goddamned wind machine. The contraption had blown our trailing cargo against the stern. Mooring rope and pieces of jetty had fouled up the prop.

Karan stood motionless, looking at the cold unwelcoming water. She knew there was only one option open to us and she gulped noticeably at the prospect.

'Hurry!' I yelled.

'You . . .?'

'Yes, yes. Now get in that damn water and strike out for the bank.'

She kicked off her shoes and did a forward roll off the gunwale. She hit the water with no more than a sibilant splash. I watched her surface, saw her naked shoulders break through a bank of scud, writhing with effort as they got into their stroke. The combination of lights and the water tinged her skin a bright emerald.

Bernard was watching her too. The speedboat veered, tightening its turn to cut her off.

My pulse began to race as I clambered on to the foredeck. I ignored the throb in my arm, aware only of Karan's bobbing head and the skimming hull lifting with increased power, casting out a mantle of spray as it homed on its human objective.

Karan kept swimming, a rather slow schoolgirlish breast-stroke. Her chin dipped with each thrust of her arms, leaving behind a rippling narrow wake. The scissors kick of her legs displaced water in erratic little swirls and splashes. She was fifty yards from the bank.

The wind machine blasted me with cold air as I balanced precariously on the foredeck. I clung to the windshield and shouted for Karan to submerge. She didn't hear me, just kept right on swimming. I didn't shout again—I screamed. This time she stopped, trod water, and turned. She saw the onrushing hull, grabbed a mouthful of air and disappeared. I watched in helpless terror as the keel slashed over the circle of ripples, the prop churning the water into turmoil. The bows dipped as they were caught by the wind. Foam smeared across the windshield then dispersed in a starburst of tiny streaks to reveal Bernard's grin of amusement.

'Try me!' I yelled as the boat canted past. '*ME*, you poxy shit-eater!'

He eased off the throttle, glanced back. Karan had surfaced, looking exhausted. She'd never survive a second run.

I veed two fingers and scooped them through the air. 'Did you hear what I said, you bloody ball-less bastard!'

He heard. The prow lifted sharply as he increased revs. He swung wide, then arrowed in. It was the same manoeuvre but this time I was the target.

I stood on the foredeck dancing and chanting obscenities. The movement didn't do my arm a lot of good, but it projected an irresistible challenge.

I had no fixed plan in my mind. Perhaps I was a little beyond caring. Instinct, I supposed, would couple the right moment with the right evasive move. I'd dive into the drink or even leap into his goddamn cockpit if the mood so took me.

The engine note started to build. My feet took a firmer hold on the Trackmark. The droning abruptly swelled to a roar and then the bows were so close that I could see the sneer on his rain-sheened face.

A brilliant ball of orange flame suddenly wiped out the picture. The foredeck trembled with such intensity that I thought the boat was falling apart from under my legs. A scorching force hit my chest and face, tossing me upwards and backwards like a sawdust toy. I was swathed in a holocaust of heat and smoke, then plunged into the punishing coldness of the lake. The variance was paralytic. I drifted down for what seemed like an eternity, but which in reality could have been only seconds. Surfacing brought choking black smoke to my lungs and a stutter of sparks caught up in a whirlwind of air. Glowing debris fell like bird droppings from the sky. A flotilla of petrol patches burned all around me.

I was pondering on the fact that the blast had carried me some ten yards inshore when a tremendous shock-wave racked my body. Bernard's boat, its stern ablaze and hanging in tatters, pitched unbelievably towards me. It seemed to come slowly. Just a glint of steely-grey belly, its bows lifting, hesitating, trembling, ramming my vessel amidships. The cockpit was liquid with fire. The fenders dribbled and flared, the windshield disintegrated as spasms of orange and gold flame tore loose along the gunwale, licking at Bernard's clothing, running like quicksilver up his neck and into his hair. He was just a screaming blur. A passenger riding in a molten angel of death.

I felt another tremor as a second explosion ripped the craft in two. The smouldering stern and half the deck broke away, mushing through the water, hissing and crackling and finally submerging under the weight of the still clinging outboard. The bows and cockpit continued under their own momentum. They scythed high over my head, their trajectory carrying them towards the wind machine.

I wiped oily smoke from my eyes and ferried myself round. The boat fireballed as it struck the half moon of safety grille, cartwheeling, twisting, jettisoning Bernard in a hideous flaming tangle of arms and legs. He uttered a bubbling scream as his body hit the top of the grille. He lay momentarily wedged on the cross-bar, then the blade caught his shoe and he teetered sickeningly into the machine's exposed sector. There was an audible splintering of bone as the cleaving propeller jammed, managed one revolution, then jammed again. The belt-drive strained and groaned protestingly. A great gush of redness percolated the gaps in the grille before subsiding to flaunt the butchered torso. It dangled upside down, half face, half skull, and a spinal column exposed from neck to pelvis.

Bile burned in my throat as I kicked for the bank. My guts were letting me know I'd seen death at its worst—a physical mechanism that didn't help my already weakened condition. I didn't feel cold any more, I just didn't feel anything. I dragged my languid body from the water and gathered my legs under me. Swaying dizzily, I tried to clear my eyes of the oil and smoke which gummed my lids. I could see Karan making her way towards me, her body thrown into harsh relief by the flames. Great orange serpents gorged hungrily at the lake's huge backcloth, buckling the scaffolding, desecrating the painted canvas with omnivorous intensity.

Karan tended my shoulder. Her hands were quick and strong as she tightened the towelling strips. The blood was beginning to coagulate blackly. She didn't say a word, just gazed silently at the wind machine.

'Don't look,' I said.

'I'm all right,' she whispered weakly. She tried to smile, a pitiful travesty of a smile in the reflected light from the lake. 'Just hold me, Simon. Please, please, hold me.'

I ran the fingers of my good hand through her matted hair and pulled her close. I felt tiny vibrations in her throat as our naked flesh fused. A brief moment of intimacy. Her moment. The image was gone, the reality was there, and the request for masculine contact told me her sexual inhibitions had been quashed.

The rain eased into a smirr of drizzle. We dragged our fatigue-drained bodies through it and emerged at the rear of E stage. A yellow glow feathered from beneath the door of an adjacent building. Six inch letters announced that it was the wardrobe department and closer inspection revealed a bent lock tongue hanging in a broken frame. I pulled the Browning from my waistband and we entered cautiously. A gun with a spent clip was only useful for frightening old ladies, but better a bluff than nothing at all.

An avalanche of garments littered the floor. Racks of metal hangers gleamed at us in skeletal silence. Nothing human stirred.

I unzipped my sodden pants and climbed out of them. 'Get those wet clothes off before you catch your death,' I said.

'But who . . .?'

'Never mind who. Just be grateful that somebody has.'

Her tongue passed over her lips as she wriggled free of the ravaged trouser suit. The saturated material hugged her thighs jealously. Two minutes later I'd donned a polo neck sweater and corduroy suit. The trousers were all waist and no inside leg and the jacket can only be described as 'roomy'. My belt gathered up the excess inches and some fresh padding around my wound filled out one shoulder at least. Shoes came in all sizes and were no problem. Karan tied the laces looking amused. I smiled a little too. Just being dry had given my morale a lift.

'Stay here,' I told her, slipping the Browning into my pocket. 'Just put out the light and sit tight.'

'Shouldn't I get to a phone, try to reach Captain Grant?'

'I left Kirk alive. I'm not risking—' I broke off suddenly. There was something very familiar about the fleecy-lined jacket which she twirled over her shoulders.

'What's the matter?'

'That looks like Frankie's jerkin.'

'It can't be. I found it in the pile.'

I rummaged in the pockets and came up with a handkerchief, a few shards of straw and a strip tab from a can of Coke. 'It's Frankie's,' I affirmed.

She blinked, looked confused.

'No time to speculate,' I motioned for the door. 'Keep warm and give me your promise you'll stay put.'

'I promise.'

'And don't say be careful.'

'I was going to say I love you.'

'You were . . .?' I bent the muscles of my face at her. 'You're crazy.'

'I love you.'

She brought a hand up to my cheek, but I backed out of the door. If I felt the touch of her skin I might wilt into her arms and never make it away from there.

I stood motionless in the drizzle. All quiet. I made a quick survey of the stage's massive steel doors; three electrically bolted, the fourth heavily padlocked. No windows, no skylights, no fire exits. The place was built along the lines of a vault, and to my untrained eye it seemed impregnable.

I paced the length of the building and came face to face with Delgado's parked Lincoln limousine. I wasn't interested in the car so much as the door it partially obscured. Metal, locked of course, but of normal size and slightly inset into the surrounding structure. I commandeered the Lincoln's ignition keys, opened the boot, and dragged out the jack. I mentally measured the door's width from hinge to lock, then barked a few knuckles raking around for a gap-bridging length of Dexion or scaffolding tube.

My shoulder screamed mercy as it held the improvisation in place. I set my teeth against the pain and worked the ratchet furiously with my right hand until the jack had expanded enough to hold the tube by itself. I released my shoulder, shook sweat from my brow, and pumped that handle until the door surround uprights creaked and bowed and the bottom of the door began scraping harshly on the concrete. The brass lock tongue glinted at me. Two more determined pulls brought it within a centimetre of freedom. I couldn't manage a third so I deployed my remaining strength to my leg and began kicking it in. The keeper gave, springing the door at the second blow.

In and up, my anxious footsteps echoing on the treads of a metal staircase. Through some kind of sound department, dodging microphone booms, chairs, benches, and sound mixing equipment. My muscles stilled for an instant as I caught my reflection in glass. Catherine, Delgado and Anthony were illuminated on the set below.

I blinked at what I saw. A rear projection machine was beaming a moving image of a stormy sea on to a huge transluscent screen. In front of this, mounted on wheels, and powered by what must have been a complex hydraulic system was the head of a giant sperm whale. Blue-grey in colour, glossy in texture, the man-made mammal looked utterly convincing as its metal innards stretched it to its full height. The mouth gaped showing a lower jaw of gleaming teeth. Water sprayed briefly from the toothless sockets of the upper jaw, running down the throat, cascading over the sides to be collected in a tank at the model's base for recirculation. The mouth closed as the hydraulics retracted. The head dipped and the motion started over again.

Delgado appeared amused by the display. He stood with Catherine on the gently rocking deck section of a mock whaler. The boat rolled realistically whenever the mechanical creature appeared and Delgado seemed to take a malicious delight in forcing the actress to within a whisker of the yawning jaws. He helped her maintain balance with the occasional nudge from a revolver's barrel.

Anthony couldn't see anything. He'd been tethered to the seat of a *Nike* crane-mounted camera and angled so that a stand spotlight was playing directly in his eyes.

The door in front of me held two side bolts. I freed them, broke cover, and pussy-footed silently down the staircase to the stage. I could feel my shoulder leaking under the corduroy. A fine tracery of blood was emerging from my cuff and pooling into my palm. I was now subject to spasmodic bouts of giddiness and violent shivering and I ached in a way I never thought possible. I wiped a fine dew of sweat from my upper lip, rested in the shadows and thought about Karan. I reminded myself of all I stood to lose if I blundered in without strategy, or hung around weak-kneed inviting detection.

I circled behind the flats. Half my strength was going to be pitted against a man twice my age. Fair, apart from the gun—apart from the chance that Anthony might get his face spread all over the camera.

I belly-crawled under the hull, past the rocking simulators, and took up a position where a portable gangway stretched from the bulwarks to the stage. Python coils of cables brushed sinuously against my legs. Several heavy rubber couplings were within reach so I stretched for them and began detaching male from female. The rear projection ceased. The whaler stopped undulating. Total silence, then the hollow slap of footsteps over my head.

'Some sort of power failure, my dear.' Delgado's voice floated down the gangway. 'I had hoped to kill a little time, keep you amused while awaiting assurance that you weren't followed.'

'If thrusting me at that . . . that *thing* is your definition of amusement then you're psychopathic.'

There was a stumble, the thump of knees hitting the deck.

'Careful, Catherine. Your tongue seems to be tangling with your sealegs.'

'Y-you pushed me.'

'You slipped, my pet. I know your mind is confused, I've made allowances——'

'My mind is not confused!'

'Of course not.'

'And don't patronize me!'

'You're watching the stage door instead of watching your feet. You're still clinging to the tenuous hope that Drake has arrived at the entrance gates and is at this moment construing some miraculous plan to get past Kirk.'

'Your Mr Kirk isn't infallible. I'll abandon hope when you bring me Simon's head on a pole.'

'That might amuse Kirk, I'll have to mention it. Anything else?'

'Get me a stiff drink.'

'I thought you didn't touch alcohol.'

'I don't. I want to throw it in your face.'

'Your ill-considered dialogue is spoiling the scene, my dear.' The remark was followed by a fairly hefty slap. It carried Catherine backward down the gangway and into a position where she only had to turn her head to see me. 'I suggest you save your snappy locutions and start considering Anthony's plight,' Delgado added.

'I . . . I . . .' She sensed me, her eyes came round.

They were large and exaggeratedly blue under the bright lights. Her skin was pale and I could see the red outlines of Delgado's fingers breaking through her cheek. I pressed the Browning's muzzle against my lips and hoped to bloody Christ she'd pick up the cue.

'I . . . want your word that Anthony won't be harmed,' she covered convincingly, forcing tears to her eyes then brushing them away impotently with her arm.

'You have it. Withdraw My Liberty at the four day declaration stage and the boy will be released alive and healthy.'

'And between then and now?'

'He'll be in Kirk's custody. Filming will go on as normal and you will continue to behave as the cantankerous old bitch we've all grown to love.'

Her voice sharpened. 'How do I explain Ant's disappearance to Luke? And what's to stop me going to the police once I've got him back?'

'Use your imagination for the first part, my dear, and think about the damage I could do for the second. Anthony's told me everything —the Mescaline, the tapes, the lipstick. The newspapers would be black with the scandal. He called me uncle Rex when he arrived. He talked and I listened. He's a very inventive young man.'

'He's a sick young man.'

'No sicker than me, Catherine. I took a rich old actress out of moth balls and filled her head with delusions of renewed stardom. I built a production around her purely as a means to an end—and then I killed to achieve that end. First Gibson, wrongly, because of your damn stepson, and then Hunter because he was fast becoming a liability. Your pictures went out with white five pound notes, but I——'

'Stop it!' she shrilled.

'Am I upsetting you?' His footsteps rattled with swift efficiency on the gangway. Catherine backed up.

I stood perfectly still watching a revolver barrel move into my line of vision as Delgado advanced. It was pointing at the actress's stomach, yet it was so close to my face I could read the word *Enfield* stamped under the hammer. An arm followed, then a shoulder, then a profile. 'Catherine the great,' he added. 'My God, the critics are going to slay you.'

'Figuratively, of course,' I murmured mildly, letting the Browning's foresight ripple over the soft flesh of his neck and bury itself deep into the hollow of his jawbone. 'Move, and you're a bullet mark on a wall.'

His mouth didn't drop open and he didn't shake or start to sweat. He remained cool and kempt; we might have been preparing for a take. Finally he said, 'I suppose you want the gun?'

He offered the butt to my left hand but I could barely move my fingers. I gave Catherine custody of the Browning then reached for the revolver with my right. There was a startled gasp as the actress suddenly drove the automatic hard into his belly. The muzzle went in as far as the trigger-guard and there was a metallic snap as the hammer found nothing but emptiness. Delgado clamped his eyes in relief and fumbled for a lozenge. Catherine made a loose, gurgling noise that trailed off into a frustrated sigh. She sent the Browning skittering across the studio floor.

'D-did it jam?' Delgado wheezed, shooting out his immaculate cuffs, smoothing the lapels of his polyester suit and doing a few other nerve soothing manoeuvres.

'Spent clip,' I said.

'Spent . . .?'

'Don't reproach yourself, it just saved your life.'

Catherine's eyes were opaque with bitterness. 'By rights he should be dead.'

'By rights so should Karan and I. We're about to join her. Out the way I came in. All of us.' I ushered Delgado towards the crane-mounted camera. 'Get Anthony off that *Nike*. We're paying Grant a visit in your Lincoln.'

The thought tightened his face muscles. He held up a pink-palmed hand. 'Let's not be hasty, Simon. There's still room for compromise.'

'Skip the speeches,' I said, 'why not admit you've failed.'

'The world failure isn't in my vocabulary. If we could just talk for a moment about money——'

'Half a million?'

He nodded. 'You see I can afford to be generous.'

'With bookmakers' money you'll never receive.'

'Intruder's fast.'

'How fast?'

'Fast enough to finish seventh in the Schweppes, even though we'd pumped him full of Terramycin.'

'Hunter must have been crazy to agree.'

'Hunter was a puppet, he did as he was told. He knew we were up against massive TV coverage and an extra large gate. Over-zealous strangling could have ruined everything.'

'So he jumped hurdles on a dope-filled horse and you rewarded him by beating him to death in a shower.'

'You saw the leg-boot explode on film. Your shrewdness killed

210

him. In time you would have pressured him into talking.' He fiddled with his signet ring, adding in sour amusement, 'Let's say you precipitated the inevitable.'

'So putting Wade up for the Princess Royal Hurdle was calculated,' I grunted.

'Of course. It paved a way to secure Chuck Busby for the big one. The change of jockey made the difference, they'd say, the professional —you know how it works.'

'You're despicable,' Catherine said thickly.

'No, my dear, clever.'

'You murdered Fiona.'

'I poisoned her drinking water with paraquat, yes. I was rather fond of the dog. It was regrettable but necessary.'

'Please spare me the pathos,' she snapped.

'Save it for Grant,' I cut in. 'My shoulder can't take time off to listen while you vomit up your morality.'

His eyes strayed from the blood spots on the floor to the gun to the spotlight and then back to the gun. He was weighing up the various possibilities. Churning over the standard clever things that screen villians invariably pull when cornered but which rarely prove viable in a real situation.

'Simon?' Anthony peered towards us, eyes dilated with terror. 'S-Simon, is that you?'

He looked mussed and sweaty from straining against the chain which secured him to the seat of the *Nike*. Catherine twisted the spotlight away. Although shaken she summoned a smile and spoke almost composedly.

'It's all right, Anthony, we're taking you home.'

He ignored her and looked at me.

'Your father must be worried sick,' she pressed on. 'I expect——'

'Dad's not here?'

'There wasn't time to reach him. Simon and I came——'

'Your mother came alone,' I corrected. 'She came because in spite of what you've done she still loves you. I followed her only because I have a fee to safeguard and an overwhelming desire to wring your bloody neck.'

He glared at me and then lowered his eyes.

Delgado stirred. 'This is all very touching,' he said.

'Key for the padlock,' I coaxed. 'Hand it to Catherine—easy.'

He did. The actress unravelled the chain with neat efficient movements. Anthony climbed stiffly from the *Nike*.

I had no control over what happened next. I suppose it was a loss of focus through fatigue coupled with a lapse of sensory alertness. I suddenly felt enfeebled and I let it show on my face. An air-wave brushed my sagging lids as Delgado powered his foot towards the *Nike*. The crane pivoted and I just stood there helplessly waiting for the rear-end to crash into my shoulder blades.

It connected heavily, taking away my legs and sapping what little strength I had left. I was aware of Delgado's hand reaching for the finger-grips of one of the crane's counter-balance weights and for a moment I thought he was going to bring it down on my skull. Instead, he drove it into my wrist and regained possession of the Enfield. I cried out with the pain, certainly Catherine was screaming and Anthony was saying something like Oh Christ and somewhere in the middle of everything a bell was ringing.

I just lay there and bled. I lay until a mud-caked chukka boot nudged me in the ribs and a voice ordered me up. Shapes gradually took on personalities and I found the Enfield's black eye-socket gazing at me from Kirk's hand. Delgado was at some kind of electric switchboard. He fiddled with buttons as Kirk brought him up to date with the situation. The bell's din abruptly ceased.

'This is known as the organ,' he informed me. 'Most things can be controlled from here—that's how Kirk came so quickly. The flashing red light over the door, Drake—do you follow me?'

I leaned dizzily against the crane. I could barely catch his words, let alone follow their implication. The blood-loss from my shoulder was getting critical. A redness was ballooning through the corduroy, the pain running beyond the wound in hot and cold repetitions.

'I think he's bleeding to death,' Kirk blew out his pock-rumpled cheeks.

Delgado said, 'Then a brisk walk to the lake should exacerbate his condition. Let him carry Harv's body. At some point the strain will kill him. Leave him where he falls and return here.'

'What about the girl?'

'Find her and deal with her.'

'Find her where?'

Delgado held his gaze for a second, then looked at me. 'Judging by Drake's attire I'd say the wardrobe department, wouldn't you?'

Kirk grinned.

Catherine's face was stretched tensely. 'No!' she shrilled. 'If you harm Karan then so help me God I'll——'

'You'll take a back seat and keep your mouth shut.' Delgado stooped for the Browning, hitching it from the floor by inserting a ball-point pen through the trigger-guard. He smiled distantly as he wrapped it in a handkerchief and pocketed it. 'Insurance, my dear. How thoughtful of you to cover the butt with your prints.'

'That's the gun that killed Harv,' Kirk pointed out.

'Really?' Delgado feigned surprise. 'How unfortunate for Harv and how ill-fated for Catherine.' He turned to the actress, his voice heavy with irony. 'Your killing him will be our little secret, my dear. As long as I have Anthony I have the Champion Hurdle; as long as I have the gun, I have your silence.'

'And when four bodies are discovered in the morning,' I said shakily, 'you'll be shit deep in trouble.'

He walked agilely up the gangway. 'For a dead man, Drake, your concern for the living is really quite commendable. Let me suggest that tonight you and your girlfriend met the two men who framed you for Gibson's murder. Let me further suggest that Catherine will co-operate in telling the police of a telephone tip-off you received; how she begged you to enlist help and how her suggestion was thwarted by your impetuous nature.' His eyes glowed with narrative pride as he motioned across the whaler's deck and towards a swivel-mounted harpoon gun. He leaned on the blued cannon-shaped barrel. 'Don't ask about an alibi, Drake, just rest assured I have one. I believe you'll recall I'm rather good at providing them.'

'Julian's slipping saddle,' I breathed.

He nodded. 'An incident which you saw on film and which satisfied you as to my whereabouts at eight-thirty.'

'I checked the time, the saddle did slip at eight-thirty.'

'And so it did, my dear Simon, so it did. The question you should have asked was whether or not I was there when it happened. The camera doesn't lie but a film splicer and cement can dramatically distort the truth.'

'Film splicer?' I repeated stupidly.

'When you saw me dash into shot it had nothing to do with a slipping saddle——' He paused and eyed me speculatively as if assessing my capability to grasp what he was about to impart. He continued, 'It was my reaction to the rain two and a half hours earlier. The camera set-up was the same, Julian behaved similarly, and any discrepancy in the position of the horse was covered fortuitously by a film flicker—not that I can really take full credit for that. It was a rather hammy piece of cutting and my splice made itself felt as it passed through the projector gate. I temporized with the broken sprocket hole excuse and of course you believed it. A perfect deception, wouldn't you agree?'

'Congratulations,' I managed.

'Thanks——' He stopped and stiffened, as if some invisible hand had been clamped over his mouth. His eyes drifted upward. Someone was moving about on the gantry.

A muffled voice said, 'You're all wind and piss, Delgado. Now me, I give it style.'

Kirk tilted the spotlight. The beam traversed the roof, rifling shadowy recesses, scrutinizing each segment of the wooden structure before moving on. There was a measurable silence then Delgado began wagging a finger towards a cloud of descending dust. A sheen of coloured silks was picked out by the light. A small face hidden behind goggles and a skull-cap emblazoned with the initials: B.D.

'*Hunter*', Delgado's face blanched as he mouthed the name.

'Who else,' came the muted reply.

I stared, astonishment erasing my weariness. I knew it had to be Wade and yet by clipping his sentences he'd managed to capture Hunter's accent close to perfection. He crouched for cover behind two gantry-mounted spotlights.

'I've given evidence to Grant,' he grated.

'No!' Delgado shook his head vehemently. 'This is some sort of trick, you're——'

'Dead? Phoney hospital bulletin. Sorry, Rex, closing night.'

Delgado swivelled the harpoon gun half-circle. 'You knew about this all along, Drake. You damn well brought him here.'

'Sure I did,' my words were shaky but audible, 'so stop waving that papier-mâché leftover from *Jaws* around and start reconsidering your position.'

'You think this is a fake? Catherine's had lunch with the director, ask her how phoney it is. Tell him, my dear. Tell him about the explosive head timed to detonate five seconds after penetrating the synthetic skin of that whale.'

She nodded bleakly. 'It's real enough,' she said. 'Special effects have filled a section of the model with entrails and other disgusting mishmash.'

'They've taken licence only with the weight of the harpoon—a mere fifty pounds instead of the conventional two-hundred.' Delgado paused, fumbling another lozenge into his mouth, his face now flushed and awash with sweat. 'I hope I'm not being gratuitously masochistic, but I'd say even that would be a slight over-kill in your case, wouldn't you?'

'You're outta your mind,' Wade shifted on the gantry.

Kirk tried to keep him circled in the spotlight but he was too agile. Three successive shots whined harmlessly into the roof.

'Save your ammunition!' Delgado ordered harshly.

Something which was almost a flicker came and went in Kirk's eyes. He took a couple of paces forward, squinting up at the gantry. 'I think there's something pretty damned weird about this character,' he said shortly. 'What the hell is he doing ponced up in jockey gear anyway?'

Delgado was reading his thoughts. A thin smile invaded his fraught features. He said to me, 'What were you hoping to do, shock me into submission? Who have you got up there, Drake? Who's masquerading as Patch Hunter?'

Wood creaked and splintered as a spotlight somersaulted from the gantry. The barn-doors flew off narrowly missing Catherine and the bulk of the thing crashed on to the whaler's foredeck. Delgado's feet visibly lifted an inch under the impact. He wrestled the harpoon gun round and shouted for Kirk to pinpoint the jockey. The beam swung wildly. Kirk began pumping the revolver as a reflex action and the stuff was going all over the place. Frankie dodged and weaved, playing tag with the light and coming murderously close to the shells. There was a snatch of strangled invective as he tripped. Kirk homed the spotlight towards the noise and the harpoon gun followed suit. Suddenly the spotlight sagged on its stand. Kirk gurgled as a *Nike* weight took him in the back of the neck. Accurately placed and effectively delivered, Anthony Taylor had hurled it with the power of a baseball pitcher.

Catherine stood for a moment, her eyes closed, taking slow, deep breaths. Her lower lip trembled fractionally as she knelt by Kirk's body, fumbling for his belt and extracting the stiletto from its sheath.

She gazed at the thin blade and began walking almost trance-like towards Delgado.

'Simon?' Anthony looked as if he was about to be sick. 'Stop her, Simon. Please stop her.'

I put my hands on my knees, my shoulders hunched in an exhausted arch. My consciousness was beginning to slide. I was in no position to stop anyone.

'Mother!' Anthony's voice was beseeching.

Catherine's stride faltered. She looked at the boy, her blue eyes glazed and vacant in the pallor of her face. She smiled. It was a word she'd waited a long time to hear.

'No further, my dear,' Delgado summoned a halt with an impassioned outflinging of his arm. 'I'm sure you'd like nothing better than to stick that between my ribs, but take another step and you'll be pinned against the far wall with the sagging realism that only the dead can achieve.'

'Words, Rex. You always were very good with words.'

'Stay——'

'I'm going to kill you,' she said tonelessly.

'Don't force me to destroy you, Catherine . . . I made you . . . I alone put you on a pedestal . . . I . . .'

His eyes held stupefaction as she advanced up the gangway. He had every opportunity to operate the trigger-mechanism, but he didn't. He just seemed to shrink as Catherine lunged the blade towards his throat. It shouldn't have stopped until the hilt was against his thyroid cartilage but somehow he managed to deflect the thrust with his forearm. He staggered away fighting for balance and losing it as his feet tangled with the harpoon's coiled hawser. Catherine took an involuntary step forward, cursing her ineffectualness and shaking from the reaction. She leaned on the barrel and it tilted. Wade's urgent voice echoed from the gantry's dusky shadows as she fell heavily against the gun's swivel arm. The word: *Trigger*! suddenly became irrelevant; drowned in the deafening roar of the harpoon leaving the barrel.

The hawser snaked towards the roof like thread spinning off a bobbin. A loop snagged Delgado's ankle and he was propelled upward, his body climbing with a twisting, writhing motion, his mouth hanging loose, his throat too constricted to utter even the faintest of cries. Wood splinters whined past my face as the barbed blade buried itself in the gantry. Coins, keys and lozenges rained down on Catherine as the producer dangled some twenty feet above her head.

A hand touched my shoulder and I looked round. Anthony Taylor stood shakily by my side. His pale uncomprehending face held a mixture of bewilderment and disbelief.

'T-that's going to detonate,' he said. 'Frankie's up there and mother's——' An explosion shook the gantry, cutting off his words as surely as if he'd had his throat cut.

My unfocused eyes picked up a fusion of movement—Catherine wandering dazedly towards the wheelhouse, Wade vaulting through smoke, glancing off the head of the whale, bouncing against the rear projection screen—and caught up in all of this Delgado's fear-crazed scream as he came down like a marionette with its strings cut. The scream died in his throat as his head struck the deck and he rolled bonelessly past Catherine to the starboard rail. He lay still, eyes open but unseeing, face locked in a rictus of death.

'You O.K.?' An initialled helmet swam into my vision. Wade was holding his side and looked badly winded.

'O.K.,' I echoed. 'You?'

'Torn a few ligaments. Us jump jocks are a hardy breed—I've had worse.'

'Simon's bleeding pretty badly,' Anthony told him.

'I'll see to Simon, you go comfort your mother.' Wade glanced at Catherine. She was staring at Delgado, her face stilled in shock. 'I think you'd both benefit from each other's company,' he added.

The boy managed a tight smile and strode towards the whaler.

'Had Delgado fooled, huh? Even had you fooled for a while, I bet. How was the accent?'

'Patch would've been proud of you.'

'Thanks.' He dragged a half-smoked butt from his silks, went to put it in his mouth, and then as an afterthought pushed it in mine. 'I managed to contact Grant, he should be here any minute.'

'Then I'll let you stay and fill him in.'

'What about you?' His lighter rasped, flaring brightly at my eyes.

'Karan can drive me to the nearest Casualty Department.'

He looked at me wryly. 'How the hell do I explain all this?'

'Just tell him the truth.'

'He won't' believe it.'

'No he won't,' I said. 'Tell him it only happens in the movies.'

Chapter Fourteen

It EXPLODED violently, ricocheted and missed my left ear by the width of a cigarette paper. Nothing too lethal, just a Bollinger cork caught on the rebound.

I suppose it was fitting I should go out the way I'd come in. Guests, rampant laughter, low schmaltzy music, and glasses filling and emptying with ever increasing rapidity. A celebration. A Champion Hurdle victory.

'Care putting yours to mine, dear?' I caught the redolence of expensive body lotion as Julian Knight posed the question.

'Putting . . .?'

'I want a light.' He waggled a cheroot between his teeth and indicated the glowing cigarette in my hand.

Karan saw my expression and giggled. I grudgingly proffered the light.

'Heaven forbid I should mean anything else,' Knight added, puffing vigorously, swaying away from us and holding the cheroot as though he was an usherette hired to escort people to their seats.

'Sarcastic sod,' I growled.

'Your face was a picture,' Karan remained amused.

'I should have laid one on him when I had the chance.'

'And when did you?'

'He mentioned something once about a holy grail—you wouldn't understand.'

She sighed. 'I'd hoped your stay in hospital might have mellowed your aggression.'

'It mended my arm not my——' I broke off as Amanda Stewart glided past. Her blue eyes made contact and projected a secretive smile beneath large stiffened lashes. Her blonde hair was fluffed in an elaborate fashion and her thighs swelled provocatively against an evening gown which could have doubled for a negligee. 'Nice dress she's nearly wearing,' I murmured.

'Now who's being sarcastic,' Karan clicked her tongue.

'Pity about Frankie,' I said, watching the young jockey straighten his dicky-bow before making a beeline for Amanda. 'If Intruder had run and he'd been the pilot it might have gone close.'

'Inflamed tendon, wasn't it?'

'That's what it said on the vet's certificate.'

'You sound sceptical.'

'You're damned right I do. It stinks. Even when the publicity broke there was no legal way anyone could stop that horse from running. I think pressure was brought to bear on the trainer by the T.S.D. I also think——'

'Yes, Simon?' Howard Grant ranged over my shoulder.

'I also think I need another drink.' I gave him a sideways smile and flagged down a waiter.

'You've been avoiding me,' he said, biting into a caviar canapé.

'I've been in hospital,' I retaliated.

'In a private bed where you refused to see visitors.'

'The private bed was Catherine's idea. As for the visitors . . . well a sick man doesn't always desire company.'

'I understand Miss Langford visited you on numerous occasions.'

'Therapy,' I murmured unconvincingly.

'Yes, I dare say.' He fingered his steely hair and tried not to notice Karan's blushes. 'Fortunately Catherine and Frankie were able to furnish most of the details, but I still need your written report and I need it by the morning.'

I grunted but it came out as a belch.

'Was that a yes?'

I nodded. 'The champagne,' I apologized.

Karan sipped at her drink, licking away a little foam that clung to her lip. 'They're forecasting a box-office bonanza when it goes on release in the summer,' she enthused. 'The enormous amount of publicity has helped of course, but Catherine's had lots more offers for lots more films, so I like to think people will be going to see her performance rather than to satisfy their morbid curiosity.'

'Even in death Delgado can take the credit for Catherine recapturing the limelight,' I said softly.

'A touch of irony,' Grant agreed, adding, 'changing to a happier note, you'll be pleased to know that Anthony has enrolled for a horsemastership course at an equestrian centre. No protests from Catherine. Should do the boy good.'

'I'm glad,' Karan smiled prettily, her hand hovering undecidedly over a salver of various delicacies.

'Try the venison paté,' Grant advised. 'It really is quite excellent.'

'V-venison?' She flinched visibly. 'No . . . no, I don't think so.'

'Simon?'

I cleared my throat and declined. 'A little rich,' I added.

His eyes were watching me closely. 'Could this sudden aversion to game be connected with a certain incident in Windsor Great Park?'

I lifted my eyebrows, struggled to produce my blank expression.

'The park authorities have been in touch with us,' he went on, 'apparently your Jaguar was found in a prohibited area with half a stag hanging through the windscreen.'

'Really?'

'Yes, really.'

'They didn't catch him, I suppose.'

'Catch who?'

'The guy who stole my car.'

'The . . .?' He worried an earlobe. 'Are you saying you weren't driving?'

'Oh, look!' Karan broke in urgently. 'Here comes Catherine now.'

Grant turned, sighed elaborately. 'I shall expect a full explanation in your report,' he said, then flexed his face to blend in with the abundance of smiles.

Flashbulbs heralded the actress's appearance. Microphones menaced her face as newsmen hampered each other in the battle for position. Questions overlapped questions and the answers were barely audible as the circle tightened and the clamour increased. Laughter crinkled the flesh around her eyes as she shimmered from reporter to reporter. Every now and then she would pause to adopt a fresh pose for the cameras. She'd offer her profile while tenderly tracing a finger over her corsage of orchids; she'd adjust her ermine cape so it clung a little more lavishly to her shoulders, or gently brush gossamer hair from her face, so that the lenses would capture every inch of that diamanté smile. Anyone else would have been overwhelmed by the reception, but Catherine revelled in it.

'How do you feel about your come-back, Miss Forrest?' asked a fresh-faced reporter.

'What come-back, darling? Ask your mother if I've ever been away.'

Laughter, clicking shutters, and Luke Taylor looking a little bewildered as Catherine clung possessively to the sleeve of his white sharkskin dinner-jacket and kissed him. She was playing a role which the years had polished to perfection and the audience was loving it. The inevitable applause erupted. Even Grant indulged.

I sipped my drink and reflected that for a short time at least I'd seen the woman rather than the actress. That circumstances had peeled away the fame, the flattery, the success, and shown me something more substantial than just an image on a screen.

'You're looking very serious,' Karan remarked.

'Thoughts,' I said.

'About Captain Grant's report?'

'Not especially.' I noticed his absence. 'Where . . .?'

'To his car. He has a surprise for Catherine, a poodle puppy I think.'

'That guy's a providence tempter. Who's in charge of the hi-fi?'

'Anthony.'

'Then let's go.' I took her hand. 'I never sit through a film more than once.'

'You don't honestly think . . .?'

I grinned and stared into her soft brown eyes. My reflection was caught in a maze of tiny fairground mirrors. 'No I don't,' I said, 'but when the Press have finished monopolizing Catherine we'll both be expected to participate in the "Oh what a cute little doggy" bit and she might . . . well she just might cause embarrassment by mentioning my fee.'

Her eyebrows lifted. 'I didn't know Simon Drake was embarrassed that easily.'

'He's not, but his boss might find the experience painful. What started out as a private enquiry ended as official Security Division business. I get paid from both ends and that has to sting.'

In a half whisper she said, 'I suppose we could go to my room, you could dictate your report and I could type it up.'

'I've had a few drinks,' I murmured with just the right amount of apprehension. 'I might forget I was once regarded as a trousered unknown quantity and do something we'd both regret.'

'Like?' She wrapped her hands over mine and leaned voluptuously against me, her breasts taut and uptilted, cushioned between us.

'Like ending up in bed with you.'

'What a gorgeous thought,' she said.